dust

dust

ALISON STINE

WEDNESDAY BOOKS
NEW YORK

This is a work of fiction. All of the characters, organizations, and events portrayed in this novel are either products of the author's imagination or are used fictitiously.

First published in the United States by Wednesday Books, an imprint of St. Martin's Publishing Group

DUST. Copyright © 2024 by Alison Stine. All rights reserved. Printed in the United States of America. For information, address St. Martin's Publishing Group, 120 Broadway, New York, NY 10271.

www.wednesdaybooks.com

Library of Congress Cataloging-in-Publication Data

Names: Stine, Alison, 1978– author.
Title: Dust / Alison Stine.
Description: First edition. | New York : Wednesday Books, 2024. | Summary: When her reclusive family relocates to climate-ravaged Colorado, sixteen-year-old Thea, who is hard of hearing, finds community and potential love with Ray, a Deaf boy.
Identifiers: LCCN 2024027051 | ISBN 9781250878731 (hardcover) | ISBN 9781250878748 (ebook)
Subjects: CYAC: Hard of hearing people—Fiction. | Family problems—Fiction. | Communities—Fiction. | Love—Fiction. | LCGFT: Novels.
Classification: LCC PZ7.1.S74675 Du 2024 | DDC [Fic]—dc23
LC record available at https://lccn.loc.gov/2024027051

Our books may be purchased in bulk for promotional, educational, or business use. Please contact your local bookseller or the Macmillan Corporate and Premium Sales Department at 1-800-221-7945, extension 5442, or by email at MacmillanSpecialMarkets@macmillan.com.

First Edition: 2024

10 9 8 7 6 5 4 3 2 1

For Henry, always.
For my dad, who loves history.
And for anyone who feels they aren't heard.

They passed down all the roads long ago, and the Red Bull ran close behind them and covered their footprints.
—Peter S. Beagle, *The Last Unicorn*

dust

1

I saw the dust before the truck, before I could hear its motor. A cloud like a dragon tearing down the road, the dust looked majestic, a plume of brown fire, because the highway was flat. Flat, flat. It spread to a point far off in the horizon, the sky so clear you could see a hawk swirling over the next town.

If there had been a next town.

I paused by the windows of the café. The truck might stop. The driver might come into the café for coffee; Louisa's special was a latte with CBD oil. The truck might need fuel from the gas station next door, which meant my boss would take off her apron and hurry over. There was a chance we might actually get some business for once.

I felt a flutter of hope. I couldn't always hear strangers, and people don't like it when you don't understand them. But I also felt starved of meeting another person. It might go the other way too. The stranger might be kind, speak loudly and clearly, let me see their mouth as they talked.

But the moment passed. The truck came too fast. It blurred past the discount grocery where my mom, Caroline, worked, stocking dented cans on the shelves. It blazed past Louisa's Café and Gas Station, the tiny public library, and the even tinier post office. It continued down the road and far away.

"Thea," Louisa said. "That floor ain't gonna sweep itself."

I looked away from the grimy front windows. That they were grimy was my fault. I was supposed to wash them, and the truck hadn't done me any favors. Dust settled over the glass, stirred up by the truck. Against my legs, my skirt felt heavy.

I had worked at Louisa's Café for a month, a little less than we had been living in the Bloodless Valley. Even so, the dust still surprised me. How it seemed to rise from the ground, skittering over the roads like the tumbleweeds that darted out from nowhere. On our drive out west from Ohio, when the first tumbleweed had hit our truck, I'd screamed, thinking we had hurt something: an animal, a child running into the road. Then the tumbleweed had scattered, broken to bits by the wind.

Tumbleweeds were dry plants, that was all, my dad, Abraham, had said. Dead.

The dust in Colorado got into my eyes, my hair. Sometimes I thought I felt dust in my teeth. I missed rain. I missed coolness. I even missed humidity. I missed my home in Ohio.

My family came to Colorado for land, cheap, advertised along with an old farmhouse in one of the newsletters my dad would read. The newsletters taught him how to live simply, told him to do more with less. Go back to the land, the newsletters urged, with their talk of earthworms for composting, woodstoves for heat. And so we went back, back to a place we had never been.

A flood had driven us away from our home.

The water coming over the hills then had looked gray, like the silt ponds from the coal mines. It had taken on their color, carried their debris, even fish, to stream through the houses in the lowlands, to stain the walls and leave.

My dad had dreamed the flood before it happened. Dreamed a wall of ashy water swelling over the fields, swallowing them. But he hadn't dreamed what happened next. Our rent was raised. We didn't have insurance. *If you don't own land, you are never free,* the newsletters warned.

So, my dad had a vision of the next place. Our new home would be yellow, dry. It would be far away: westward, sitting at the foot of mountains like a child. Floods wouldn't reach us all the way in Colorado. But *no* rain would.

And we came because we were poor, and this was a place poor farmers went: to the Bloodless Valley in southern Colorado where you could have a parcel of land for almost nothing, the newsletters swore. And what they didn't say: where nothing grew, not without a fight.

In the valley, we had no neighbors. Dust was my company. My sister, Amelia, who was nine. Dogs. Our chickens, which my dad wouldn't let us name, and which Amelia and I had named in secret: Taylor Swift, Billina, Lana Del Rey.

My dad hadn't wanted me to work at the café, either, but we needed the money. Self-sufficiency apparently took a while. So, first my mom, then I, got jobs in town. What town there *was,* little more than the handful of ramshackle buildings the truck had blown past.

"Where do you think he was going?" I asked as I pushed the janitor's broom across the checkered café floor.

"Who?" Louisa asked.

"That truck?"

"Sand Dunes National Park, probably."

"Maybe not," the lone customer at the café said, a man older than my dad, who sat at the counter, staring into a mug Louisa kept refilling. He wore his cowboy hat low, shading his eyes. His hand on the mug handle was creased with lines. "He was driving a little fast for a tourist."

"Where else is there to go?" I asked.

"Lots of places, if you know them."

I cast a look at the man, his dark eyes turned down to his coffee. He took another slow sip. How could I get anywhere? I couldn't drive. My parents wouldn't even let me practice. Colorado wasn't like Ohio where I could walk to town; where I had ridden the school bus for a time, rattling over the hills.

But I had not been in school for two years.

In Colorado, the town felt as small as a speed bump, buildings spread far apart on the plain, unending road. My mom and I went to the café, to the store that sold damaged goods at a discount to farmers like my dad, and to our home: that skeletal ranch. My parents wanted me and Amelia to *call* it home, even though it didn't feel like it. That was it. My dad didn't even want me to cross the road the café was on. There was nothing for me over there, he said.

And besides, that highway was dangerous.

I glanced at it as I swept. The public library seemed so small, the windows dark. The post office looked like the fake storefront of a movie set. So tiny, I wondered how there was room inside for an employee and a customer.

Louisa said something. "Don't just _____ that dirt around now."

Something like that. I fought to make it make sense, to order her words, feeling the pressure of not responding in time, which grew heavier with each passing moment. It was too late to tell her I hadn't heard. It would be worse now, more awkward, if I asked her to repeat herself, to fill in the blanks.

I was born half deaf. The left side of me was silence, and I felt I heard about half of the sounds swirling around me. Half I could only guess at, or didn't know I had missed at all. I realized I had not heard something with Louisa, but it took me a moment or two of puzzling out the sounds to make sense of them. Sometimes I never could decode what someone had said. Most nights, I had a headache from trying.

My boss, older than my mom, her hair pulled severely into a black bun streaked with gray, had a habit of looking away when she spoke. She talked as she moved. And she moved constantly, doing over and over the little work the sleepy café seemed to require: stacking napkins under the counter, pushing through the swinging door in back to retrieve something from the kitchen or storage room.

It would have been easier if she had looked directly at me while speaking. I could have seen her lips move. But I had mentioned my hearing to her briefly, only in passing early on. I was quick to reassure Louisa that it rarely caused any problems, and didn't mention it again.

My dad didn't like it when I told people.

I was supposed to just pretend I could hear.

They could after all, everyone else in my family.

I went behind the counter to fetch the dustbin. The man sitting there tipped his hat to me. He was dressed nicely—what passed for nice around here—in a clean shirt with pearly white buttons and jeans with no dirt on them. Everyone wore cowboy boots or high rubber muck boots, I had noticed. Everyone, like this man, kept their hats on inside.

Louisa appeared behind me. I hadn't heard her approach. "Another refill, Sam?" she asked the man.

He pushed his cup away and stood up from the stool. "No, thank you. I should finish my rounds."

"When's your boy coming home?"

"Tonight."

"Planning something special?"

"Grilling _____. You want to come over? I know he'd like to see you."

Louisa shook her head, talking as she dumped the coffee mug into the dirty dish tub. "Oh, no. Ray doesn't want to have dinner with an old woman. You _____ have your time. I'll see him around here soon enough."

Sam stood and stepped carefully over the piles I had swept. But his eyes looked the way my mom's did when she gazed over our long dirt driveway, at the land beyond our farm. It was filled with nothing but a spiky, clumpy weed called sedge. She missed home, I thought. We all did, except my dad.

What was Sam thinking about? And who was Ray? His boy, Louisa had said. The man looked Louisa's age—and he acted like there was another reason he wanted her to come to dinner.

I brushed the piles into the dustbin, then emptied it into

the trash. Every day I swept, and every day the dust came back. I turned to see my mom standing by the door that led to the kitchen and outside. "Ready to go?"

I nodded, untied my apron.

"How's business?" Louisa asked her.

My mom had that look again. "Oh, about the same. Plenty of quiet so I can get a lot done."

"That's one way to think about it."

"Does it ever pick up?"

I knew my mom was worried about losing her job. She had just gotten it. I was worried too. How could Louisa afford to pay me even the little she did?

My boss had been born here. She had a house out back behind the café, rows of photographs taped behind the counter of smiling cousins and nieces and nephews with black hair like hers. She had family. My parents had no one. I had no one, either, no connection to this flat place. If my parents could not get plants to grow in the valley, could not afford to pay for our water from the well, I was not sure we had enough money to go anywhere else.

"When it cools off a bit," Louisa said, "we'll get more tourists coming through. They need snacks and gas, and they've got to stop somewhere." She grinned at me and my mom, like this was a fun joke we were in on.

But it didn't feel like a joke to me.

When my mom and I stepped outside, the heat hit us. I didn't understand what people meant about dry heat, the warmth of the desert without the humidity back in Ohio. It was still hot in the valley, unbearably so. It felt different, but no less awful.

Colorado had the kind of heat that seemed to get inside you through the pores of your skin. A heat that had a feel, gravelly like sandpaper, from the dirt that would blow, stinging my eyes and mouth. The heat had a taste like stale crackers, sticking my tongue to my mouth. My eyelids felt hot, like fingers pushed into them.

And the heat was only going to get worse—even I, new to the valley as a weed, could tell that. Louisa had a tiny TV on the counter by the espresso machine. She switched it on during slow times and we would watch the news together. A lot of news was about the weather, told in the deep, serious tone of a horror movie.

Maybe Louisa knew some things about me, without me having to say anything. It was a small valley; the arrival of a new family, even on the outskirts, and people might talk. How we girls didn't go to school and wore long dresses most of the time. How we bathed in an old metal trough my mom dragged into the back room. How we didn't even have power out there.

It might have surprised Louisa to learn my family had a TV. We had electricity too once my dad fired the generator up, which he did for a few hours every day to get the AC running, cool the fridge, and sometimes even to watch that TV. But we watched together as a family and only the shows my dad approved of: black-and-white dramas, classic musicals, cartoons.

Louisa let me watch the news. I felt she would have let me watch whatever I wanted—soap operas, music videos, things I barely remembered from before—but I hadn't asked. The news unfolded on the café's small screen. Floods, mudslides, fires, temperatures rising everywhere.

Like here in the valley.

My mom started the truck but left the driver's door open to let the heat escape. She cranked the windows down. "Give it a minute."

We waited as the engine rattled and the air conditioner steamed. After a moment, my mom said it was safe to get in the truck. But the seats still burned my legs as sharp as a slap. The air pouring in from the vents felt warm and stale.

Even the air didn't want us in this place.

We left the AC on and the windows cracked as my mom drove onto the main road, the only road we ever took: Highway 17. The temperature gauge in the dashboard read 103. Hot wind out the windows whipped my face. The road sounds were too loud for me to really hear the radio, and there were hardly any stations, anyway. My mom didn't want to listen to news. She wanted to believe my dad, and that was it, what he told her passing for law.

It was a long drive from the café to the acres of flat, brown earth with an even browner, flat house on them that my parents had bought sight unseen. I knew the trip pretty well by now. There was nothing—so much nothing, I had it memorized. Wire fences bisected fields. There were sections where the fences had bowed or been broken by animals or crashed cars. There were rust-colored gates and telephone poles. Sparse green clouds of brush. And the real clouds, huge and white, stretching endlessly in a sky that always seemed to be blue.

Nothing else until we hit the Alien Watchtower, the viewing platform someone had constructed in the middle of a far-off field. There was a museum accompanying the tower, a shrine where people left things for the aliens, and a labyrinth. That was what the sign advertised, anyway, a sign in the shape of an alien, pointing the way. I had glimpsed it from the highway only. I was not allowed to see any of it close-up.

But that was it, the only thing to look forward to on the drive home, to break up the landscape. Unrelenting, that's what I would have called it to my friends back in Ohio, Ellee and Angie. If I could have written a letter to reach them. It was hard to convey just how plain and monotonous the valley was, and it felt shameful to admit to my friends how bored and lonely I felt, my mood as flat as the land.

And that was why the snakes stood out.

Most of the trees visible from the road grew far back by the low squares of houses or sheds, the mountains always in the distance like a jagged blue collar. Out here, trees were more bushes than real trees. Scraggly, undergrown. Trees needed water to live.

But two trees, their tops only slightly scorched brown, stood by the highway, behind a stretch of wire fence. Today, something hung from the fence.

On our drive out west, when we had hit the first tumbleweed, I had screamed. Amelia had screamed at the sight of her first prairie dog, thinking it was a stray, that we should stop for it. I shouted now. I couldn't help it. "Mom!"

She tapped the brakes, the truck wobbling on the road. "What's the matter? Are you hurt?"

"No. On the fence!"

She barely looked.

She knew, then. She knew they were there.

"They're snakes," she said.

We were already passing them. My mom had not stopped or even really slowed. I craned over my shoulder to try to see them more clearly. Lashed to the top of one fence rail, two tied on another.

"They're dead. They found them dead," my mom said.

"How do you know?"

"Old-timers at the grocery store—they told me. It's bad luck to kill a snake. They have to find them _____ way."

"Why are they there?"

It wasn't natural. The snakes had been knotted with rope. They twisted in the hot breeze, against the fence like heavy, dead windchimes.

Now my mom looked surprised. Like I should have known this, like Louisa or someone should have warned me. "It's a superstition," my mom said, "to make it rain."

Dear Ellee,
 I hate it here.

2

Everyone came out to see the truck, except my dad. The first few weeks I had worked at the café, I thought my sister just missed me that much. That the dogs did too. But now I felt the truth of it was: there was just nothing else to do out here. Our return to the farm marked the highlight of Amelia's day, the only change in the long hours my sister spent wandering around, trailed by dogs or goats or chickens, or in the dark house, pretending to study.

As soon as my mom parked, Amelia hopped up on the truck's running board. Her long, reddish-brown hair swung straight around her shoulders in two rope braids. Her eyes were as green as I remembered grass being after rain, and her dress was an old one of mine.

"What's the matter?" she said. "You look upset. Did something happen?"

I thought of the snakes. "People are messed up."

"They're not _____," my mom said. "It's just an old wives' tale."

"Whose wife?" Amelia asked.

I couldn't tell her. She loved animals, even if reptiles weren't her favorite. And she wouldn't believe me if I said the snakes had been found already dead, like my mom swore. I wasn't sure I believed it myself.

We were all alone on the farm. If we had neighbors, we didn't know them. We couldn't even see any other houses from our own, except for a small glint of silver on the horizon, which must have been a hanger or garage where no one lived. We were on our own out here, the way my dad wanted. I tried to stuff down my anxiety.

"It's nothing," I said.

I couldn't let my sister see I was rattled. I did a lot of pretending for her.

My mom reached into the back seat. "Louisa sent some day-old treats."

She lifted the package of stale muffins, a Danish or two. My boss always seemed to throw in at least a couple of cookies for Amelia. She had never met my sister, but kept hinting she would like to.

Amelia hopped off the running board. Dogs yipped and swirled around her. The small rusty one, the medium white one, the two big yellows, the fuzzy spotted brown, and the shaggy gray. The dogs we had inherited, all except for the spotted brown dog, Wednesday, who just showed up. The others had come with the land, which had come from the bank, repossessed when the farmer before us couldn't pay the mortgage.

Sometimes I felt bad for him, whoever he was. We had profited off his bad luck. But maybe we had inherited his misfortune too, a curse that came with the deed.

My parents said the property was cheap in part because the house on it was unfinished. Plastic sheeting flapped on the back. Some of the walls inside were just frames. There was a leaning shed on the property, and the remains of a second shed Amelia liked to play on. It was her dinosaur, half-buried in silt. She called the old wood poking out of the ground *bones* and pretended she was going on an expedition every time she went out there, trailed by the dogs.

Amelia always had a strong imagination, and it was not like there were any playgrounds around. No parks. No school that we would ever see the inside of.

Though my parents said they were doing everything for me and my sister—this move to Colorado, living simply, what they called *unschooling*—they never asked us about anything at all. I had started to believe my whole life was just waiting around to be old enough to leave, to make my own decisions, to have a life at all. I was wasting days.

Now I was wasting them in an actual wasteland.

We had two fenced pens. One pen we used for the goats. One we were supposed to use for the chickens, who also had a little wooden coop, but my sister kept letting them out. She said they liked to wander, but that they would never go far. Soon, we would need another pen for the pigs my parents wanted. My dad was building a barn that right now was just a pile of lumber, protected by a tarp in case it rained.

Which it never, ever did.

Two metal doors were buried in the ground behind the

house and shed. My dad said we were not allowed to go near those doors; we could fall inside the storm cellar, a bunker that seemed to open into the very earth. If the storm cellar was anything like the rest of the house, it would be dusty and dim—even worse because it was underground.

Then there were the fields, running alongside and behind the house, fenced but full of mostly nothing. The plants of the fields wilted, their small leaves pale and sandy. We had arrived in summer—too late to plant many crops which needed to be put in the ground early, but my parents hadn't thought of that. Still, my dad was outside all the time, as if he could change things just by standing around.

"Where's your dad?" my mom asked my sister.

She didn't need to answer. He was always in the fields.

My mom said, "Thea, see if your dad wants a treat. And he should drink something."

"He's been outside a long time," Amelia said sagely.

"Yes, ma'am," I said.

I walked behind the house, a couple of the dogs following me. There were so many, Amelia had decided to name them after days of the week. We had six, every day except Saturday. Amelia said she was saving that name for last, for when a new dog decided to join us, because it was her favorite day.

Weekends used to mean something. Sundays made me nervous, knowing I had school the next day, and probably homework to complete at the last minute. But what I wouldn't give to feel that again, I thought, the apprehension of waiting for the bus, going into the loud and crowded building. To feel the ordinary nervousness of getting an answer wrong or missing something said in class or in the hall. I barely remembered what that was like, being in a crowd, being one of many in a classroom.

I didn't want to tell Amelia that I doubted Mom and Dad would let us take in another dog. Even if we only fed them scraps and the generic dry food my mom could get for free once it expired at the store, the dogs still needed water.

Water cost money.

I was trying not to get too attached.

It was an hour's drive to a well. We hauled the water from it in a big plastic tank in the bed of the truck. Then we filled the cistern back at the house, where it was pumped inside. The generator powered the hot water heater. Otherwise, we would have to heat water on the cookstove, which took forever. Amelia and I couldn't take baths whenever we wanted, and we had no shower, just that dented tub. So much water went to the chickens, the goats, the dogs, and the crops. The land lapped up the water, greedily. And still the plants looked small.

My dad stood in the fields. All around him, the plants were scrubby, smaller than they should have been. Dirt showed through the rows. My dad looked still as a scarecrow, hands on his hips, gazing away from me. In the distance, the mountains seemed calm and endless. When my parents had first said *Colorado*, I thought they meant mountains. But the valley was dry nothingness. *Bloodless* was right. It was a trick, how close the mountains seemed, how huge. I felt we would never go there, never see their trees or snow.

"Mom wants to know if you're hungry," I said.

I tried to keep my interactions brief. I didn't really talk to my dad unless I had to, unless my mom made me. Things had never been great between me and my dad, but since the move, they had only gotten worse.

"Louisa sent some baked goods," I added. "Mom says you should have some water, at least."

He shook his head and glanced at me finally. "Shouldn't waste _____."

Since the move, my dad had started drinking beer. It was strange to see the tall bottles in the generator-powered fridge. Before, my dad drank only on special occasions: Christmas, his birthday. My mom never drank at all. But now, he said beer was cheaper than soda, less precious than water.

"Do you want a beer then?" I asked.

I'd said it to try to hurt him. Even a simple conversation was useless, like trying to find a spring in the woods. My dad had changed everything about our lives—and changed himself too. In Colorado, he spent more time alone. His rules got even stricter. We had to go to bed earlier; we couldn't use the generator in the evenings. He yelled at me all the time about listening.

But he was the one who never heard.

He rubbed his face, his hands making his cheeks more dirty. "I'll come in. How was work?"

"Fine."

A truck almost stopped but then didn't. Someone named Ray is home.

He started walking to the house. Behind him struggled the barley and potatoes, butted with white-flowered heads of buckwheat. My dad called them *volunteers,* crops we hadn't planted and weren't sure what to do with. Nearer the house, only the beans seemed to be flourishing, creeping up the stakes we had stuck in the ground. Their thick green vines reminded me of the dead snakes.

How long before the old-timers took the snakes down, before they realized their superstition hadn't worked? The clouds were stubborn white and bone-dry. It was such a joke: perfect weather—if you didn't mind the heat and if you didn't need to farm.

I hurried to walk in step with my dad. I kept him on what I called my good side, the side I could hear. He didn't like it when I misheard or missed something. He liked it even less when I reminded him. My mom said he just didn't like to think about it, that it made him sad.

But I could tell I made him angry too.

"If you want me to check the long-term weather forecast, I could at the library," I said.

"I can check the weather on my phone just fine."

He had a phone. Amelia and I didn't.

"I don't want you at _____ library," he added.

"But I could research why it's so hot, so dry." We had no internet on the farm, no way of knowing. "If people are doing anything. Maybe there are farmer meetings." I knew there were—Louisa had told me—but my dad might be more likely to attend if he thought we had discovered them ourselves.

"I have all the people I need to talk to _____ here," my dad said, patting my arm and trying to smile. His smile looked forced, and his hand left an imprint of dirt on my arm. "My family."

"I just think someone might be able to help—"

"I said no, Thea. I don't want you in that library. On the

internet, filling your head with garbage. Spending too much time on screens. You go to work and home, that's it."

"Yes, sir."

The internet was garbage. TV was garbage, unless it was a show my dad picked. Public school was garbage. Only at home could we be free. My mom would teach us what mattered: math, reading, and the important skills, survival skills like cooking, growing food, and running a farm.

But how good were we at running a farm? Back home, we had a small but healthy vegetable patch so fertile we sold at the farmers' market and gave the neighbors extra. The earth was rich and old there. The land, green from all the rain. Mist rose from the hills in the morning and the ground steamed.

Until the flood came, when it disappeared under a lake.

But in Colorado, my dad was trying to do more, so much more, with less. That was what the newsletters promised, after all. The land in the Bloodless Valley seemed like such an opportunity, my parents said, the chance of a lifetime. Almost as far as we could see belonged to us, my dad liked to say.

What good was that if all we could see was barren, dry land?

No trash service came out here. We hauled our trash to a dumpster off the highway. There was no recycling, either, though we repurposed as much as we could. My mom, Amelia, and I turned metal cans into planters, milk jugs into birdfeeders. But for all my mom's resourcefulness, we had not been able to sweep all the dirt from the house, to clean the months—maybe years—of grime from the floors and walls. It stuck, that dirt. It stuck to us.

My dad mumbled something, and when I looked questioningly into his face, he didn't repeat himself. Instead, he got angry. He glanced away from me—he must have known I hadn't heard him—and said, "Go help your mother." He veered off to wash up, toward the bathroom at the back of the house.

I didn't understand why my mishearing made him mad. I hadn't asked him to repeat himself; I hadn't said anything. I had only looked at him. My mom never stormed off in a huff like my dad did. Louisa didn't scold me if I missed something she or an actual customer had said.

"I suspect some of my hearing's going as well," she had admitted when I told her my first week at the café. "Though of course it's different for you."

How was it different? I wouldn't know. I had never met another person like me, a *young person,* as Louisa called me, who couldn't hear too.

But Louisa, I had noticed, despite often forgetting to look at me when she talked, touched my arm gently when it seemed like I hadn't heard her. She never approached quietly—I had been startled often by my parents when I hadn't sensed them. When had Louisa learned to do these things?

And why can't my dad? I thought as he banged into the house. The screen door rattled in its frame. That door, like most of the house, wasn't attached very securely. One strong slam and it might fall off.

Nothing was what we thought it would be: the house, which my parents had only seen from pictures before buying, the baked-dry land. The farm seemed unfriendly, like it would always be a stranger. I didn't want to call it home. And my dad was angry all the time. Even the sky seemed to annoy him. It hardly ever changed. It never gave him what he wanted.

I glanced up at it reflexively as I went around the house. I had learned the valley sky usually held only a few clouds, if that. It was bright blue, clear, and constant as a heartbeat. The sun hurt my eyes—it was always out.

But not this afternoon.

Clouds obscured the sun, more than I had ever seen in the valley. A strange, hazy light fell over the yard. And as I watched, the clouds started to change. They moved, boiling like water. The sky turned from grayish blue to brown. Then the wind picked up. It felt different in a way I couldn't explain. I just knew it was off, wrong.

My mom opened the front door of the house. Amelia stood behind her, my sister's eyes white. "Get inside, Thea," my mom said.

She widened the door, and the wind came from behind me, pushing with a howl like coyotes from the woods back home. Hair whipped my face. The gates rattled on their pens. Bits of the house that were loose, shingles and the siding, banged loudly like dishpans crashing.

The clouds had darkened. The deepest tips of them seemed to reach down from the sky, fingers of the storm trying to find us, grab us. Across the highway, I saw a wave of yellow and brown. It swept across the road, coming diagonally and fast.

Dust.

3

My mom had been holding the door wide, but the wind ripped it from her. The screen crashed open. "Thea!" she said.

I raced inside, the wind at my shoulders. My mom, sister, and I wrestled the screen door back, closing it and the storm door behind it. It took all three of us.

"What's going on?" My dad came from the back of the house.

It looked dim inside—and dim out now too, as though it was much later in the evening. The sky had darkened. I tasted grit in my mouth.

"It's going to storm," my mom said.

"The animals!" Amelia cried.

In the shadows of the house, I tried to count the dogs, wiggling all around us, stirred up by the commotion. But outside, there were also the goats and the chickens. Had they fled to their shelters in time?

"The animals are fine, Amelia," my dad said. "It's just a storm. It's natural. It's normal."

It didn't seem normal: how quickly the clouds had turned colors like a bruise. How the wind had picked up, a gust nearly hard enough to tear the door off its hinges, to shove me off my feet. It didn't seem natural, not for anywhere.

"It's a dust storm," I said.

"Those happen here."

"Like this, though? This big? This fast?"

Nobody answered me. All three of us stood at the window. We watched the dust sweep across the farm. We waited for rain, which never came.

Dear Angie,

I'm not sure if this letter will ever reach you. I've been writing to you and Ellee in my homeschool workbook. It's not like my parents ever check it. I've asked my mom if we can go to the post office and actually mail something, and she keeps forgetting or finding excuses. I know my dad wants us to have a clean break, to think of the valley as our life now, and not be yearning for more. Or missing home.

But we don't really go anywhere except work and the farm. Is he embarrassed about the way we're living? Or does he just not want my friends—or anybody—to know?

It was a long list, the list of things my dad didn't believe in. He didn't believe in the government interfering in his life or the lives of his family. He didn't believe the schools had much to teach me and Amelia, certainly not more than our mother could. She had been an early childhood education major, before she left school to marry him. He was already working by then, had dropped out of college his first year—and she didn't need more. *Life comes from living,* my dad liked to say.

My dad didn't believe in taking handouts even from family. With Colorado, he moved us far away from them. Maybe relatives would stop giving us stuff we didn't need, like new clothes and plastic toys.

The older he got, the less he believed in—or, the more firmly his beliefs became embedded in him like an ancient tree whose roots could buckle sidewalks, rip up a road from beneath. Except the thing he was destroying was me.

He didn't think I needed another language because I couldn't hear. Or any school. I wasn't special, he told me, just like he told my little sister she wasn't. I would be expected to work the same as anyone. And if I didn't hear something he or anyone said, that was my fault, not his. I needed to pay more attention.

The world's not gonna bend to you, Thea, he'd say. *It's not gonna slow down or stop.*

I didn't want the world to stop. I just wondered, what did he mean—another language? Were there lots of kids like me? Sometimes I thought about getting to talk to people who might understand. Did they feel alone too, like their life was a house and they were only allowed in one room?

Most of the time, I told myself I was fine. My room contained Amelia, the dogs, and now the café. But other times, I felt like tearing down the walls with my bare hands, kicking until I made a hole in my room wide enough to crawl through, to escape. I felt the world I might have known spinning off, a coin on the ground I just couldn't reach. It flipped away from me.

My dad didn't believe our lives should contain more than our family. He didn't believe the world was any different than when he was young: the weather, what we could expect and how we could grow food. He had read books, heavy old ones like *The Farmer's Almanac* and *The Country Living Bible,* along with newsletters about homesteading and simple living that he saved carefully, like someone else might have saved important letters. He said farming didn't change much. You cleared the earth. You planted seeds. You watered them. Farming hadn't changed for hundreds of years, he said.

But it seemed like it was changing now, I thought the next morning as I got into the truck with my mom. This early in the day, the heat hadn't yet sizzled down from the sky, but the air felt heavy and stale.

The evening before, it hadn't rained. Not at all. It was like no storm I had ever seen. Dust came from the clouds—that was it—and the wind rushed across the farm in a big dry wave. I imagined after my mom and I left, Amelia would be tasked with cleaning the corners of the house, dumping dirt from the animals' troughs.

My dad believed in hard work, physical labor. He believed that everyone had their jobs, their roles in a family. He had learned from his books, books that became more important to him after the floods.

But I thought he had taken too much from those books, twisting an idea of simple living. He couldn't control what happened back in Ohio. None of us could. So now we would start over, and try to control even more. We would make our own world, he said, and wouldn't rely on anyone.

We also wouldn't rely on technology. The electric grid might fail in another emergency. Our appliances might break in a solar flare, and we didn't want to be left defenseless. So, we would cook on a woodstove, eat what we had raised, tote our water by hand. Amelia and I didn't need phones. We didn't have to participate in all that, he said.

The outside work was my dad's domain: farming, hunting—though there seemed to be nothing *to* hunt in the scrubby brush, which looked like scars on skin. Nothing could hide there except skinny, long-legged jackrabbits. And according to my dad, my mom's role was as a teacher, a nurturer of us girls and caretaker of the house: doing all the cooking, cleaning, laundry, and inside chores, work that also fell to Amelia and me, being daughters.

We were supposed to have school for at least four hours a day, I knew that.

But we were supposed to do a lot of things.

My mom said I could study in the evenings, after work. But chores took up most of that time. Watering the gardens, feeding and watering the animals, cleaning up from dinner. With any time left, I was supposed to help Amelia with her lessons.

I helped her more than I did my own schoolwork, and though on some level, I didn't mind ignoring algebra in favor of helping her with easier multiplication tables, I felt the nagging sensation that I was losing something I might need.

That with every evening I didn't study, something was slipping away from me.

When we left Ohio, my friends Ellee and Angie had been studying geometry and precalculus in the homeschool group, the group that had once been *ours*. Would I even get to that? My mom said teaching was a kind of learning. What was I learning, though?

She turned the truck onto the highway. The engine grumbled. So did my stomach. We avoided lighting the cookstove in hot weather, and I had only eaten half a cold Danish from the day-old bag. My mom had just had leftover coffee herself.

Dirt and gravel grumbled beneath the tires. Dust flew alongside us, keeping pace like a dog or a ghost. When we parked behind the café, I knew the dust would catch up to us, swirling into the truck. I closed the door again as fast as I could, dust twining about my ankles. My mom went one way, to the store, and I went the other, into the café.

"Have a good day," I thought I heard her call to me before the back screen door of Louisa's thwacked shut.

I was often too late to catch the ends of sentences, which people tended to mumble, trailing off. I didn't answer right, which is how I knew I had gotten it wrong. Amelia said I nodded and smiled. She said she could tell when I hadn't heard because my smile took on a frozen quality. I wondered what I looked like in these moments, and why my sister always noticed when my parents did not.

In the back of the café, I stashed my backpack with its water bottle and a sweater I probably would never need. I tied on my apron. I mumbled a hello to Louisa, thinking she was in the kitchen. But when I swung through into the main room to right the upside-down chairs from the tables and swivel the closed sign on the door around to open, I saw her standing at the counter.

I had heard nothing from the café and thought it was empty. I slapped a smile on my face. My dad said the world couldn't scare me.

"We had a special order," Louisa said. A brown paper sack sat on the counter. She pushed it toward me. She finished filling a cardboard cup at the shiny espresso machine and fastened a lid on top, pushing the cup toward me too. "Would you mind delivering this?"

"Deliver it?"

Louisa had never said anything about delivery before.

Though I was already sixteen, my parents wouldn't let me get my driver's license. I wasn't sure when they ever would. They wouldn't let me practice, though the long, empty roads in the valley seemed perfect for it.

"I can't—" I started to say.

"Just run it across the street for me."

Only the post office was over there. The post office and the library, where I wasn't allowed to go.

As if reading my thoughts, Louisa said, "To the library. Captain forgot his breakfast."

"Captain?"

Louisa tapped the folded top of the paper bag. She had written on the bag in black Sharpie: *Captain* with a smiley face below the name. That didn't answer my question. "It's prepaid, so just run it _____, okay?"

"Okay."

I didn't want to tell her all the things I couldn't do. I couldn't drive. I couldn't use the internet, or watch TV at home without my parents. I couldn't contact my friends back in Ohio (how could I, without the internet or my own phone?); I could only write letters I buried in my schoolwork, letters that were more to myself than to them. I couldn't go to school. I couldn't hear.

I couldn't hear.

I grabbed the bag and coffee and crossed the road.

I looked over my shoulder once, feeling like I could sense my mom watching from the store. She would see me; she would tell my dad. They would not understand—he would not: I was just following Louisa's orders. She had been so insistent about the delivery. It seemed unlike her, the boss I had known so far: easygoing, forgiving, apparently unconcerned about the little business the café did.

But behind me, the grocery store windows looked dark, as grimy as the café. I couldn't see my mom. I couldn't see anyone inside the library, either, the windows tinted against the sun. I noticed a metal emblem on the side of the building, a square yellow sign with a black line on the bottom and a circle with triangles inside.

All the buildings in this not-town, this hardly-a-town, seemed so small. Toy buildings on a model railroad, like someone could smash them with a fist.

Hands full, I opened the library door with my shoulder. Cool air washed over me. Air-conditioning. It felt like a miracle. Despite the tiny size of the library from the outside, the inside opened up into a two-story room that felt airy and bright. A desk stood to my right, and before me were rows of shelves, a little seating area with a table of computers and worn-looking chairs and a couch.

Three people were in the library, not counting me. An older man slept under a newspaper on one of the ratty armchairs. A younger man placed books from a rolling cart onto a shelf. And a man stood waiting before the desk, his back to me. He wore hiking shorts, a nylon shirt, and boots that looked expensive. Nice, new active clothes. They were missing the dirt that seemed to glom on to everything I wore out here. The man had his hat on backwards and his sunglasses on inside. They were polarized, glassy rainbows.

"Hello," the man called out. From his tone, he sounded like he had been waiting a while. "Does anyone work here? Anyone?" He brought his hand down hard on a silver bell on the desk. It clanged with a high and sharp ping.

The man below the newspaper, who had been snoring, stopped with a snort. The person stocking the shelves didn't even turn around. Sunglasses rang the bell again. He banged it repeatedly.

Ping ping ping.

Someone appeared through a door behind the desk, a man with pale wispy hair and glasses. He wore a striped blue-and-yellow bow tie—in this heat—though his shirtsleeves were short and he went without a jacket. "Can I help you?"

"Finally," Sunglasses said. "I need _____ directions."

"This isn't a gas station," the librarian said, "but we do have maps."

"You're funny. I need directions to a dispensary."

"We don't have those."

"Every place in Colorado has those."

"This place doesn't."

Nobody at the library seemed to have noticed me standing by the door. I spoke up. "Louisa's Café has CBD. A CBD latte—that's our specialty."

Sunglasses turned. "Hello there. Who are you?"

My parents tried to shield me from strangers, keep me away from anyone who might correct their views, interfere with their teaching, ask questions. But I knew when a man was looking at me. It was like the snakes; I couldn't escape it.

He took in my appearance and smirked. "Nice apron."

I had forgotten I was wearing it. At least it helped hide my long dress. "I work there," I said. I raised the cup and paper bag, as if they were evidence. Some of the coffee had spilled.

"Where is this café of yours? Can you take me _____?"

"It's not mine. It's Louisa's."

The librarian said, "It's just behind you. You should go there. _____ now."

"So much for friendly locals," Sunglasses said. But he was leaving. He brushed by me, his shoulder bumping into me, causing more coffee to slop onto my hand.

What did he see? A girl in old-fashioned clothes. A girl with hair cut by her mom so it made a jagged curve at her chin. My hair was the color of Colorado dirt, wavy like the leaves of our struggling plants. My eyes were not green like Amelia's, but muddied brown.

I didn't move again until the door closed behind the man. No one did. Then the librarian pushed up his glasses. "He's Louisa's problem now."

"Poor Louisa," I said.

"She can handle it."

"Now she'll make eight dollars."

"I hope she charges him ten," a new voice said.

I turned to the main room. The older man had resettled himself in the chair, finding a comfortable position to sleep again. But the person stocking the shelves had stopped his work and was looking our way. He was my age, I thought, or close to it, with hair that fell long about his tan face, the front parts getting lost in high cheekbones and dark eyes. There was something about his voice that struck me. It sounded familiar.

He sounded like me.

It was as if his voice was half-hidden, rough and soft at the same time. The librarian looked at the boy, then something happened. The boy set a book back onto the cart and moved the fingers of his hand quickly, motioning to the man.

The librarian smiled. His eyes returned to me. "Is that my breakfast?"

"Are you Captain?"

"Captain, my captain."

I set the bag and the cup on the desk, then wiped my hand on my apron. "Sorry I spilled some."

"Not to worry. And thanks for delivering."

"Louisa was pretty forceful about it."

"Well, we're far too busy at the library for me to go over there _____. I couldn't _____."

I looked around. The man had fallen asleep again and was snoring deeply. The boy had resumed restocking the shelves. *Too busy?*

"You're new here," the librarian said. "Your family lives at Cuthbert's old place?"

"I guess so. The house we moved into is unfinished." Could there actually be a story behind its thin walls and bare sides?

"That was Cuthbert. He never could finish a damn thing."

"He's gone now."

"Of course. Headed back to California or Michigan or wherever he came from. Most families can't make it _____, not from elsewhere." He looked at me over his glasses. "Not you, of course."

"We just moved from Ohio. My dad doesn't really know how to farm here."

I was not sure why I was telling so much to a stranger, except he seemed like a kind stranger, and he was the first person I had talked to in weeks who wasn't my mom, dad, Amelia, or Louisa. I was hungry for conversation, desperate for it. And I could follow much of what Captain said. He looked at me when he spoke. I felt a rare lift from being heard.

"Few do know," Captain said. "Especially since we drove off the people who farmed here first. Let me introduce you around. That's Elmer, taking a power nap, like most mornings. And that's Ray, our volunteer."

The boy waved. He had an awkward way of hunching his shoulders, as if his body had grown too tall overnight and he was still unused to his arms.

"I'm Thea," I said. "Thea Taylor."

"Welcome to the valley, Thea Taylor. We can help you here at the library. You can study the weather. What to _____." Captain indicated the computers. "Though it's hard to really know what to expect these days. Just the unexpected."

The computers looked dark and still, and they were outdated,

I knew, like the computers had been at my former school: humming desktops with heavy, clunky backs.

"Do you want to get set up with a library card? We can log you in. You can check your email and social media at least."

"That's okay." How could I tell this librarian with his kind eyes and thin yellow hair like corn silk that I didn't have social media? I didn't know if anyone would be emailing me, not anymore. It had been too long, with too much silence on my end. "I should get back to the café."

Captain put his hand over his heart solemnly, as if he was going to say the Pledge of Allegiance. "I cannot, in good faith, let you leave this library without getting a library card. I'll get it started for you. It'll just take _____. Where is that paperwork?" He looked on the desk, riffling through several stacks of paper, then disappeared through a glass door which led to a closet-sized office. There was another metal door in the wall beside it.

I wanted to go back to the café, but it seemed rude to leave the librarian like that, when he was expecting me to wait. I wandered away from the desk, into the main room, my fingers drifting over the shelves.

Would my dad let us check out books? What if they were older books, stories he and my mom approved of, like *Little House on the Prairie* or *The Lion, The Witch, and the Wardrobe*? I had read those books before, but I wouldn't mind reading them again. We had gotten rid of a lot before we moved, including boxes of chapter books. I could read to Amelia, help her with her vocab. I saw the library had *The Last Unicorn*, a favorite.

I stopped. The boy at the cart was looking at me.

"What was your name?" he asked.

There was that slight hitch in his voice, the tone I thought I could recognize whenever I spoke, though I didn't know why. Amelia didn't sound like me. Neither did my parents. Even I could tell sometimes I sounded different than them.

"Thea," I said.

"Ray."

I held out my hand, but he didn't take it. Instead, he made a movement with his fingers, like the one he had made before.

He was signing.

Ray knew sign language.

I tried to ignore how my heart was beating into my chest. I dropped my hand. I felt unmoored, almost dizzy. "What's that?" I asked.

"My name sign."

"What's a name sign?"

"For me, the letter *R*." He showed me again. How could his fingers move so swiftly, so smoothly?

"Why do you have that?"

"Someone gave it to me. I'm hard of hearing," Ray said. And when I didn't respond, he said, "Deaf."

My heart beat so fast, so hard, it hurt.

I should tell him. I *had* to tell him. What were the chances I would meet someone like me who looked to be my age? Everyone I had ever run into who was deaf—a cashier in a store back in Ohio, a substitute at school when I had been allowed to attend—was elderly. They weren't born this way, as I had been. They weren't young.

I found my voice had dried up. All my words were gone. My head pounded, and I could not say it, could not tell him.

Everything I might have said swirled inside me, like that dust storm, words and questions crashing against my rib cage, knocking against my throat, which had gone tight. My parents had taught me not to say anything. To hide. To pretend I was fine. And I *was* fine. I was also different.

I was like Ray.

Here in this tiny town in the desert was the first person I had met who was deaf like me.

4

I didn't know if I could identify myself to him, this stranger, if I should. I didn't even know what to call myself. Ray had said he was hard of hearing. But my dad called me *impaired* whenever he explained what he described as my *flightiness* to people in public.

It was only desperation that would cause my dad to speak up, when it was painfully obvious something was off about me and they looked at him with questions in their eyes. I had missed a request. I had made a mistake, answered strangely. Or stayed silent, which was also a mistake.

She can't, you know, he would say, excusing me like I had done something wrong, like I was embarrassing him, when all I had done was not hear. He made a motion at these times, a kind of waving at his own ears, as if a stranger would know what that meant. Like it was rude, somehow, to say it out loud, or to name it—to say anything at all about my hearing.

I was here, I reminded myself. I was at this tiny library.

In front of this boy who had signed to me, while behind us a librarian by the name of Captain was filling out a library card for me. And out of the tinted windows, the wind picked up. Dust skittered over the lonely road.

"I should go," I said. I turned so quickly I knocked into a shelf. Several of the books on the end display spilled onto the floor. "I'm sorry."

The books were new, titles I had never heard of, their covers bright, glossy, and hopeful. There was so much I didn't know, so much that had been kept from me and from my sister. Ray said the sign was a name sign and that someone had given it to him. Could someone give one to me? How did you learn to make your hands move so fast, so sure? But the librarian had learned. Captain seemed to know what Ray had signed to him. He had smiled, recognizing some word or phrase.

Ray bent to help me pick up the books. Our fingers brushed and I straightened up immediately.

His brown eyes met mine and I blurted it out before I lost my nerve: "What did you sign to the librarian? When that man was in here before?"

"*Rude*," Ray said. "I signed that he was rude."

"Well, he was."

Ray smiled. "Yes, he was."

"And Captain knew it? He knew what you said?"

"Captain knows a few signs. Useful for when you don't want abled people to know what you're talking about." He smiled again, knowingly.

But I couldn't smile. I didn't know. *Abled people?* Did he mean people who could hear more than I could? Or—the thought came to me as sudden and hopeful as a bird—more than *we* could?

Then Ray pulled out a phone from his back pocket. That made him different from me, worlds away. He unlocked the screen, lifting his eyes from the phone to meet mine again. I didn't know if he was going to ask if we could exchange numbers or text, or if he was looking up something that had nothing to do with me.

It didn't matter. I didn't have a phone—I wasn't allowed to—so I was out of this conversation.

I mumbled a goodbye, and this time I exited quickly. Out of the main room, to the atrium by the desk. Captain had returned with some papers. But I headed straight for the door.

"Wait!" Captain said. "Your library card. You just need _____."

He was waving the paperwork, and he might have said something else, but I didn't hear it. And I was already gone.

The café looked empty. Sunglasses had gotten his latte and left. Or probably, I thought as the door crashed behind me, never came in at all. He had taken one look at the outside with its dirty windows, its handwritten signs, the gas station next door with pumps that wouldn't even take credit cards, and driven off into the sunset.

Behind the counter, Louisa stared. I must have slammed the door harder than I meant to.

"How was the delivery?" she asked.

"Fine." I ignored my heart, still beating fast.

"What did you think of the library?"

"It's fine." I felt the hot spike of adrenaline. I knew later I would pore over that moment in the library, second-guessing myself, thinking of our hands touching, his eyes. Had I done the right thing by leaving? "Did you want me to deliver something else?"

"No. I just wonder if _____?" Louisa said. "If you met anyone?"

"I met the librarian. And a snoring man. And some tourist who said he was coming here for a latte but I guess not."

Rude.

I remembered Ray's hands. The sign was like a finger scraping across a tabletop.

"Is that all?" Louisa asked, kindly enough.

"No, that's not all." She wasn't going to stop until I said it. "I met Ray."

Louisa grinned, satisfied.

"Is this . . ." I fumbled for the words, "some kind of setup? I'm not allowed to have a boyfriend."

I wasn't allowed to have anything.

"No. We just thought—you're the same age, and we thought you could use a friend. Ray spends summers here, with his great-uncle. The rest of the year he lives in Denver with his mom. And he's learned to sign, from the kids at school in _____."

"The librarian knows signs. Do you?"

"A little."

"Why?"

"Well," Louisa said. "We were trying to be helpful, to make Ray feel welcome when he first came here. Sam, his great-uncle, thought it might give him options. You should talk to Ray about it."

"I can't sign," I said desperately, even though Ray had spoken to communicate with me, and we had understood each other. I needed Louisa to know for some reason. I needed her to understand: I did not have what Ray seemed to. I did not have another language. I did not have family—a mom, a great-uncle, she had said—who understood me, who *tried*. Lost. I was lost. "I don't know sign language."

Louisa turned back to the counter, then remembered she needed to face me when she spoke. "Maybe he can help with that."

Over the course of the day, which was slow and hot, as they all were, Louisa dribbled out bits of information about Ray. Information I hadn't asked for, but felt strangely hungry for, like the dogs gathering for scraps after supper.

Ray was sixteen, but he had been driving since he was twelve. Many farm kids did and Louisa was surprised, frankly, that I hadn't learned yet. His parents had divorced when he was little, and his dad lived far away and wasn't much interested in being a dad, so his mom sent him to Sam when school was out. He went to a public school in the city with a center program for the deaf and hard of hearing. His mom was an artist and worked as a park ranger in the summer season, toting watercolors and easels up mountains in between giving tours and directions to tourists. She couldn't watch him and work when he was a kid. Then, Louisa said, Ray just got used to coming to the valley.

"And we got used to having him around. Especially Sam."

Sam was a rural outreach agent, driving all over the valley checking in on people on their farms and homesteads. He made sure they had enough water when it got hot, wood when it got cold.

"I'm surprised Sam hasn't been out to see you yet," Louisa said. "Your family's probably next on his _____."

More than anything else Louisa had said in her long day of talking at me while I refilled the sugars and married the ketchups and swept and swept, that comment made me feel strange. Nervous. And ashamed.

What would Ray's great-uncle think if he visited our farm with its unfinished house? The fields of dust and all the dogs? And my sister with dirt on her face? My little sister left on her own while my dad tried to coax nothing from the ground. She played on the fallen-down shed or somewhere else probably dangerous when she was supposed to be doing lessons. Would Sam understand we were both supposed to be doing them?

Louisa hadn't asked too many questions when she gave me a job. It was still summer. But what would happen when September rolled around and I didn't have to stop working?

I knew whatever Sam did for the county, my dad would not accept his help, be it firewood or seeds or advice about farming. We were on our own, the way my dad wanted. He wanted to farm using the old ways, relying on gadgets and electricity as little as possible. And refusing to rely on other people too.

"Ray got so bored when Sam went out on his rounds," Louisa was saying. "Sam would take him out wherever he was going, but the kid just sat in the truck, you _____? It's a long drive out to some of these homesteads. Poor kid was spending all day _____. So, we got the idea that he should volunteer at the library. That keeps him busy. A kid needs to have something to do, someplace to go." She gave me a look.

"Does the library really need a volunteer?" I pictured the single room. The one patron, asleep.

"Every place could always use a little help," Louisa said. "Every person too."

At lunchtime, Louisa would let me have my pick of the bagels, sandwiches, and pastries. Sometimes there was soup if she had felt particularly ambitious the night before, but I was not sure who would want hot soup in this heat. Louisa didn't always plan her items well, missing out on holiday-themed cookies and not even offering iced coffee or tea this summer. She was both no-nonsense and distracted. *A dreamer,* my mom would say, who lit candles in the summertime and was busy making suncatchers she said would be ready for sale in the fall, when I imagined there wouldn't be as much sun. At least, I hoped there wouldn't be.

It was hard to think about living here for that long. I still felt like the valley was a phase, something my dad would grow out of, a temporary pause in my real life.

I gathered a ham-and-cheese sandwich and a fizzy juice from the refrigerated case and went out back. I couldn't picture myself living in this place through another season.

Behind the kitchen, in the dirt parking lot between the café and the grocery store, sat an old picnic table. Louisa had chained it to a metal fire barrel, in case anyone tried to steal it.

"No one's stealing you," I said to the table as I sat down.

The barrel was so rusted, its sides looked like lace. Dust

whipped through the lot. Little swirls of it peppered my parents' truck, parked there. I wondered when the truck, already a bit banged up from fender benders before we had owned it, would start to be damaged. Could dust cause dents? I felt this dust could.

The grocery next door where my mom worked was called Second Chance. It sold *second-chance goods,* as my mom had explained to me and my sister when she first got the job: dented cans, packages of pasta or boxes of cookies about to expire. Those items that had already expired, she brought home to us.

Most of the cereals and dish soaps and jars of preserved goods in Second Chance were from brands I had never heard of, like Lucky and Good Home and Sunshine. The vegetables and fruits looked wilted—but so did the plants in our fields. Farmers shopped at the store, always needing a break.

The fluorescent lights of the store burned so brightly, my mom had a headache most nights after work. Like I did, from listening. When she brought home bread, we always had to check it for mold. (We had not realized this the first few times, and my dad said this was yet another reason we should bake our own.)

But sometimes, my mom brought home big bottles of soda with names like Bright and Dr. Pop. We were never allowed to have soda back in Ohio. In the old stories of pioneer life my dad loved so much, people drank buttermilk or spring-clear water, cold and fresh. Water was a luxury in the valley, though.

My dad said soon enough we would be growing our own food. Soon, we would have plenty of fresh vegetables, enough to sell at a farmers' market, enough we would have to give the extras away to neighbors, like we used to.

What neighbors? I had thought.

From the picnic table, I watched the dust spiral. The whirls ran into the door of the grocery and broke apart again. I wished I could move like they could, just twist myself out of here.

Second Chance was to my right. Inside the store, my mom ripped open boxes and put away dry goods under the lights that hurt her head. On my left, past the truck, Louisa had her house. It was one story—everything seemed to be ground-level out here, closer to the dirt and with basements or storm cellars burrowed deep inside—not too much smaller than ours, even though it was only her who lived there. The house had white siding stained by dust, striped metal awnings over the windows. There was a table out front with an umbrella, like at a pool. The umbrella tilted sideways, askew from the wind.

Louisa had wind chimes hanging on hooks along her house, twisting and pinging with a sound like rain. She also had plants, bushy herbs in bright pots. I recognized lavender, mint, and rosemary. Maybe she was an optimist, a dreamer, because *her* plants were growing, thriving.

I knew my dad needed help with the farm. It was too much for him, too much for all of us. And he was wrong about the weather. The climate had been changing, even back in Ohio. There, the temperature had dropped too cold for too long in the spring. Snow fell well into May. Then, the weather turned baking hot too quickly. And when the rain came, it overwhelmed. It swelled the river, rushing through town.

A hundred-year flood, the newspapers said.

But it had been less than a hundred years since the last one.

My parents had overcorrected and moved us to a desert—a desert where the original inhabitants had been forced to leave,

Captain had said. When we had first moved to the valley, my dad had pointed out all the ditches and canals. From the air, if we had flown, instead of driving the many-days trip, we would have seen wells all over the ground, patching the land in green and yellow circles like a quilt. There were thousands of wells in the valley, my dad said.

He didn't know what Louisa had told me: that some people had wells on their farms, some had river rights—and we on our little farm had neither. He didn't know that years of pumps and irrigation had drained the river, and the snowmelt from the mountains amounted to less and less every year. Farmers held meetings about it at the Grange down the highway, meetings I thought my dad should go to.

The farmers debated things like: who had a right to the river? Who had to pay for it? Who was draining it? That last question had an answer, Louisa said: factory farms and big corporations. And drought and rising temperatures meant the water level was shrinking every year. The river was drying up.

Louisa talked about these meetings to me, kept the coffee pots warm long into the evenings for the farmers who were going to attend. She never charged them for a cup. Or for refills.

The Bloodless Valley stretched wide, clear into New Mexico. Farms dotted it, and some were big businesses, big money-making industries. National beer companies got their barley from the valley, my dad made sure to tell us on our drive west. He jokingly (not too jokingly, I thought) called the beer in our fridge *local*.

He didn't tell us—maybe he didn't know—what that really meant. That some people owned water and some didn't, Louisa said. And some businesses were using a lot and some farmers weren't allowed to. Nothing could grow without water, I knew that. The ditches and canals, even when my dad had first pointed them out, they all looked dry.

I finished my sandwich. I balled up the wrapping, and took it and the empty can inside. In the café, a man sat at the counter. I recognized him, the brown-eyed cowboy. He was in his sixties or so, with earth-colored skin and friendly lines around his eyes.

"This is Sam," Louisa said. "I should have introduced you before."

"Ray's Sam?" I asked.

The man smiled. "I like being referred to that way. I *am* Ray's Sam. Louisa was just telling me more about your family, that maybe I ought to go out to your _____?"

I dumped my trash and pitched the can into the recycling. "I'm not sure."

"Do you know what I do? I'm sort of outreach for the county. I go around seeing if families need anything. We can offer a lot, for free—help with heating _____, a ride to the doctor or _____ prescriptions. Maybe you folks need some help getting started out _____?"

"My dad won't want that."

"The man that built that house of yours didn't last a year."

This stopped me. I had my hand on the rim of the trash can. I was about to ask Louisa if I should take it out back and put a new bag in, but I froze. I thought of our rickety house. I thought of the dogs that had just shown up, most of them thin, like they hadn't eaten in a while.

"Why did the owner leave?" I asked.

"I'm not sure. Money running out? _____ support?"

"We don't have family here."

"That's not the only kind of support," Louisa said. "You're not alone, even if your dad thinks he is."

Her words and the words of the man with the wrinkly, dark eyes, Ray's great-uncle, made me feel the best I had since coming to this place. Stronger, somehow. But Louisa and Sam hadn't met my dad. He could go for hours without speaking to any of us, and none of us, my mom, my sister, were allowed to ask what was wrong, if something was upsetting him. A question like that would send him into a rage. *Can't a man be alone with his thoughts?*

He would storm off into the fields, to stare at them some more, or head off hunting. And then it would take even longer for him to come back inside, to come back around and talk to us again. He wouldn't apologize. He never apologized. He would only say he was tired. He was always so tired.

Eventually some kind of switch would flick in his brain. He would realize how gruff he was being, how distant and cold. He would see how Amelia's eyes had reddened, or how my mom had turned back to the dishes in the sink, not even meeting his glance anymore, not even trying.

Everything is going to work out just fine, he would say then and pick Amelia up, swing her around the room, even though her tight smile told me she didn't want to be carried. She was getting too big for that.

Louisa and Sam didn't know that my dad believed a man's whole world was his household. He was the head of that world, and no one—not my mom, not my boss or a librarian or the county outreach agent or me—could tell him how to run it. How to rule it. He ruled without objection, without doubt from us, his family, though he seemed to be full of nothing *but* doubt, I thought sometimes, the way he stared at the sky and hoped for anything but sun and dry heat to come from it. He waited for the traditional ways from his books to work. He expected us to listen with no questions.

I had questions, though. A lot of them.

Louisa said, "You know Captain came in while you were at lunch?"

"Captain?" I turned to face her so I could hear.

"He said they could use someone else over at the library. He's ordering new books and needs some help organizing _____. Another young person who knows what young people read."

"I don't really know what young people read," I said.

"Someone to help Ray. Maybe a few hours a week?"

I didn't understand what she was offering. "My job is here."

"And you're wonderful at it. But, look around, my dear."

I did, taking in the counter with only Sam sitting there. Several of the stools beside him were so disused, dust flew up if you sat down on them. Louisa told me she was afraid she would never pay off the espresso machine, and she sent home more pastries with me at the end of the day than we ever sold during our open hours.

"I can spare you," Louisa said.

"Am I being fired?"

"No!" Louisa laughed and Sam took a sip of his coffee. I could see the sides of his mouth turning up in a smile. "I'm only saying if you want to spend time at the library, feel free _____ there when it's slow here. You're helping the community out."

"Helping Captain and Ray out," Sam said.
"It won't count as your break."
"I don't really think I should."
"I won't tell your folks," Louisa said.
And then there was no reason not to.

5

It was called *unschooling*, my dad said. He had read about it in his books, in his newsletters that arrived at our house folded like prayers. He read about it more and more the first year of the pandemic, when school had stopped briefly. He thought, *What if it stopped forever?*

The flood the very next year provided another perfect excuse. Our school buildings had been damaged. Who knew how long until mold would bloom in the walls? *What a tragedy*, the newspaper wrote, *for local children just recently back at school to be ripped from it again.* School was dangerous, my dad thought.

Better to never send us back. Better to try this new idea, which was actually an old one. Unschooling. Homesteading. Working the land and doing it alone. *Not contributing to the "grinding machine of capitalism,"* he said, quoting.

We would go for hikes, learning about the flowers and

plants we saw along the way. We would take field trips to the capital city, Columbus, and go to museums, art galleries, the zoo. We would read, write journal entries, work on recipes in the kitchen. I could help out with the farm more, learning about science, weather, agriculture, with my hands actually in the earth. I wouldn't be stuck in some stuffy classroom all the time.

And every Saturday, we would go to the farmers' market in town, where my parents had a stall (really, a tent attached to the open bed of our truck). We sold vegetables, jam, and hand cream my mom and I made. My sister and I would work on our math skills by making change.

With unschooling, I could explore, really get into the things *I* was interested in, my dad said, not just the dry old subjects some school board made me learn.

But the reality was, I learned the subjects my dad wanted me to learn, which wasn't really science, art, culture, or history at all. I read the books he wanted me to read, as old or older than the books we had been reading in school: *Lord of the Flies, The Scarlet Letter, A Separate Peace.* Books he remembered from his youth and that we already had at the farm, or ones we could easily pick up used. My parents didn't want to spend a lot of money, not on teaching us.

I resisted the unschooling idea at first, refused it. And then eighth grade happened to me.

And at first, there did seem to be some benefits to this idea of unschooling, things that almost—I told myself—made up for not being in school. I could sleep in as late as I wanted, get snacks from the kitchen whenever I was hungry. I could spend more time with Amelia and be outside under the trees, rather than in a classroom with the windows painted shut.

At first, my parents wrote a schedule on a whiteboard in the kitchen. Mornings were for chores and reading. Afternoons, we would go for a nature hike or journey into town for an adventure, then work on math in the kitchen.

But in only a matter of weeks, that schedule fell apart. My parents were too busy to take us to town or on a hike. There was too much work to do on the farm, work that soon overwhelmed any learning. We saw the homeschool group only for social activities, never anything educational like lessons. Amelia and I spent most of our unschooling days cooking, cleaning, weeding, and sleeping.

I had stopped sleeping in since I got the job at the café. I rose early to get a ride with my mom, and even in that hazy hour, hurried to get some chores done before we left, watering the plants nearest the house, making sure the chickens were out of their coop and grazing.

What was I learning?

Sometimes I thought of the arguments I would make to my dad, the points I would raise. I went over them in my head when I was alone, pulling weeds or scattering chicken feed.

I had already known before how to take care of plants and animals, that was one point. Yes, Colorado was a brand-new place with different wildlife, history, and certainly weather, and I would have loved to learn more about those things. But my parents were not teaching them. There had been no mention of nature hikes, not since we moved so deeply into nature.

There had been no field trips, not since driving to the nearest Walmart would take hours.

And Amelia and I had not met—not even glimpsed—any other kids in the Bloodless Valley.

Not until Ray.

It was easier not to question my dad. I argued with him in my head. But when he was around, I fell silent. All my arguments seemed to die in my throat. To spend time in the library, any time, like Louisa had told me I could, like Sam and the librarian encouraged me to do, was to stand against my dad. If he found out, I would be punished.

The thought came to me as my mom drove us to work: *What could he do to me, though?* He had already taken me from school, from my home and my friends. What was left?

Your job, the answer came as clear as the Colorado sky.

I watched the fences and fields of wheat race by, and tried to dismiss the thought. We needed my paycheck, small as it was. We hadn't yet found a farmers' market to sell at, and besides, we had nothing *to* sell. The only money coming in—to pay for food for us and the animals, for gas for the truck and generator, for water—came from me and my mom.

I sat up in my seat. Something had changed about the boring drive, shifted. The road looked different. Dirtier, somehow. My mom drove over sandy-colored stretches. It was like a beach had somehow drifted onto the highway.

"What happened here?" I asked.

Her eyes didn't leave the road. "I don't know. Maybe they had a storm last night, closer to town."

"A dust storm?" I asked.

But if she answered me, I didn't hear it.

I would go in then, I decided. I would help at the library. And if I had a chance at the computers, to check the weather, to see if I could reach my old friends like Ellee, so be it. And if Ray, the boy who was hard of hearing, was there—well, there was nothing I could do about that.

At the café, as soon as I dropped off my bag and turned over the chairs and the CLOSED sign, I told Louisa I was leaving. I barely even glanced around. I knew I had to go before I could lose my nerve, before I could talk myself out of it.

This early, only Captain was inside the library, placing a new trash bag in the can by the door. I hadn't even considered the possibility that the building might not be open.

But it was, or Captain pretended it was. "Glad you're here," he said brightly, as if he had been expecting me, as if I had an appointment. "I have your library card all ready. I just need a signature from you."

I signed it, then asked, "Can I get on the computer?"

Captain looked around the yawning, empty room. "I think we can manage that." He helped me log in, pointed out the search browser. "I'll just be at my desk, if you need me."

I wanted to immediately check my email, but I was afraid. That I might have a bunch of messages. That I might not have any at all. I couldn't bear to look. I did a search instead.

There was nothing about our valley, maybe because the dust storms had just happened or maybe because the area was so small. We didn't even have a newspaper. Maybe no one outside of the valley knew what was going on here. I read about dust storms in the west and southwest. They happened suddenly, could be miles wide and thousands of feet high, and contained not only dust but particles of debris. That was what made them so dangerous.

I thought of the pelting sound I had heard two nights ago, when gusts had struck the windows of our house as hard as fists. Like most sounds, it had been difficult for me to place, to know where it was coming from. And no one would expect dust to have a sound.

I looked up from the screen to see Elmer, the snoring man, had entered the library, looking more bedraggled than before. He coughed with a chest-knocking noise that made his shoulders shake. Then he said something about power lines. They were out, he said. Down near his place.

I hadn't even looked around when I had gone into the café, I realized. I had just left Louisa alone. I felt a weird sense of unease, that these storms weren't just storms but previews of something bigger, like how it had rained for days and days before the flood at home.

I stood up from the computer. Captain and Elmer glanced over at me. "I have to go."

I was through the little lobby and out the door before they could say a word. I hadn't logged out of the computer. I hadn't even taken my library card.

In Louisa's Café, Louisa was alone, washing tables. The whole room had a kind of patina to it, yellow-gray like a flashback in a movie. A tint of dust. I had barely noticed when I had dashed off to the library. Louisa, too, looked muted, gray.

"I'm sorry for leaving," I said.

She turned. She saw it was me and smiled as she patted her

face and the small white hairs that had escaped from her bun, trying to put herself together. She switched so quickly into pretending everything was fine. I did that too, for Amelia. So did my mom, for both of us.

But the eyes couldn't lie. Louisa's looked watery and red. "It's all right," she said. "Don't you worry about me, kid."

"Did you have a storm last night?" I asked. "Is the dust bad here?"

"It's worse at my house."

I took a rag, dampened it at the sink and started to wipe the counters. They were coated with a skin of dirt, as if the café had been abandoned for years, a forgotten place we had just stumbled upon.

Louisa returned to swiping the tabletop. "You go on to the library whenever you want. I mean that."

I squeezed the rag. "Louisa, I was reading about dust storms. I read that Arizona has three big ones a year."

"Could be."

"We've had maybe two already this summer. Will we have just one more?"

She paused. Her eyes were tired, and she had more of those straggly white hairs than I remembered. I imagined trying to sleep alone in a house, like she did, to survive by myself through a storm. She had no one to tell her everything was going to be all right. No one to lie. All her wind chimes must have rattled and jumped, her plants tipping over, pots smashing or filling with dust.

"I'm not sure what we've had," Louisa said. "And I'm not sure _____ we're having. But something feels different this summer."

I scrubbed harder. I knew back at home Amelia was doing her own scrubbing and sweeping while her lessons languished.

It wasn't home, I reminded myself.

It was just a place we lived.

Unschooling. It should have been called *unspooling*.

That was what I did. I came apart. I unrolled, everything I had learned loosening and spiraling away from me like a spool of thread dropped down a flight of stairs. I forgot, not just equations and long division and who won what old war, but how to talk to people, how to pretend like I had heard them, how to fit in at all, how to make friends.

I still remembered going to school. How tired I often felt in the mornings, hauling myself out of bed, getting dressed, and waiting at the end of our long driveway for the big, wheezing school bus. Often, fog rolled off the green hills and if I watched it long enough, I could see the fog move like a person, a great misty ghost. The bus would always surprise me, breaking through that white wall. It burst through the fog like a football player jumping through a paper screen held by cheerleaders—one of the stunts at the Friday night games the older kids would talk about.

I imagined going to one of those games: what I would wear, who I would sit with. I sat in the back of the bus in a seat by myself, an eighth grader near the high schoolers but wholly apart from them. I stared out the bus window, at the fog fleeing our approach, and tried to listen.

I tried hard.

Those snatches of conversations I could overhear, the chatter from the older kids, would be my only taste of high school, as it turned out. I would never go to a football game. Never letter in a sport or in anything—debate, choir. I would not get to join clubs.

I would be pulled from school. Never to make it beyond the middle school: that squat brick building where the bus dropped us off first, before the high schoolers. Never go to a dance. Never take driver's ed, or pull an all-nighter studying for an exam. I would never take calculus, or physics, or French, or anatomy: the class the high schoolers tried to scare the younger kids about, spinning tales of pigs, the bitter smell of formaldehyde. I would never get college counseling from the overworked, underpaid guidance counselor who told most kids in my town just to apply to Ohio State or JV Tech or nowhere at all. Never experience senior skip day, or write a term paper, or climb a long rope to the rafters in the high school gym.

My parents said, when I first protested leaving school, that I could learn all of those things at home. And in theory, I could.

But I didn't.

My mom turned down the driveway. We had fallen into a pattern of not really speaking on the ride from work, both too exhausted. I knew all I did was complain to her, and she wasn't going to change things. She couldn't. But I still felt frustrated by how she just agreed to every whim of my dad's. They were his dreams, nobody else's.

Now she squinted at the windshield, leaning forward. "Does that sky look right to you?"

It was barely 5 P.M., five in the summer. It wouldn't get dark for hours. But as we watched, the sky churned with a single huge and shadowy cloud. The cloud was wider than the road, larger than the house. And dark.

It hadn't rained once since we had moved here. I wondered if I even remembered what that was like. The drumming on the roof, the silver race of drops across the windows, the relief of cool air. Would our half-built house hold up in a rain?

"Make sure the animals are secure," my mom said.

She parked the truck and hurried off, maybe to find my dad. In the yard, Amelia rushed to me. Wind lashed her hair across her freckled face, and she was breathless with excitement. "Do you think it's going to rain?" she asked.

"I don't know." The air felt strange to me, not cool like before a rain, not tinged with ozone, that sizzling electric scent. It hadn't rained here the night of the storm when it had turned all windy and dark. It hadn't rained at all, only gotten dustier. A cloud had swept across the farm, leaving grit in its wake. "Are the animals okay?"

"I put them inside. All except for the chickens."

"What's wrong with the chickens?"

"It's so strange, Thea. They already went in. You know how they roost at night to sleep?" Amelia knew more about chickens—more about all animals—than me, but I just nodded. "I guess it's so dark, they already went inside. They're roosting in the middle of the afternoon!" She laughed, like this was some new trick of the chickens. But it didn't seem funny to me.

It seemed wrong. Everything was: the big cloud, like fog but thicker, faster. The way the air didn't cool down at all. It still felt hot, motionless and dry. The air hurt, as the heat did.

Inside the house, the dogs were all barking. Amelia had locked them in the laundry room, which wasn't much of one. We had no dryer (that was what the line strung from the house to the fence was for) and the washing machine didn't require electricity. It required someone—me, my mom, or Amelia—to push a heavy pedal up and down. There was space in the room for the dogs, though I bet as soon as my dad came in the house, he would kick them all outside.

But then the wind picked up, howling like a hungry man.

And rain wasn't what came from the sky.

It was dust.

We counted the dogs, pulled down the shades, and closed the curtains in the house, waiting for the sky to finish darkening and the shadows to fall over us. The wind never gave up. My mom thought we should go back to our bedroom, but Amelia couldn't stand being without our parents in the howling darkness. So we dragged in quilts and mattress pads, piled them on the living room floor. We spent an uneasy night in there.

I remembered huddling in the basement of our old house when tornado warnings had beeped across the TV. Back then, I would usually fall asleep to the crackling radio and the hum of the hot water heater, comforting in their way. But tornados passed. It was a moment, an evening, then a tornado moved on, whirling away to someone else. So did floods, swelling some valleys and not others. In the morning, when I would awaken to our home still intact, I would feel grateful we had been spared.

Dust was not a tornado, not a flood, and we were not spared.

When I awoke cramped on the floor, two dogs weighed me

down, curled up on my legs. I woke because I heard coughing. And I hadn't slept well, my back aching from the hard floor and my mind churning with some kind of deep, unsettled feeling, an anxiety I had carried with me through the night. A bad dream?

I sat up, one of the dogs grumbling but not stirring. No one else was awake, not even my mom, who usually woke with the dawn.

But there *was* no dawn. The sky seemed different. Dark and gray. When I slid out from beneath the quilts and dogs and went to the window, lifting a corner of the curtain, the sun looked hazy, as if it hid behind a veil.

I heard the coughing again. A small, high sound.

My sister.

6

Sometimes I felt I had sisters before I had my sister. I had girls I felt as close to as Amelia, who had come into my life when I was six. Emily and Frankie, June and Isabel. Girls I fingerpainted with in elementary, girls I sat next to on the bus and at the long tables in the cafeteria. Girls who shared their Lunchables and Uncrustables. I only had whole-wheat sandwiches that definitely still had the crusts on, but I would trade my mom's homemade cookies.

On the weekends, I went over to their houses, split-levels in neighborhoods with trash pickup and newspaper delivery. And my friends would come out to our small farm in the woods, to wade in the creek or "boot skate" when the weather turned cold, to snuggle the kittens that always seemed to be born in the barn. When we were young, it seemed not to matter that my friends had things I didn't, like flat-screen TVs and internet.

But in middle school, that started to change. My friends got phones.

We shared secrets. Emily's parents were getting divorced, and her dad had a girlfriend already. Frankie's food allergies were worsening, and her mom was going to make her sit at a special table in the lunchroom, separate from everyone. June was afraid to fly on a plane but her family had a spring break trip planned. Isabel had a crush.

I only had one secret. It was about my body. It was something I hid because my parents had warned me to, taught me to. I kept it close as a talisman, tight against my chest. But like the jewelry we would get at the mall, saving up allowances and Grandma money for a heart-shaped necklace we would wear to prove our devotion, my secret was staining me. Poisoning me.

I thought I should tell.

It would help the other girls feel close to me, I thought. I was one of them. I too struggled.

But as soon as I said it, in eighth grade, late at night during one of our sleepovers—I couldn't hear on one side, I struggled in school to follow the teachers' instructions, even to follow my friends' conversations sometimes—I knew it was a different kind of secret.

It was deeper than Emily's parents' divorce and June's fear of flying, even Frankie's food allergies. It was somehow shameful, embarrassing, or it appeared to be for my friends. It was my fault, as none of the other girls' secrets were.

They scooted away from me, on the carpet downstairs in Isabel's basement. Their hands moved to their faces, covering their mouths so I had an even worse time hearing them. They didn't understand. They didn't believe me. And they were so, so sorry for me.

That seems really hard, Emily said.

I just wish you would have told us, Frankie said.

It's like you lied about who you are, Isabel said.

I hadn't lied. Nobody had ever asked about my hearing before, not even my oldest, only friends; I just hadn't volunteered the information. And all the times I had misunderstood, been left behind in a conversation, said the wrong thing, or been shut out?

I just thought you were a bitch, Isabel said.

The word stung. It was the first time a word like that had been directed at me. She had thought that? Did the others? Why hadn't anybody said anything?

Well, you *never said anything,* June said.

There's no lying in the friend group, said Isabel, who was, by virtue of being the oldest, the prettiest with her fluffy blond hair and blue eyes, and the one with the nicest basement, the leader. *We can't be friends if you lie.*

I didn't lie, I said.

But you did.

That was the reason they gave. I was deceitful.

Isabel turned around to text something. That was the clue, the signal for the others to pull out their phones too. They scrolled silently while I just sat there.

My parents said a phone was too much money, too much of a distraction. They said it would hurt my brain. Isabel laughed at something on her screen. A ping as another girl got a text.

It spread through the group like Telephone, my least favorite game because it ended with me. I couldn't pass on the secrets of my whispering friends; I couldn't hear them.

I was not to be trusted. I was *really* the sneaky girl, the one who was pretending all this time.

I was pretending only to get by.

But I couldn't say that. I didn't even know it yet.

The Monday morning after our basement confessions, my friends weren't on the bus. I remember thinking this was strange—maybe they were all out sick? Later I found out Isabel's mother had driven them to school without me.

My friends didn't speak to me during class, but we didn't have many chances once the bell rang. I wanted to pass a note through the rows of desks as the teachers droned on, but I didn't know what I would write.

Are you mad at me?

Did I do something wrong?

Did I do something?

You didn't do enough, I could picture Isabel answering, the head of the mighty five-headed dragon.

At lunch, which was to be one of Frankie's last lunches not at the peanut-free table, I set my tray beside Emily and June. They moved their trays away. I sat down, and they took their trays and rose, moving to another table where they sat laughing, sharing Uncrustables.

Gone were Emily and Frankie, June and Isabel.

And gone was me. My parents pulled me out of school, discovering—though I certainly didn't tell them—in the way of adults that I was being bullied. Something had happened to me, and whoever was to blame (was it my fault for speaking up, telling my friends?), I would be the one punished.

Urgent phone calls took place in the kitchen. My parents spoke in stage whispers late into the night, when I was supposed to be sleeping. I couldn't hear the words, not really. Only my name, hissed.

Then one morning not long after the incident, I woke to find a row of freshly sharpened yellow pencils by my place at the breakfast table. It was my first day of home school, *un*school, my mom announced.

My dad had always wanted to do it. They had both been reading so much about it and well, now, after the pandemic and the flood, it was time. All the arrows seemed to be pointing this way. My bad experience in middle school was only the latest catalyst, and the last one.

When you're looking closely enough, everything is a sign.

It would be an adventure for the whole family, my mom said. My new life was beginning. My old life was over. Overnight.

I hadn't known my dad wanted to unschool, not really. I didn't even know the word. I hadn't paid much attention to the newsletters arriving, the books he studied with their covers of kids frolicking in long grass, grinning in flower crowns, holding up chickens. He studied newsletters and books with names like *Return to Eden, Mother Earth Monthly, The Back to the Land Plan,* nodding off over them after dinner.

I thought they were just about gardening. I didn't know they had anything to do with us, those smudged sheets with black-and-white illustrations like the Vermont Country Store catalog.

But in their pages, he had first found the seed of unschooling.

Later, he would see an ad in one of the newsletters for a farm.

Everything was a message telling him to go.

The school wasn't a safe place. My friends had turned away from me. Now we would turn away from the school. His newsletters would tell him how.

At noon the next day, Sam blew through the café door. He had a jitteriness about him.

"I've been running all morning," he said as he set his hat on the counter. Dust circled its rim like powdered sugar. "Some families lost power in last night's storm. How about you, Thea? Is your power out?"

Our power was never on.

I shook my head. "We have a generator."

"I'll get out to your place soon, I promise. It's just this storm. I've been sawing tree limbs to _____ off the roads."

Louisa moved to the shelf where the mugs sat. We had had to rewash them all to get the dust out.

But Sam said, "I can't stay. Got to grab some lunch and get back _____. Ray is waiting for me in the truck." He went to the sandwich case.

Louisa said, "Thea, you've done enough work this morning for a whole day."

I glanced at her, uncertain how to respond.

Sam knew, though. Some look passed between them, subtle enough I wouldn't have noticed except I was staring at them. "Do you want to tag along?" he asked. "We could use the help and Ray would love to hang out with someone _____. Most of the homesteaders are older. Loners, who don't like to talk _____."

"And Ray loves to talk." Louisa was already setting out another wrapped sandwich, filling three cardboard cups with the iced tea I had only just convinced her to offer for sale.

I was not sure *I* liked to talk, what I would say to Ray or Sam, or how long we would be gone. But the thought of sitting next to Ray brought a strange warmth to me. It spread through my chest and limbs, as if I had stepped outside into the baking air.

"I have to be back before the end of the day," I said. "If my mom comes—"

"I'll be your alibi, don't worry," Louisa said.

Ray waited in the front seat of Sam's old yellow truck, staring out the dirty window. When he saw me, he grinned. I had made him smile. I had brought a smile to his face. *Me.*

My face was moving by itself, turning up into its own grin. I probably looked ridiculous, I realized a second too late, wishing I had thought to check my reflection in the café restroom or at least the shiny espresso machine. Why did Louisa think Ray and I might get along? Was it just because we both couldn't hear? But I had had less in common with my good friends from home.

Ray opened the door for me and scooted over until he was in the middle of the wide front seat, leaving room beside him. That meant he and Sam would be on my deaf side; I wouldn't be able to hear them if they spoke. There was a squashed back seat in the truck, but it looked like the knees of anyone sitting there would bump right against the driver, and the seat was already crowded with gear, anyway: jackets and work gloves, water.

I didn't know Ray or Sam very well. Did they know about me? How much had Louisa said? And how different were things for Ray, who could sign, who had the support of his family? He had two languages when I barely had one.

I didn't want to make a big deal out of things, to remind them I was different. Silently, I took the seat beside Ray. Our legs touched then sprang apart. Sam stuck the tea into drink holders and I closed the passenger side door, which squeezed me and Ray close together again—and this time, with the door closed, there was no space in the cab to break apart. Sam started the truck, which came to life with a roar.

It would be a silent drive then, too loud to talk.

But as we headed out onto the highway, Ray asked me a question. He touched my arm in order to do so, to alert me to turn.

The feel of his hand sent a pulse through me. I fixated on his knee, bare in shorts, then reminded myself he was talking—and I couldn't make out the words. He was asking how my family was, or how we did in the storm?

I thought fast and gave an answer that wouldn't seem too out of nowhere, I hoped. "My sister has started coughing."

"Asthma's pretty common _____," Sam said, his eyes never leaving the road. He didn't turn toward me so I could see his lips. He said something else, something . . . *before*. Maybe: *Did she have it before? Or, did I?*

I shook my head.

We drove for a time in silence. Then Ray tucked his hair

behind his ear and I saw it: the hearing aid. It was small, barely visible. What a pair we made, both on each other's deaf sides. Or, maybe Ray wore two hearing aids. I had so many questions. How well did they work? Were they worth it? My dad said insurance wouldn't pay for hearing aids. Not that we had insurance.

Ray must have felt me looking at him. He glanced over, smiled again. I looked quickly away. The highway was grimy, dust piling on the sides, tumbleweeds bouncing onto the road.

"We'll head out to Helen's," Sam said. "She lives alone and it's always the loners I try to check on first. Helen's not the kind to ask for _____."

I nodded. Ray said something to Sam and they laughed. A joke I wasn't in on. I knew it wasn't about me, but it didn't matter. I couldn't keep up.

I wasn't worried about my mom and dad finding out I had left the café. They didn't want me at the library, on the computers, I knew. But riding out with Sam and Ray seemed like more of a gray area.

I was going to help. Community was something that had mattered back home, where we had shared our food. Where our neighbors had left hand-me-downs on the porch. And where I had friends, good friends like Ellee, who I had met once my parents pulled us from school and we met up with other homeschooling and unschooling families.

Unschooling had meant no more bus for me. No more cafeteria, recess. No more chances for my former friends to make fun of me, to shut me out at the lunch table, to turn away from me in class, or to whisper in the halls. Whispers I could never really hear or respond to.

And at first, I had felt relieved. My parents had fixed my problem. They had made it go away. Made my old friends, my life, vanish like magic. I wouldn't have to face those mean girls again. That feeling of relief and escape lasted a day, maybe two, before the loneliness came.

But my changed world wasn't entirely solitary. I made fewer friendships, but they were deeper. Ellee and Angie: fellow homeschooled girls.

They were the kind of kids we would have made fun of in my old friend group. Ellee had braids tied off with actual yarn. Angie wore glasses as thick as ice on the pond. My old friend group wasn't friendly, I would grow to realize. They weren't kind. I had become friends with those girls in the way of little kids; we were placed together on the bus and in the kindergarten class. We had grown used to one another over the years. I had grown accustomed to, but not immune to, Frankie's sarcasm and Isabel's barbs, which hurt like prickers and stuck in my skin. Comments that would burn later for a long time. Words that left scars.

My new friends were different. They sought me out, coming up to me at the first homeschool group meeting my mom made us go to, shortly after I left school—Amelia along with me—in the basement of the Presbyterian church. Standing in front of the long card tables, patterned with covered dishes, I felt a motion at my side. I had turned to see two girls.

You're new, the girl with glasses said.

Want to hang out? the girl with braids asked.

And then we did.

It was easy as breathing, like we had always been a trio. We shared a similar secret after all, the thing that would have made my old friends turn up their noses at us, turn away to whisper. We were homeschooled and unschooled. We were weirdos.

We would be the weirdos together.

Right away, I told my new friends my other secret, not wanting a repeat of how I had lost my first friends. I couldn't hear. The ear my new friend tried to whisper into, to share some joke about the casserole her mother had made for the potluck, I wouldn't be able to understand her.

I was born this way, I said.

It's not a big deal.

I just wanted you to know.

That's cool, the girl with glasses named Angie said.

I think there's pie, the girl with braids named Ellee said.

She linked her arm in mine, on the right side, and we went together to the dessert table. The pie was blueberry, I remembered that. It stained our teeth and we all smiled, then laughed at our smiles, as if our teeth had been blacked out.

I wondered when those memories would stop being painful. Even the memories that were sweet, kind moments like the evening in the church basement when Ellee and Angie and I first found one another, felt like aches now, like a broken bone that had healed. But every time the weather changed, like a bone every time it rained, it hurt again.

I was lost in my thoughts, a coping mechanism I adopted when conversations moved on swiftly without me, like a current. I hadn't noticed when Sam had turned onto a side road. The truck was heading down a long dirt driveway. At the end sat a house, its walls the same blue as the distant mountains.

It was strange that my dad, who valued privacy and freedom so much, had wanted to move to this valley. You could never hide here. No trees offered protection. There were no hollers to disappear down like in Ohio, no cliffs or valleys except the main one. The blue house and its occupant looked exposed, laid bare to the hot sun, and to any visitors, like us.

Sam parked the truck. He opened his door and I opened mine.

Ray got out after me. "You're quiet," he said.

"You were on my deaf side," I said automatically. I didn't want him to think there was another reason I had ignored him.

Then I realized what I had done. I had told him about me. Did he already know? Had Louisa or Sam told him anything or everything? He didn't seem surprised. He didn't even blink.

Instead, he looked me in the eye. "I won't make that mistake again."

7

The door of the little blue house was propped open, and through the screen we could see a woman vacuuming in shadows. When she saw us, she straightened and waved. She turned off the vacuum, kicked the cord out of the way, and came to the door. She held it open for me, even though she didn't know me.

"Come in, come in." Her voice sounded like music and water.

She ushered me inside, followed by Ray and Sam. We wiped our shoes on the doormat. Still, only the center of the home was swept clean, the wood floor emerging out of dust.

The front door of the home looked straight to the back, which was a wall of windows displaying the mountains and pastures. The white walls along the hall held paintings and black-and-white photographs in frames. I saw dried flowers in a vase, some kind of white and purple-blue blossom, its petals fanning outward like a lion's mane.

What struck me most about the home were the rainbows. Light from the many windows bounced off of glass bulbs dangling from the sashes. The bulbs hung on strings. They were teardrop-shaped, cut like fancy jewels, and the light that came from them seemed to be every color.

"I'm Helen." The woman held out her hand to me.

I shook it. "Thea."

"Thea's family is new here," Sam said. "They moved into Cuthbert's old place."

"Oh, you poor thing. Have some lemonade."

Did the woman know about our half-finished house, the undersized crops? Maybe it was my appearance, bedraggled from the road, that made her eyes crinkle with sympathy. Possibly I looked worse than I thought. I tried to run my fingers through my hair.

"Sit, sit," Helen said.

I walked into the light-filled living room, Ray beside me. I took a seat on the sectional couch and he took the place right next to me, not close enough that we were touching, as in the truck, but near enough that it seemed deliberate. It was a large, U-shaped couch. He could have chosen anywhere.

He sat on the side I could hear.

Sam went into the kitchen with Helen. I looked around so I wouldn't have to look at Ray, so close that if I crossed my leg, it would brush him. If he reached up to tuck his chin-length hair behind his ear, as I had observed him doing often, his arm would graze mine.

Ray had hair long enough to hide a hearing aid, but he didn't seem like he wanted to, always brushing the dark strands out of his face.

All the time I thought: Was I behind? Was I missing something? Had I heard the wrong thing, answered incorrectly?

Could people tell? I wondered what it might be like to live with my deafness out in the open. I wouldn't have to say anything to people. They could just look at me—if they were perceptive—and *know*. Would that be better or worse than always pretending?

"You okay?" Ray asked me.

I found an excuse for my silence. "Just . . . checking out the rainbows."

"They're prisms," Helen said. She and Sam had returned from the kitchen, carrying a tray with a pitcher and four tall glasses of lemonade.

I took a glass, its sides silver with frost.

Helen was an age somewhere between my mom and Louisa. From some angles, when she turned, the sun from the big windows striking her, I could see the girl she had once been with an upturned nose, light hair, and freckles. It was the opposite with Amelia. Sometimes I thought I could see the teenager my sister was growing into and the adult she would become. Like a hologram, like some kind of message from the future that flickered out as soon as it was received.

Helen was still blond, though her hair was thin and less yellow than I imagined it had once been. She wore a blue sundress under her apron, frillier than anything in my mom's closet. Helen must have liked blue. Her house and her clothes were the color, the same shade as the mountains turned under the clouds. But speckled across her apron, her sundress, even the skin of her hands was paint, a rainbow of drops and dribbles so small I hadn't even noticed them at first. They were as fine as sand.

I looked back at the prisms, twisting slightly in the air conditioning. Heavy-looking drops of glass, strung on wires.

"Do you know what prisms are?" Helen asked me gently. Her eyes looked patient. She walked over to the window and pulled at one of the strings. The other prisms rocked on their cords, crashing into one another with soft knocks. She bent close to me and I scooted forward on the couch and peered at the crystal she held in her hand.

It looked like a big fancy earring, or like a doorknob I had seen for sale at a flea market once, cut into a dozen angles.

"Light colors travel at different speeds inside the glass," Helen said. "They get bent in different ways, and so when they come out of the glass, they come out _____ as a rainbow. Or, many rainbows." She looked around the room. Rainbows painted the ceiling, her potted succulents, her face. In her palm, the prism turned, heavy as an egg.

"Why do you have so many?" I asked.

"I guess I just like watching the light change." She straightened, reached out to unfasten something at the top of the window. The string holding the prism pooled in her hand, slack, and she held it out to me. "You should take this."

"Oh, no." The prism looked expensive, and besides, Helen hardly knew me.

"I have plenty. And Ray already has one."

I glanced over at him on the couch and he nodded. "It looks cool in the mornings, all the _____."

I tried not to imagine Ray in the mornings: where he slept, how he slept.

I took the prism. It felt cool. Helen wrapped the cord into a circle, then closed my fingers across it. Her fingers were warm and she wore many rings, turquoise and coiled silver, though nothing on her ring finger. I felt so alone on the farm, but at least I had my family. We had one another. Helen was by herself, down this long driveway. So many pictures on the wall, and I didn't see a single one with people in it.

I would have to hide the prism from my parents. It was a record, evidence. They would know if they found it: I had disobeyed. I had gone somewhere, met someone, taken something my dad would want me to refuse. A fancy-looking, delicate, and ornamental thing. It would have no place in our home where everything served a purpose. Even Amelia hardly had any toys. And every dress she wore was once mine.

I put the prism in my pocket. Helen and Sam had seated themselves in chairs opposite the couch and were talking about the weather.

"I'm all right," Helen was saying. "I still have power and that's what matters. I can clean _____. I guess it's a sign my windows need replacing."

"Anything we can do for you while we're here?" Sam asked. "Fix or take a look at? Is the roof over the kitchen leaking again?"

"Well, it's been so dry, I wouldn't know, would I?"

They laughed a little, but I leaned forward to ask, "When was the last time it rained, ma'am?"

"Oh, please don't call me ma'am. I'm just Helen." Then her face grew thoughtful. "I don't really remember the last time it rained. Do you, Sam?"

He shook his head. "It's written down somewhere in the office. Or Gus would know."

It didn't seem to bother them, like it did me. Rain was so infrequent they couldn't even remember it.

"Water is something we don't _____ here," Helen said. "Not without money."

And money was a thing my *parents* didn't have.

They had moved around a lot before I was born, my mom and dad, always looking for better opportunities—a fresh start, my dad said. Both born in Ohio, they moved away together, trying the hills of West Virginia then rural Pennsylvania. Humid places with forests and farmland, where it was easy to grow food. My dad used to joke that there were so many orchards in Pennsylvania, Big Foot probably lived there, the creature making his home among the thick rows of apple trees, simply picking up soft, fallen fruit whenever he wanted to and snacking.

Once my parents knew they were going to have their first baby, they wanted to go home, my dad told me. Home was a place where anything could grow, including me and Amelia. My dad thought it was the right thing to do. But the flood must have made them feel like even home wasn't safe anymore, like they had to move again. We had traded a swamp for badlands.

Sam followed Helen around the house as she pointed out things that needed repair or that she was working on. The place seemed pretty solid to me, especially compared to my family's farm.

"Helen looks like she has it together," I said to Ray.

"She does, but she's alone. After an emergency, Sam checks on people with no family."

I thought of my parents and Amelia. "Are many people alone in the valley?"

"Actually, yeah. If you want to be alone, the desert is a good place to go."

"Why?" I just wanted Ray to keep talking to me, here on the couch, so close our knees almost knocked together like the prisms at the window. He hadn't heard, so I repeated myself. "Why live out here?"

"A lot of reasons," he said. "It's beautiful and the land can be cheap, if you get a _____. And it's remote. Nobody's going to drive out here to see you unless they *really* want to. Some places don't have internet and phones don't work great. It weeds out people." He moved closer on the couch. I felt a jolt of warmth, like a lightning bolt or sun beam as his eyes focused on mine. A laser, that was the feeling. "Some people say it's different in the valley, though. That there's like a vortex deep under the ground pulling creative people here."

"Do you believe that?"

"Well, my mom hasn't moved here yet and she's an artist. Though, Helen did." His expression grew thoughtful. "Sam's more scientific. Me too. Maybe I get it from him. Rocks, that's my thing."

"Rocks?" And then I knew what Ray's eyes reminded me of, their deep gloss. Not just the stream back in Ohio, shining and dark after a storm, but the stones inside the water, the smooth ones I would reach for.

Ray picked up something on the end table. It was a rock about the size of his index finger, grayish brown but translucent and shaped like a pillar, rough on the end. "Do you see this?" He turned it in the light and I saw the way the stone contained veins and shades inside shades. "This is smoky quartz. It's from here."

"Maybe this is the place to be if you like geology."

"What's your thing?" he asked. "What are you into?" He placed the rock gently back on the table.

I felt the light and warmth which had sparked when he had inched closer to me wither a bit, cooling. My stomach dropped. I didn't have a thing. I didn't even have a *school*. I was boring, uneducated. I didn't know myself. "I'm not sure yet," I admitted.

"I read a theory once, about San Francisco. Everyone who makes their home there is a lost citizen of Atlantis, and one day when a big quake happens, they'll return to the sea."

"That's dark."

"Well, I don't believe it."

"Is there a story like that for here in the valley?"

Ray got a line in the middle of his forehead as he thought. "I don't think so. Just the vortexes and aliens."

"Aliens?"

"You've seen the watchtower?"

"We've driven by it." I thought of the alien pointing the way, the sun-faded sign.

"People say that's a good place to _____ them. I mean, the sky is pretty big out here." He tucked the hair behind his ear. Maybe it was a nervous habit, more than anything. And was it my imagination, or did his skin flush slightly, like clay, as if he couldn't believe what he was telling me. "It's just a story."

I didn't want to break the closeness between us. I didn't know anything about geology or prisms—or many subjects in which I was sure I was terribly behind. But I always had books, even if I could only read the same books over and over; I could talk about stories. "What if the story is, everyone who settles in the valley is a lost citizen of Oz, and one day a dust storm will come so powerful and strong, it will return us all to the Emerald City?"

I knew it was a tornado that had picked up Dorothy and Toto—and in the neighboring state of Kansas, not here. But maybe it was near enough. I had never felt closer to the heroine of that story than now. Lost, adrift in a strange land, alone. Except Dorothy wanted to go *back* to the west, her place of plains and lonely farmhouses; I would have given anything to escape it. Still, we both longed for home.

"That kinda checks out," Ray said.

Sam and Helen returned. "Ready for our next stop?" Sam asked.

I wasn't worried about time. We hadn't even eaten lunch yet, and the sun was hot but not too high. I headed to the truck with Ray. Passing the porch, I noticed a little round table with a folding chair and a wooden easel. Rags hung off the end of the easel, and a canvas was propped on the rail. I couldn't see the painting, which faced the house. On the table was a skull, its jaw too long to be human. Maybe a deer.

Ray noticed I was staring. "A still life," he explained. "Helen paints things she finds. Sometimes, Sam brings things to her."

"Like what?"

Sam overheard us. I often forgot some people could do that, listen in on conversations that weren't directed toward them, and answer easily, effortlessly, as Sam did, "Oh, bones and feathers. License plates that fall _____. You never know what people leave." He got in the truck and rolled down the window to wave as he started the thunderous engine.

Helen waved back, a lone figure on her porch, the first living artist I thought I had ever met, called to the valley.

The next stop surprised me.

Another small house, another long driveway. But this time the person who came out onto the threadbare porch to greet us—or, to see what all the fuss and stirred-up dust was about—was someone I knew.

"*Elmer?*" I stared in disbelief through the windshield. His shaggy hair and scowling expression made him look like a lion guarding his den.

"See?" Sam smiled over at me. "You've already got friends here."

"I'm just surprised he's not asleep at the library."

He pointed through the window. "Maybe he couldn't _____."

Parked on the side of the house was an old truck I had seen in the library lot. But most of the truck was hidden by branches and a canopy of downed leaves. A tree had fallen on Elmer's truck, knocked down by the storm.

"Looks like we got here just in time." Sam closed his door and went to the back of the truck. I turned to see him pulling a chain saw from the bed.

"Your great-uncle's prepared," I told Ray.

"Always."

"My dad would like that about him."

"I think they would get along. Sam gets along with most people."

But that would never happen, I knew. They would never

meet. Besides, I was not sure Sam *did* get along with everyone. At least not with Elmer.

When he saw it was us in the truck, even with the chain saw to help, Elmer waved his hands in disgust and headed back into the house, flinging the door wide behind him, so hard it slammed against the outside wall. He wasn't going to hold the door open for us like Helen. I doubted there would be lemonade.

"Did he know we were coming?" I asked Ray.

"Probably not. Elmer's one of the ones who doesn't have a phone. Or, he never answers it. But he needs us."

We got out of the truck.

8

My legs had cramped from the drive. I stood around in the yard, uncertain, as Ray and his great-uncle unloaded equipment. They were practiced. They knew how to help each other without saying a word. But there didn't seem to be anything left for me to do. I took my sandwich and iced tea from the truck and walked up to the porch.

The house looked dirtier than Helen's house had been, and I was not sure it was all from last night's dust storm. The storm had only deposited yet another layer of grime on a house that had always been grimy, collecting dirt like paint. The porch felt unsteady under my feet, tilting.

So did the house when I stepped through the open door, seeing only shadows. It was more of a cabin than a house. Once my eyes adjusted, I saw one large room with the dark mouth of a fireplace, and a door that might lead to a bathroom (or maybe not—I wouldn't put it past Elmer to have an outhouse). Small windows let in light above the kitchen sink and along the side wall. Otherwise, the only sun came from the back and front doors, both standing open.

Elmer stood at the sink, looking away from me.

"Are you all right?" I asked him.

He mumbled something.

Great. Elmer was a mumbler.

I wondered if he was also the type of person who would get angry if I asked him to repeat himself or speak up. Or, if he wouldn't do either of those things, but simply huff away from me, like my dad did. Elmer seemed grumpy enough.

I held up the sandwich. "Hungry?"

We sat out back behind the cabin, at a picnic table Elmer had placed there. Maybe he had made it himself, based on the rough appearance, drips of sap frozen on the logs like beads of dew. I wondered if he had made the cabin too. It wasn't *that* shabby, I saw as I peered at it in the sun. Just small and dusty. There was a garden plot where things actually seemed to be growing, and Elmer had bird feeders hanging.

Anyone who fed the birds couldn't be all bad.

I sipped my watery iced tea and Elmer ate my sandwich. From the front yard came the whine of the chain saw. I imagined in a moment we would go help Sam and Ray. Or, maybe Elmer would not be able to help so much. I had noticed the way his shoulders hunched as he ate, his stiffness when he tried to fold his legs under the table, as if even those small movements hurt.

He stopped eating. "Where's your sandwich?"

I shook my head and slurped the tea.

"Kid, you can't give away everything. I'm not a charity case."

"I'm not, either."

He held the sandwich out to me, already half gone, but I took a bite from the other end and he grinned. Gray stubble dotted his face. His shirt was worn flannel with the sleeves ripped off, and there were certainly some missing teeth in that smile. Maybe Elmer was okay.

A shuffling, a voice behind me.

Ray stood on the back porch. I tried to make sense of what he had said. Across from me, Elmer was standing awkwardly: my cue to rise. We walked back through the cabin together. I noticed now the twin bed in the corner, made snugly with gray flannel blankets. And I saw the books everywhere, stacks of paperbacks piled tight and high against the cabin walls. One book lay open on the bed, several more on the kitchen counters. A desk pushed against a side wall held its own book stack, and a typewriter, fresh paper at the ready.

Sam stood by Elmer's truck, which was starting to emerge piece by piece as he and Ray hacked away at the fallen tree. "We just need your help with this big _____. You'll have a head start on your firewood this year, Elmer."

"Well, I could have sawed it myself, except my chain saw is out of gas. And I can't get gas because my damn truck is buried."

I stood beside him and Ray, lifting a portion of the tree when Sam told us to. The tree was heavy and scratchy, snagging at my arms. We hefted, then dragged the tree away from the truck and set it down in the dirt.

Sam prepared to saw the tree into sections, but Elmer said, "I can take over for a bit. Why don't the kids rest awhile in the shade and eat something? Thea." He looked at me. I didn't even know he remembered my name. "The rest of that sandwich is yours. And I have fresh molasses cookies inside."

"Wow, Elmer bakes," I said to Ray as we sat in the shade of one of the backyard trees, enjoying the cookies. They were soft and rich with brown sugar sweetness.

"People are full of surprises," he said.

"And the typewriter? There's no computer, but he has a typewriter."

"Elmer is a writer. Why do you think he's always at the library? Not _____ for sleeping. Or my excellent company."

I thought of the books in the cabin. "Has he published anything?"

"Lots of things."

"What does he write?"

"Thrillers, I think. Horror books set out west."

"Out here?" I didn't think I had ever lived in a place before that was written about in a book, a published book. Surely Ohio had been—but we didn't read those stories. Not anything by living, breathing, contemporary authors. I didn't know any of the writers of the books my parents allowed us to read, but they seemed long gone, the stories set in older times. Simpler years, as my dad liked to say, and in easier worlds than ours: when tapping your heels three times could get you sent home.

Ray didn't answer me. Maybe he hadn't heard. He reached into his pocket and pulled something out. When I saw it was his phone, my heart sank.

It sank deeper when he said, "I should get your number." He pulled up his contacts. "We could text."

My throat had gone dry. I could only shake my head.

He was looking at me, concern and confusion in his eyes. "I know reception's probably bad where you are, but—"

"No," I said. "I don't have one."

He didn't hear me, so I repeated myself.

"Don't have reception?" he asked.

"Don't have a phone."

His eyes widened. Now they were deep as a well, one in which I would disappear, be swallowed whole. It marked me as so different, not having a phone, more different than my funny clothes or the fact I didn't go to school. A phone with texting and a notes app *would* have made my life easier. I needed this, needed it more than my dad needed internet, or my mom needed a vacuum, though I believed we needed those things too; they could all help us.

"It's okay." Ray put his phone away.

It didn't feel okay, though.

We finished the cookies, brushed the crumbs from our clothes, and stood. In the front yard, Sam and Elmer had sawed the tree into chunks. They were placing the pieces onto a stump and splitting them into logs with an ax.

When he saw us, Sam turned and rested the blade against the stump. "Thea," he said. "What do you know about chopping wood?"

He was breathing hard. Elmer stood on the porch, stacking the wood in a pile against the house.

"A lot," I said. "My dad had me learn when I was little."

"I figured as much." He indicated the ax. "Want to give it a whirl?"

"Sam!" Ray said. He tucked his hair behind his ear and shot his great-uncle a look.

"It's all right. I chop wood all the time. And I wore these." I flexed my toes in my worn sneakers. They pushed against the fabric.

I didn't say that closed-toed shoes were the only shoes I had. These were getting too small and the laces had ripped and been knotted together. But they would last me. They had to.

I took the ax from Sam. On the porch, Elmer wiped his forehead with his shirt hem. Ray just stood tensely, watching.

When chopping wood, you had to get into a rhythm. My dad had never let me play sports, but I knew about being in a zone. Chopping wood was like that. As my dad had explained it: if you thought about it too much, you messed up. If you messed up, you might lose a toe. Elmer's ax was sharp, I noticed, the blade glinting. Despite the dusty cabin, he kept up what mattered. A dull blade was more dangerous than sharp. My dad had taught me that too.

I stood with my feet balanced, raised the ax, then brought the blade down evenly. If you let gravity take over, let the ax work like a pendulum, it was smooth. It felt natural, like the ax *wanted* to sing into the wood, wanted to split it open and find the deep red heart. And then there was the sound. The crack I could always hear clearly, loud and sharp as ice breaking. It let me know I had found the true center. My ax had made its mark.

"Well done!" Elmer said as the log split, the two sides falling off the stump.

I kicked them away and reached for another hunk of wood.

Sam applauded. Out of the corner of my eye, I watched Ray watching me. He said something to Sam, but I couldn't catch it. Maybe he was protesting me being put to work with the ax. Or maybe telling Sam about the phone thing, expressing just how much of a weirdo I was. Ray went to sit on the edge of the porch.

I had to focus on the ax to stay in the zone. I raised the blade, let it drop again. I chopped until I started to get sloppy. My arms burned, but it was better than thinking about how I was different, how I was wrong. I couldn't sign. I couldn't hear. I couldn't...

"I think that's enough," Elmer said. "You don't have to do everything, you know." He surveyed the porch, where the wood pile looked high, the logs almost reaching the top of the cabin wall below the eaves.

I glanced back at the fallen tree. Not much left now. Only a bit of chopping for Elmer or someone to do, plus gathering the sticks for kindling. I had liked the work. This was the first time I had felt useful since coming to Colorado, like my presence here actually mattered. Maybe this was the secret to fitting in, to feeling not so alone.

Helping.

I set the ax down. Once the blade was out of my hands, I realized my fingers ached, my palms hot and blistered. My hands would hurt tomorrow. If my dad noticed, I would have to make up some excuse. I glanced at the road.

There was a cloud hanging over it, more brown than white.

"Is that a bad sign?" I pointed it out to Sam.

He gazed at the cloud. "Not necessarily. But I'm glad we got the tree _____ and the truck _____."

"I can't thank you enough," Elmer said.

"Just don't write a book about me."

Elmer got a funny smile on his face. His grin looked lopsided when he smiled. I wondered if that was why he didn't do it so much. "Maybe I already have."

I sat down on the porch beside Ray and he offered me the rest of his iced tea. We sat in silence as Sam and Elmer said goodbye. I didn't want to talk about the phone, but I had so many questions for Ray.

I asked one of them. "Why do you sign, if you can hear?"

"I don't hear everything," he said. "My friends don't. Being deaf isn't just like one kind of experience, and no one thing is going to work for everybody all the time."

"I don't think my dad wants me to learn ASL."

"Why not?"

I had heard him, but I just shook my head.

"He could learn it," Ray said.

I tried to picture my dad studying videos with me, poring over a book at the kitchen table. I couldn't imagine it. My mom, maybe. But not my dad.

"It seems hard," I said.

"You can do it. So can your family." He pointed to Sam, leaning on Elmer's truck as the two men talked animatedly. "Sam learned and he's really old."

I tried to smile, but I felt sad for some reason. Left out. "How did you learn?"

"Kids at school. But there are community _____. As long as you learn from a deaf person—that's the most important thing."

The idea of someone hearing knowing more about sign

language—much more—than I did made me feel even more alone. Like a boat was leaving, into the water, and I was stranded on shore with no way to get home. Nobody knew who I was, how to reach me. Even Dorothy had the Lion, the Scarecrow, and the Tin Man. Who did I have?

"The Grange had a night class on ASL last fall. They might again this year, especially if Sam suggests it. I'll ask him, okay?"

I nodded.

In the truck, I started to worry.

The dashboard clock read almost three, later than I had expected. Beside me, Ray was drifting asleep, his eyes fluttering closed from the heat. I didn't want to wake him, but I had to ask Sam, "Is that clock right?"

He shook his head, and for an instant, relief flooded through me.

Until he said, "It's an hour behind. I never changed it after daylight savings. Don't know how to and don't see much of a point. I'd only have to change _____." Sam sensed my unease. "We'll get back before your mom's done with work."

But so many things could go wrong. If we got a flat tire. If the truck overheated. Then I saw something that made me forget my worries, that replaced them like a curtain coming down. The truck was heading for a brown wall. A cloud had lowered and covered the highway, right in our path. The cloud was dirty, the color of nicotine teeth.

"What is that?" I asked.

Ray had been slumped on my shoulder and he jerked awake.

"It's dust," Sam said.

"Can we go around it?"

Sam was concentrating, his hands gripping the wheel. "There's nowhere else to go."

Fences ran beside the road on both sides, wire-thin but barbed. We hadn't passed another road, a turnoff, for miles. Maybe since Elmer's place.

"Kids," Sam said. "Close _____."

Ray knew what to do. He lurched forward, snapping the air conditioning vents closed, then hit a button on the dashboard for recirculating the air. Sam's truck was so old, I wasn't sure the button did anything. Sam said something about the windows. I reached for the crank at the passenger side window, twisting it up as tight as it would go.

"Hold _____," Sam said.

The panic already inside me had started to boil. I couldn't hear his directions. I didn't know what was happening. Ray touched my arm. I turned to see his face and he puffed up his cheeks with air, nodded at me.

Hold your breath.

I did and we drove through the cloud.

9

It was a moment of nothingness. Only swirling, dirty tan. I felt like I was plunged underwater in a pond. A slurry of darkness and dust. I had a memory of the stream at our old house, swimming in the summer.

I should have closed my eyes. It would have been less terrifying than barreling into the cloud. I glanced over quickly at Sam. His eyes were stuck to the road. He kept on driving dead ahead. I remembered hearing a race car driver on the radio once say you should drive right through a crash on a course, straight into it. Because by the time you got to the crash site, the cars would have spun out to somewhere else.

I felt movement at my side, and Ray's hand was there. He reached for me, grabbed my fingers. He squeezed and I held on tight. It felt natural, necessary. I clung to him like a rope.

Then we were through the dust cloud. We burst through it back into sunlight and the straight black road. I thought I had never felt so grateful to see the Colorado sky again. Boring, plain, and blue. I let out my breath with a gasp.

Ray did the same. "What *was* that?" he asked.

His question scared me almost as much as the dust had. Ray was *from* here. He had lived in the valley for years, every summer. "You don't know?" I asked.

"Nobody does." Sam didn't look away from the road.

Ray held my hand until the café. Once we were safely through the cloud, I could marvel at it, really feel it: his fingers, the secure grasp, the heat. He didn't have to hold my hand anymore, but he chose to.

I realized I didn't want him to let go. I felt tethered, like his hand meant I belonged. But once we stopped at the café, I had to get out, I had to run and break the link between us. I untangled my fingers, instantly missing his warmth and that feeling. That feeling like I mattered, like I was part of something, belonged with someone. I hopped out of the truck, looking back once over my shoulder.

I had really just met him. He had held my hand, this boy who liked rocks, who seemed to like me. He waved to me. I slammed the truck door and ran.

Inside the café, as soon as I pushed open the door, I could hear voices, nothing as distinctive as words. But my mom was seated at one of the tables, holding a mug. Louisa sat across from her. My mom's mug no longer steamed. If she had hot coffee or tea it had cooled. She had been waiting for me.

"There she is," Louisa said brightly. "How was chopping wood?"

I tried not to let the panic show on my face.

"Sam texted me, told me you _____ late."

Lucky Sam, to have a phone. And lucky me, that it worked.
"Great," I said. "I mean, I'm sore."

"I told Louisa you've been chopping wood for years," my mom said.

"Lots of trees down?" Louisa asked.

I nodded, still stunned.

"It was kind of you to let her go help," my mom said.

"Oh, of course. It's not like it's rush hour around here." Louisa stood and retrieved the stale pastries she had packed up for me. "I'm telling you, bring your sister next time," she said as she held out the box, making direct eye contact with me. Her eyes seemed to hold another message. What was it? That I could trust her to cover for me? That we had gotten lucky, this time?

I had the prism from Helen hidden in my pocket. Was it my imagination or was it weighing me down? Like the lie of omission Louisa and I had just told my mom. I hadn't been just with Sam. I had been with *Ray*. I had held his hand.

That secret felt heavy, like those clouds that never rained.

I didn't take the prism out again until nightfall.

Amelia was already in bed by then, in her twin across our room, and I was supposed to be getting ready myself. For once, I didn't mind how early our parents made us go to sleep. I felt exhausted. The ache on my hands from gripping the ax had bloomed into blisters. My neck burned and my shoulders did too. I thought I worked hard every day, but I didn't work as hard as Sam. And probably as Elmer, either—just the work he had to do in order to survive out there alone.

My mom had looked over in concern when I had winced getting into the truck, using my sore hands to pull on my seat belt. But blisters were easy to explain away. She knew I had been chopping wood.

Why then did her eyes linger on me before starting the engine? Why did they look so questioning? Not disapproving even—more like she wanted to talk with me about something but could not bring herself to. Whatever it was, she didn't ask and I didn't offer. We rode home in silence, like we always did.

I pulled down the quilt on my twin bed, flush against the wall. Before I changed, I slipped the crystal from my pocket and tried to secure it under the pillow.

But Amelia saw it. "What's that?"

"What?" I said.

"I know you heard me." She pointed at the pillow. "*That*."

I could lie again. I had lied already, by not telling my mom how I had been gone all day, meeting strangers. Louisa had stretched the truth for me. But I had other secrets, big, beating ones that grasped at me and begged me to share. Secrets about the way I was feeling.

Hope. For the first time since we moved to the valley, I was feeling hope.

I pulled out the prism and Amelia gasped. I shushed her.

"Is it a diamond?" she asked.

I came to her side of the room and sat on the end of her bed. She scooted up to make space. "It's a prism," I said. "It has all these sides and they reflect light. It makes rainbows."

I held it out to her and she took it, marveling as she peered at its many sides.

"Did you find it? Did you dig it _____ like a scientist?"

"No. Someone gave it to me."

In the dimness of the room, Amelia's eyes were like little white saucers. "*Who?*"

I looked toward our door, which was closed. My parents went to bed early, as all the books told them to, as all farmers should. *Early to bed, early to rise.* Even so, I was afraid of being overheard. I sometimes spoke louder than I meant to, unable to hear or control the level of my voice. I leaned in even closer to Amelia to whisper, "Some friends."

"What friends?"

"I met someone. A guy."

"A *guy?*"

"Sh, sh. And his great-uncle who helps people in the valley. He drives out to homesteads and chops wood for people, helps them with groceries and fixing things. That's what I was doing today."

"The guy gave you a diamond?"

"Prism. And no, a woman we helped today did."

"Why did she give it to you?" Amelia asked.

I watched the prism in the shadows, turning in my sister's hands. "I guess as a thank-you? I think she was just being nice."

"There are nice people here."

It often took a moment for words to sink in, for me to make sure I knew fully what was being said—that I understood enough to answer, anyway. But those words from Amelia took longer than most. I considered them. I felt them in my chest.

There *were* nice people here; it was just hard to meet them.

We had to search for one another purposefully, seek one another out like shade.

Amelia started to give the prism back but I stopped her, folding her fingers around it. She had so little. Few toys, no dresses that were her own. Everything was a hand-me-down from me. Everything was worn-out, used, and gray. But the prism would sparkle with light in the daytime.

"You keep that safe for me," I said. "For us. Until we can hang it on our window."

She nodded, the movement like an animal in the dark. We both knew, knew without speaking a word, it might be some time before we could do that.

The next day was Saturday, but like any other day, we rose early. Even our weekends were workdays. My dad went outside, and my mom and I were busy in the kitchen while Amelia fed the animals. She would gather the eggs, and sing to the chickens as they fussed about her, trying to pet each one before coming back into the house to help us with breakfast.

I washed the kitchen table. A film of dust always collected on the surface at night, as if the table grew a dry moss, as if time moved differently here, sped up like a nature film. I had learned to reclean every morning, to wipe out every cup or dish before using them. That was just what we did here in the valley, I thought.

But what if it *wasn't*?

Sam had said the dust cloud we had driven through was not normal, not like anything he knew. What if the dust was changing?

Maybe meeting Elmer and Helen—maybe holding Ray's hand, a comfort I kept remembering in the night—had made me bold. I set the wet rag slowly down on the table, then said to my mom, "I've been thinking. What about Amelia coming with us next Monday?"

She didn't look away from the stove. "Coming with us _____?"

Where? "To the café and store."

I had guessed correctly, based on what my mom said next. "To work? Why would your sister want to do _____?"

"Well, she's bored here." That wasn't the right thing to bring up, I could tell instantly. I hurried to say more. "And lonely. And we're needed, our help is needed."

"Amelia is just a child. Too young to chop wood."

"But she could keep Louisa company at the café if I volunteer or something again." I paused. I thought of the pictures of the nieces and nephews. "Louisa's pretty lonely too."

I felt maybe I had reached my mom, gotten through. Her face looked like she was considering it. But then she shifted to the stove and stirred aggressively at the big pot of cornmeal mush. Turning her back to me while she talked meant the conversation was basically over. For me, anyway.

"_____ one-time thing," my mom said. "The storm."

I came around to her side of the stove. I would look at her, even if she wouldn't face me. "Some people say it's different. That something's happening this summer."

My mom raised her eyes. Heat from the cookstove had flushed her skin. Little baby hairs stuck to her temple, frizzing like weeds, like Louisa's hair did. "What people?"

The screen door slammed at my back and I jumped.

"Sorry." Amelia set a basket of eggs on the table, then answered matter-of-factly, "Sam and his nephew and a nice lady. Those are the people Thea met."

It was so easy for Amelia and my parents to overhear, to catch a conversation I would never have a hope of picking up. Amelia had heard our mom through the screen door, effortlessly. She smiled at us. She didn't know she had revealed a secret.

My mom's face erupted into questions. "What does Sam do again?"

"He's that outreach agent for the county," I said. "Louisa told you. He drives out, checking in on people, farmers. He can check on us. He offered."

"No," my mom said. She seized my arm. "Your dad won't want that. Strangers coming here?"

"He's not a stranger. Not anymore. And it's Sam's job to make sure people are okay. It's hard living so remotely. He said people struggle." I wanted her to know it wasn't just us. We weren't the only ones fighting to keep the lights on, to have enough gas for the generator and water for the plants.

"That's who you were out with?" my mom asked. "Louisa trusts him?"

"He's a good person."

She removed her hand from my arm and went back to stirring the mush. "What's this about a nephew?"

My mom missed nothing. It must have been nice.

"Great-nephew," I said. "Ray. He's my age."

She looked up from the pot sharply but said nothing. Behind me at the table, Amelia began to carefully count the eggs in her singsong way. She kept messing up and having to start over.

It was difficult to hear the next thing my mom said. She said it so softly, looking down. "And you met a nice woman?"

My mom was lonely. Like Amelia, like me.

"Really nice." And even though it wasn't true, Helen was older, I added: "Your age."

"I'll think about something for you and Amelia to do together, away from the farm," she said.

It wasn't exactly a win, but it wasn't a loss, either.

It was water day. The work would take all of us. My dad would drive the truck. At the well, my mom would take over, backing the truck up to the metal holding tank while my dad fastened the output hose into the bolt container, the giant plastic bin that sat in the bed. Amelia and I were to be stationed at points along the hose, to check that it was fastened tightly, ensure water was flowing, and most importantly, to make sure the hose did not leak.

It had leaked before. We had lost water that way. And money. My parents had already purchased a new hose after one failed our first trip to the well, a not small expense.

We had left the dogs at home, though the pets of strangers barked as my dad turned onto the dirt road leading to the well. He didn't have to turn far. There was already a long line.

"Are we late?" Amelia tried to peer around the front seats.

"No," my dad said. "This is our usual time."

Ahead of us, a big truck grumbled as the driver shut off its engine, trying to save gas. A few trucks down the line, people were getting out, gesturing to one another. The wind didn't carry their voices to me, but their faces looked angry.

I turned to Amelia, but she was too busy staring out the

window to tell me what anyone was saying. Someone walked down the line, an older man with a white beard and a sunburnt face, waving a red handkerchief. He said something to the driver of the truck in front of us and its engine started back up again. Then he came to our truck. He looked like the person sent to deliver bad news. He wiped his forehead with the handkerchief and my dad rolled down the window.

"Sorry about this, folks," the man said. "But the water's out."

My dad stared at him. His hands still hadn't left the steering wheel, hopeful we would move in the line eventually. "Something wrong with the pump?"

"No. Wish it were that." The man tucked the handkerchief into his back pocket, where it stuck out like a bloody tail. "The well's dry."

My dad's hands fell into his lap.

My mom leaned to the window. "Sir, how can it be dry?"

"I don't know, ma'am," the man said.

But he *did*, I felt. He did know. He just didn't want to tell us.

"Who took the water?" I asked.

The man couldn't see me clearly in the back seat. He squinted, peering inside. "What's that _____?"

I thought of what Louisa had told me, about the farmers' meetings, how so much of the river was sold to people who didn't even live here, for their businesses they managed from far away. "Somebody bought the water. Who was it?"

"That's enough, Thea," my dad said.

"What company was it?" I asked.

My dad's hands had returned to the wheel. The man with

the handkerchief took that as a sign to step back. He hadn't answered me, hadn't even listened to me. And my dad was turning us around. We were giving up, as the trucks in front of us had done.

"Dad," I said. "We need that water."

"There isn't any water, Thea." He gripped the wheel tighter than before. He said it again to himself, "There isn't any water." It seemed like he was trying to talk himself into it, trying to believe it.

In the rearview mirror, his face looked pale. His lips moved again but I couldn't see what he was saying. Maybe the same sentence again and again. *There isn't any water...* His blue eyes, the source of the lightness in Amelia's pupils, appeared to shrink, overwhelmed in white, like he was drowning.

But there wasn't any water.

"You heard the man," my mom said to me.

At any other time, her choice of phrasing would have stung. She knew I couldn't hear. She knew and she forgot, as my dad always did. It was so convenient for them to never consider the detail that marked my life. Of course, *they* didn't have to remember. But it was with me always.

This time, I had heard the man, though. I felt sure of it—and I had a feeling about where the water had gone. "They sold the water, I bet," I said. "To a business."

Amelia was listening. "What kind of business?"

"Probably one of the huge ones."

"That's not fair," Amelia said. "The water has to last for everybody."

"They have money to make, I guess."

"That's enough, girls," my mom said.

My dad wasn't saying anything.

Once my dad had told us proudly about the big farms that worked out of the valley, businesses so massive I wondered how they could even be called farms. The beer company. The egg farm. They were nothing like our farm, with rocks we had pulled from the ground by hand, and plants we still watered with hoses and buckets. Nothing like Louisa's potted garden, or Elmer's vegetable patch. Growing took water—even giant corporations couldn't get away from that basic resource. The bigger the crop, the more water it needed.

My dad had turned the truck around. It wobbled with the awkward, extra weight of the plastic tank in the back. But the tank was empty. We were facing the road again, headed home as everyone else in line was too. We were giving up, returning to our farms and homesteads dry. My dad still looked pale, and I thought, though I couldn't hear it, he was still mumbling to himself about the water.

The next day, the locusts came.

10

A buzzing woke me. It was strange for me to be disturbed by a sound. I could always roll over and put my ear that could hear against the pillow, muffling it. But I found when I opened my eyes, I had already done that. I was facing the space between my and Amelia's bed, the pillow squashed firmly into the side of my face.

It made no difference. I still could hear something.

Like the wind, but wrong.

I sat up in bed. Across the room, Amelia slept on. The light behind our curtain looked dim, still shadowy, like it did before dawn. The first hint of the sun would usually wake us in the mornings—if our mom hadn't already—blazing through that thin curtain.

Something else was blazing, though. A noise.

A rustling. A flapping, like the wind striking our laundry out on the line, and there was a strange droning sound too, almost mechanical. I followed the sound out of the bedroom, grabbing a sweater as I shut the door.

The sound was in the hallway. It was in the kitchen. It was everywhere.

At the front door, I hesitated. It still looked dark out. But the sound came from outside. It seemed to be coming from all around, though that could have just been me. If my mom called my name, even in our small house, I would never find her; she would have to come to me. Why did I think I could discover the source of the buzzing? Still, I slipped on my shoes from the tray near the door and clutched a flashlight.

Outside, I was startled to see light. It was dawn, *past* dawn, past time to rise. Why hadn't my parents woken me up? They were both awake. They stood outside in the yard before me, staring up at the clouds.

Not clouds.

The shapes in the sky were pinpointed with black dots, like a painting I had seen in a museum once. In the sky, the dots all moved together, like a great churning mass of starlings. But they were too small to be starlings.

"What is it?" I asked.

My mom whirled, seeing me. She reached out her arms and folded me up into them like I was a much younger child, wrapping me in her arms as if she could protect me, keep me away from that noise. "They're bugs." She had to speak close to my ear.

Bugs? I tried to peer into the swarm. I didn't know bugs could be so loud. That they could mass and move together in one dark, undulating bubble. And as I watched, the bubble burst. It scattered, zigzagging like a comet.

It landed in our field.

My dad, who had been frozen, staring transfixed, ran. It was the field of potatoes, which, like most of our crops, was struggling already. The insects landed all at once and they kept landing, waves and waves of sputtering wings.

"What are they?" I shouted to my mom.

"Locusts!" she said.

Then my dad was among them, screaming and waving his arms like a man in a wind tunnel. Wild. I became aware of the dogs barking. Several of them leapt into the field after my dad, their jaws snapping.

My mom shook my shoulder to get my attention. "Get quilts from the _____," she said.

I ran back inside. Amelia was awake, blinking in the kitchen, her long nightgown creased and her feet bare. I rushed past her into our bedroom, then into our parents' room, filling my arms with the quilts and sheets. I thrust the bundle of bedding into Amelia's arms.

"What's happening?" she asked.

"Take this outside to Mom. We have to cover the fields."

"Why?"

"Just take them!"

My voice startled both of us, but she obeyed, leaving the front door open in her haste to get out. The sound was louder now.

Locusts would descend upon fields and devour them in minutes. They moved like one mass, eating vegetable gardens, grass, plants. A lot of plants, though I couldn't remember which ones. Locusts had been in the Laura Ingalls Wilder books we had been allowed to read; they had consumed that fictionalized family's livelihood.

These locusts had landed on our potatoes and maybe they wanted our other vegetables too. The sound of their wings seemed to be everywhere. It was hard to think in the midst of so much sound.

But I slammed the front door shut after Amelia. I ran into the kitchen, opening cabinets and taking things out, even though my hands were trembling. Below the sink were empty plastic spray bottles. My mom would fill them with lavender oil for cleaning. I took them and screwed them open.

We had a slender jar of garlic oil on the counter. My mom had made it for pasta. I dumped its slick contents into the spray bottles. When I ran out of oil, I reached into a hanging basket for the white heads of garlic. I pulled them open, crushing the garlic with my fists. I took a knife from the drawer and cut the cloves as best I could. The garlic stung the knicks and burst blisters on my skin from chopping wood, but I shoved the cloves into the spray bottle too.

Deer didn't like spicy things. Maybe locusts wouldn't, either. My dad didn't really so my mom didn't cook with them—but Louisa had been introducing me to new flavors. Some of the sandwiches in the café were spiced with jalapeño, chamoy, tajín, or green chiles. She kept a jar by the cash register of mango lollipops dusted in chili powder, and sold long sticks of sweet, chewy tamarind.

We had none of those ingredients at home, but I had seen, at the very back of the fridge, an old bottle with a crusted red top. Chili garlic sauce.

I pulled it from the fridge. I opened the top and dumped all the sauce into the bottles, every red drop. I had filled four whole bottles. I screwed the sprayers on tight, shook the bottles, then ran.

Outside, smoke mixed with dust and the massing insects. In the time I had been in the kitchen, my dad had lit a fire, a bonfire of brush and junk. The flames were orange and greasy. Smoke drifted over the fields, hazy and black. I couldn't tell if it was driving the bugs away. They teemed in heavy clouds. My dad, mom, and Amelia all wore handkerchiefs over their faces.

My mom rushed to me and said something. I couldn't tell what it was, only that her eyes looked worried. I thrust one of the spray bottles at her.

"Garlic and chili oil!" I said.

I wasn't sure if she heard me, if she even knew what I was trying. My dad fed the flames, and my sister threw a sheet over the herb garden. I waded into the fields, setting the extra bottles on the ground. Before me, the field was alive, writhing with locusts. They moved down the plants like tiny machines. Chewing, chewing, like eating was their job, their only purpose.

Maybe it was. I had never seen anything like it.

I sprayed a plant. The liquid coming out of the bottle looked slick. A scent rose in the air, even above the scent of fire: spicy, peppery garlic.

A bug slid off the plant before me.

I moved down the row, spraying the next plant, the next.

Something brushed my back and I turned to see my sister taking a bottle. We sprayed the fields together. We covered them with cloth. My dad filled the air with smoke and kept an eye on the fire to control it. Fire could spread so quickly here. When my spray bottles ran out, my mom sent my sister to the shed for Neem oil, an organic pesticide. We refilled the bottles.

Something worked. Or maybe, nothing did and the bugs just ate their fill. They departed as they had arrived: swiftly and all together in clouds that seemed to have a single brain, to move as one.

There was silence. So odd and loud after the locusts, it seemed to ring.

Silence—and picked-over fields.

My mom pulled her handkerchief down. "Get out the tub. I'll get some water boiling. You girls should wash all this _____."

My dad was walking toward us. He looked exhausted. "What was in the bottles?" he asked me.

"Garlic oil and chili sauce. I found it in the fridge." I looked at my mom quickly. "I hope you don't mind, I used it all."

"Why did you choose that?"

"A lot of animals don't like garlic. And pests don't like spice. So, I thought if I combined them . . ."

My dad put his hand on my shoulder. "That was good thinking."

I waited for him to say more. Maybe to ask how I knew about the spices. Maybe to thank me or even congratulate me? That was a vain hope, I realized almost immediately. It would never happen.

My dad dropped his hand from my shoulder and walked away. He couldn't stop his mouth from falling open as he surveyed the fields. What was left of them. *Good thinking* was the only praise I would get.

For a moment, I felt he had seen me, really seen what I could do, what I was capable of. But the moment was over, almost as quickly as it had begun. Now he saw only ruin. No water—and now, not nearly as many crops.

We didn't talk about how many had been ruined or destroyed, how many had been saved. But his hand on my shoulder had felt heavy, like the world pushed us both down.

When my mom drove us into work the next morning, the fields lining the sides of the road looked flatter somehow. Harsh. Stripped of their crops, they had been stripped of color too. They were brown fields now. Dead.

The wheat had been mowed down. Those fields looked like mouths with their teeth broken out. I hadn't realized how much wheat had been planted in the valley until now, when it was eaten all up. The locusts had loved it. The dirt, newly exposed, stirred in the breeze. It seemed to be drifting.

We had spent most of Sunday cleaning up. Amelia and I had to wash every linen in the house. *Everything will be fine,* my mom said in the morning. She always said that.

But instead of merely wiping dust out of the mugs and bowls in the kitchen, I had to dump out the husks of dead locusts. They felt light and papery, as brittle as the garlic casings. I knew what Amelia would be doing while I worked at the café: sweeping even more locusts out of the house. That wasn't fine.

Neither was what Amelia had said after we had watched the great clouds finally depart, headed off to ruin someone else's fields. She touched a dead bug gingerly with her shoe and asked, *Are we going to have to eat them?*

Thanks to the blankets, the spray bottles, and the smoke,

we hadn't lost everything. But our farm was a stone poised on the edge of a cliff. Any motion, even the slightest wind, could send us teetering over the edge. We didn't have room for error. We couldn't spare even a few rows of beets and scrawny potatoes. We had already not been able to buy water.

My dad had said we would drive to a different well soon and try to buy water there. He seemed to be talking himself into things. It would be farther out, he said, a longer trip requiring more gas. And in the meantime, we had wasted water trying to rinse off the smoke and oil. An extra bath for each of us. That took gallons.

When I came into the café, Louisa had a weary look I was starting to recognize. "How did your farm hold up?" she asked me.

She didn't need to name it. Everyone linked by the long road of the valley must have seen the buzzing clouds. The locusts didn't obey property lines or fences. Most crops grew shoulder to shoulder.

"We're okay," I said. "My dad built a fire, and we sprayed some natural stuff like garlic. Did the locusts get to you?"

"My herbs," she said. "Just a small garden I had."

"But it was beautiful." I pictured the pots along her house. The plants had looked so healthy, full and green. I had meant to ask her *how*. How did she get them to grow? Now I would never know.

"It's all right. It was just a hobby."

Everything could be taken away so fast. Someone's home, their friends, how they made money to live, or even, like Louisa's garden, just something they liked to do. It could all be stolen, fast as a wind whipping through the valley.

Louisa had turned away from me and was busying herself with some work that didn't need to be done. I lingered by the counter, thinking of the smiling children whose photos were taped just below it. I had never seen any of those people in the café, never seen them in real life. Louisa hadn't introduced me to anybody, except Sam.

"Those photos," I said.

She turned back to me as if it was her—not me—who needed to read lips, to look at my face when I spoke.

"Your family?" I asked.

"That's right. Nieces and nephews. They all moved away."

"I'm sorry."

"That's all right," Louisa said. "That's what happens. Kids grow up and they go from the valley. There isn't much opportunity here anymore. No water, no future."

"Do they ever visit?"

She shrugged. "They're busy."

Maybe this was the reason she was so quick to be my alibi, to be my friend. We needed each other. I noticed the espresso machine gleamed, so shiny I could see my reflection like a mirror, and Louisa had been folding the same rag into a smaller and smaller square. Then I saw there was a cup on the counter and a full paper bag.

"Do we have a delivery?" I asked.

"I thought you might want to spend some time in the library," she said. "And Sam and Ray will have their hands full, checking in on folk. They might need you."

"Is that okay?"

"It's always okay, my dear." Louisa scooted the bag across

the counter. "The coffee is for Captain. There are four toasted bagels, _____ haven't had breakfast."

I picked up the items and thanked her. As I left the café, I noticed she had taped a sign on the door of the gas station.

CLOSED FOR BUGS.

Captain took the coffee eagerly and pointed me toward one of the computers. Elmer sat before another. He nodded at me, a solemn, secret look on his face in the way of strangers who have suddenly grown closer, who know things about one another now.

I booted up the computer, but before going to a search engine, I hesitated.

It had been weeks. More, maybe.

My dad said we didn't need email, that it was a distraction. He didn't know what it meant to me, and might to Amelia. We didn't have social media. We didn't have our own phones. This was our way, our only way, to be connected, to reach back home.

I took a deep breath, then checked my email.

The screen filled with bold. Message after message. Beyond the spam and the notices from my old school district—I tried not to be upset about these, not to dwell on subject lines about ice cream socials and orientations and yearbooks, their dates long past—I had emails from my friends.

What's up, Colorado?

Really miss you.

Just trying again.

As the weeks passed, one person had kept trying, kept writing, despite receiving only silence from me. Ellee.

I was afraid to click on her emails, scared of what they might contain after so long. Then I heard Elmer beside me, typing with two determined fingers almost as loudly as he snored. When I snuck a glance at his computer, I noticed he was researching how to conduct a lie detector test.

I turned back to my own screen. Seeing Elmer type, his tongue sticking out of his mouth in a concentrating move I was sure he did not know he did, it gave me courage. Locusts had swarmed our valley—and in the morning, Elmer continued to write. Louisa was keeping people fed and nourished. Captain had the library open. I could certainly make myself read an email.

I clicked on a message.

I scanned the first few sentences before relaxing enough to really read it, to make the words make sense.

> Hey T! Send me your address when you get the chance? I've got a surprise coming up for you. I hope you're just busy having a bunch of fun and making a ton of new friends. Don't forget us though.

These were not angry words. Ellee wasn't mad. She just missed me.

I read on. She wrote that she understood I probably wouldn't have access to a computer, out there in the valley, the way my parents were living, at least not all the time.

But she would keep writing until I did.

Relief flooded through me. I felt stinging in my eyes, and my stomach felt wobbly, as if someone had shoved the kickstand of a bike out from under me. My friend hadn't abandoned me. She wouldn't leave me behind forever, even though my family had picked up and left her.

Something rustled at my elbow.

Elmer was holding a handkerchief out to me. It was neatly folded and looked clean. I took it and he nodded at me. Then he went back to his loud, careful typing as if some girl wasn't trying not to cry next to him in the library.

I wiped the corners of my eyes with the handkerchief. The fabric felt soft and smelled of sunlight and laundry detergent, flowery and different than the kind my mom made. I set the handkerchief to the side of the computer. I started to type.

> Hey Ellee. Thanks for not giving up on me. I wrote you letters, but I never got to send them. I really, really miss you. It's been hard to get to a computer, but I should have access most weekdays now. It's hot and dry, and I thought there was nothing even living out here, but last night proved me wrong.
>
> I have a job.

I paused. I typed:

> I have friends.

11

I finished my email to Ellee and sent it. The tears came stronger and hotter than before. I removed my fingers from the keyboard and quickly swiped at my face.

Beside me, Elmer leaned close and said loudly, "What do you know about profiling killers?"

I couldn't help it. I gave a small laugh. "What do you know about locusts?"

He sat back and studied me. He didn't say anything about the tears. He asked, "Rough night last night?"

I said what my parents had taught me to say. "Others had it worse."

"That doesn't mean you didn't have a hard time too."

There came the tears again.

"I don't know too much about those damn bugs," Elmer said, "but I suspect this man might. Or might maybe point you in the right direction. He's real good at pointing."

Captain stood by the computer, a stack of books in his

arms. "Louisa thought you might be interested, Thea." He set the books on the end of the table. "These are historical."

"Historical?" I asked, grateful for the distraction.

"Continents like Africa have had issues with locusts recently, whole swarms devouring crops. But we haven't had them here lately."

I scanned the spines on the stack. "Define *lately*."

The books had titles like *The Great Depression. Surviving the Dust Bowl. The 1930s Southern Plains.* They were thick and smelled musty. I pulled the top book off the stack and leafed through, flashing by pictures in black and white. Images of a desolate farmhouse. A child, a girl, standing beside a thin man, a dune towering behind them, as if they were at the beach. A grain silo buried up to its middle.

Buried in sand.

"What is that?" I squinted at the picture of the silo. Nothing seemed to be in focus. But I still couldn't look away. The images were powerful, grabbing me.

"It's dust," Captain said.

Dust?

I stared at the pictures. The little girl looked like Amelia. She had thin pigtails and a long, slack dress. The man wore his pants high and his hat low. Both their faces were fuzzy in the old, reproduced image. But it didn't look like they were smiling.

"What happened here?"

Captain and Elmer exchanged a look, which was how I knew I had said the wrong thing. This was a thing I didn't know. I hadn't learned it. But other kids my age likely had.

I was behind. I was twice left: deaf and unschooled. In

many regards, I had only an eighth-grade education, even though I should have been entering my second year of high school in the fall.

"Is this an event people my age would know?" I asked. "Would they learn about it in school?"

Elmer said, "Colorado kids. They have to take Colorado history. But you're from Ohio."

I appreciated him trying to give me an out. Louisa would have told him I wasn't in school, or maybe Sam, who had likely found out from her. I thought of how fast the rumor mill must have spread in the valley. For being such an isolated place, news traveled quicker than a highway truck. "My parents haven't been super great about the history lessons," I said. "Or any lessons, lately. And they're my only teachers, so . . ."

"Well . . ." Captain selected a book from the stack. "Books can be your teachers now."

I took the volume. "*The Dust Bowl.*"

There must have been something in my tone, some query or expression of wonderment. Captain answered without me even asking, "It was a series of severe storms _____ the 1930s."

"Dust storms?"

"That's right." He opened another book in the stack, flipping pages. "There was terrible drought, and the way people farmed _____, breaking up the grassland of the prairies to plant them with crops, it just made everything worse."

I thought about the drive my mom and I made to work every day. I pictured the fields of wheat just outside the library window, fields that were brown and dead after the locusts. "That doesn't sound different than the way people farm now."

"It's not. And so, back then when the wind blew"—Captain

searched for a page—"there were no grass roots left to hold the soil in place. All the dirt blew away."

An image came into my head: a swirling snow globe. But it wasn't snow that circled in the orb, glistening and white. It was dust. Brown, choking dust.

"Where did the dirt go?" I asked.

"East," Captain said. "As far as New York City, the Atlantic Ocean. The dust coated big tanker ships out there." He was glancing through the book. "Back then, they called the storms *black blizzards*."

I could have asked: *How did I not know this?* But I knew why I didn't. History was a dangerous subject. History could cause me to ask my parents questions. Questions like: If the weather was hotter and storms more severe, what was causing the change? If the land in the valley had been owned for generations by farmers of color, as Captain had said, why did only white people own the big farms and wells now and profit from the river? If technology had been invented to help with farming, why would my dad not use it?

"One of the dust storms was so severe, it covered the Statue of Liberty." Captain opened a page wide and held it out to me.

Sailors in white uniforms stood on a bridge. The photograph had been taken from behind the sailors as they stared at a huge, dark cloud. The cloud blocked the sun. It nearly obscured the familiar skyline of New York City, almost completely enshrouding the spire of the Chrysler Building.

I thought about the strength needed to take that photo, to take it and not run; getting the image down—the evidence—so that people would know and believe the danger of the storm was too important.

"The day the worst dust storm hit Colorado, it was called Black Sunday." Captain held open a different page.

Another picture, this one of a tiny farmhouse in front of a mountain. I took the book from him and examined the image more closely.

It wasn't a *mountain* behind the house—a low, modest home that looked a lot like my family's—it was a cloud of dust, boiling and dark. If there had been a second photo taken in the next moment, the house would have been engulfed, everything blotted out by that poison cloud.

Words jumped out at me from the page.

Coughing spasms, headaches, dust pneumonia.

Amelia had been coughing. A lot.

Someone moved behind the book. I glanced up to see Ray. It was a relief to turn from the dark images and troubling words to a friendly face. He rested his arm on the table to lean down and speak to me. I focused on his arm, his skin that had deepened even more in the summer sun—and not on his mouth as I should have.

I had missed his question. But he repeated himself without being asked, "Sam's going out on some rounds. Do you want to come?"

"I'll have to talk to Louisa."

"That was our first stop. She said okay."

I rose from the chair. Elmer had turned back to his monitor and was googling *truth serums + do they work?*

Captain asked, "How many of these books would you like to check out, Thea?"

Check out a book?

I looked at the stack on the table. The photographs from

history, the words and the stories that seemed to speak to my life, to my sister's, even now. I had watched the small perimeters of my life shrink. First, my parents had taken school away. The girls who had bullied me there were a bad influence. Then books became a bad influence, the wrong books, computers. The world was a bad influence because it kept moving on, and my family didn't; they chose not to.

I touched the spines. The books felt slick, protected in plastic covers that crinkled when my finger grazed them, the sound of unwrapping a gift.

"You can borrow more than one," Captain said. "As many as you want for two weeks. Then you have to renew them."

I selected the book called *The Dust Bowl*. "I'll just start with this one."

It was not that I didn't think I could read more in those two weeks.

It was that I didn't know if I could hide more.

Captain took the book. "I'll bring it over to Louisa's and she'll keep it safe for you."

It made me feel a little guilty, so many people working to ensure I could come to the library, see Ray and Sam, read. Everyone coming together to cover for me. As Ray and I left the building, heading out to Sam's truck, I brushed that feeling away.

12

Ray took my hand in the parking lot. We were free from the adults, as supportive as they were, free from anyone's view until Ray opened the truck door and Sam was there, a smile on his face. "Good morning, Thea."

"Louisa's going to go out of business, giving us all this free food," I said. I put the bag with the bagels on the back seat so I could sit in front.

"I'll have you know, I paid for that," Sam said.

"Really?"

"Well, she wouldn't let me. But I snuck a twenty in the tip jar when her back was turned."

Ray joined me in the front seat. Before, I had been so nervous, riding in the truck with the window down, unable to hear anything over the wind. But I was starting to feel more comfortable in our silence. The road did its own speaking. The wind and the sun struck my face.

And Ray had held my hand. He might again. It seemed like ages ago that the locusts had swarmed the sky and the dust clouds had darkened it. Not this sky with its limitless blue. It seemed like it had happened to someone else. I wasn't expected anywhere for hours and I could ride forever, I thought as Sam turned off the highway. The truck bumped down a side road, then a driveway with potholes as wide as mouths.

When he turned off the engine, I asked, "Where are we?"

I felt we weren't too far from my parents' farm, but this was a house unlike the other houses we had stopped at, unlike anything my mom and I had passed on the road. Maybe unlike any house I had seen. It was a dome.

The round shell of the roof was covered in dozens of frames like windows. A weather vane perched on top. Beside the dome and all over the yard were structures that looked even more strange. They were machines: black boxes on tripods, devices perched on high poles. Fans spun at the back of some of the boxes like propellers. I wondered if there were whirling or beeping sounds coming from the machines, sounds too low for me to hear.

"This is the meteorologist's house," Sam said.

I noticed a rain gauge then: bone dry. Wind chimes hung from the few skinny trees, but they were still.

"He's retired," Sam said. "Everybody around here is. Or hiding."

Hiding certainly described my dad, shrinking from the rest of the world, its modern devices and the things it wanted to teach me and Amelia.

Sam rang the doorbell and we stood out on the porch. I imagined, though I couldn't hear it, the sound echoing through the high, strange house. The dome would be a nightmare for me, voices bouncing off the ceiling, seemingly coming from everywhere. Was this the glimmer I had seen from our farm, the flash of silver? It wasn't a hanger or a garage after all.

"He's not going to answer unless he knows it's you," Ray said.

"I know." Sam stepped away from the door and walked around the side of the house.

"Why isn't he going to answer?" I asked. When Ray didn't respond, I repeated my question.

"Gus is anxious. But he's also worried about his neighbor." Ray turned from the door and pointed.

Past the field of machines, I saw a much smaller house, old and neglected. "What's in his yard?"

Ray didn't hear me. All around the house, along its long driveway, propped in the dirt and in its scattered trees, were squares and rectangles painted with bright letters. They were signs. Crude, homemade signs.

"The neighbor has thoughts," Ray said. "A lot of thoughts." He recited a few of them. "'The end is nigh.' 'This is the world's dying breath.' Those are some I remember. He has dozens, though. And he keeps making more."

I thought of the pictures in the library books, the dust cloud covering New York City. The black blizzards, Black Sunday.

Maybe the neighbor wasn't far off.

"Sam's never talked to the guy," Ray added.

"Really?" Friendly, outgoing Sam—I couldn't imagine him

ignoring someone who might need him. I could tell, even from this distance, the house looked partially built like our house. Or, partially collapsed. Its sides had turned gray under blistering sun exposure. The roof was missing shingles. All around the house, the fields had gone to seed, bare dirt and spiky weeds. Farrow.

"Sam thinks the neighbor has guns. He saw him with a shotgun, anyway. _____ to the door with it when Sam first pulled in to introduce himself," Ray said. "So, that was it. As far as Sam got. He turned back. Didn't try again."

I stared at the little, shabby house with its signs all around. It looked lonely against the backdrop of grand mountains. "What's the neighbor's name?"

"We don't even know."

The door of the dome opened then, and a man stood in the doorway. He was very tall, thin and slouched, like the kind of person who had been hunching his whole life, trying to make himself seem smaller, to take up less space. But he filled the doorway like insulation in a wall. He wore glasses he adjusted while opening the door for us. He was lanky and huge, like a kindly spider.

"Gus." Sam had returned and looked delighted.

"I knew you'd come. I have so much to show _____," Gus said, already turning away, back into the dome house, assuming those on the doorstep would follow.

Sam said, "You remember my great-nephew, Ray. And this is our friend Thea."

Our friend.

Gus turned back, his body all angles. "Hello, Thea. Come in."

I followed Ray and the giant, spidery man inside. The door opened up into one big room, the dome above us like a bonnet. I could see a kitchen in one curve. A saggy couch and a steamer trunk used as a coffee table sat in the center. The air smelled of dust and old wood. Papers and books had been stacked on the trunk and on the kitchen counter. The sides of the dome were mostly clear, except for some vinyl covered sections, which made the air feel hot and the light bright. More instruments were lined up before the windows.

One machine, perched on a table, was different. It looked like a crystal ball: a large, clear orb on top of a brass stand. Liquid filled the orb and something floated in the water. Silvery white threads had formed near the top, like frost on a window.

Gus noticed I was staring. "It's a storm glass, invented by Royal Navy Admiral Robert FitzRoy, captain of the HMS *Beagle*," he said. "That's the ship Darwin was on, you know. Developed to predict the weather at sea. Barometric pressure makes the liquid crystallize in _____. The patterns mean different things, _____ weather coming."

"Is it accurate?" I asked.

"It's historical. Rudimentary. But, sometimes."

I studied the crystals at the top of the orb. They looked like etchings on glass. "What do these crystal patterns mean?"

"Dust," Gus said.

It had dirtied the windows of his dome, which were also smeared with insects. Locusts had thrown themselves at the panes, flecking them with green.

The people I had visited with Sam, like Gus, they lived alone at the end of long driveways, their homes like secrets. Sam's visits were more than just checking in on temperatures and firewood, I realized, less maintenance and more social calls so that the people living on the outskirts might feel like they belonged.

My sister needed a Sam visit then. So did my dad.

Sam and Gus talked, words like *clouds* and *Gulf Stream*. I felt myself drifting, unable to follow. Ray was standing by the windows and I joined him.

"Does Sam visit any families?" I asked Ray. "Families with kids?" I was thinking of Amelia.

"Sam visits all types. Other homeschoolers, if that's what you mean. That's what your family does. Right?"

Had he been told by Louisa or Sam? How much had they mentioned? "Not exactly," I said. Would Ray be able to connect my old-looking clothes with other old ways—the hand-cranked grain mill, the herbs drying on rafters, my dad shrugging off the current world like a sweater he refused to wear? "We're supposed to be learning all on our own."

"Are you?"

"Sometimes. But a lot of things seem more urgent, at least to my dad."

Ray was looking at me with only interest in his eyes, but I couldn't talk about it or explain it. I didn't believe in what my dad was doing; I didn't know where to begin.

I glanced out the windows I could barely see through. "We should wash these for Gus."

Gus protested, but eventually relented, telling us where to find the outside hose and giving us buckets and sponges. It was harder to scrub the insects off the windows than I expected. The heat had baked them on.

I scoured an especially large chunk off a plane of glass, plunged the sponge into the bucket. Then I kicked at the bucket, sloshing gray soapy water over the ground.

"Are you all right?" Ray asked. He signed something, but I didn't know what it was.

I didn't know what anything was. I wasn't just going to be good at signing, or even to get it, to understand it. The whole world kept reminding me how ignorant I was.

"I need a break," I said.

"I'll go see what drinks Gus has." Ray disappeared around the side of the house.

We had made headway on the windows, cleaned a space halfway up from the ground. I could see in now, see Sam and Gus moving about. But the top of the windows still looked grubby, blurred like that storm glass.

I was close to Gus's instruments, posted in the yard like other people might have bird baths or feeders. Only one sort of made sense to me: a pole with a shelf on it, like a music stand. A black marker was attached to the pole by a string.

Maybe Gus stood out here with binoculars and made observations about the clouds. I was not really sure what meteorologists did. Not really sure what a lot of people did. But I had guessed right about the stand with the shelf. Gus had left his binoculars sitting there.

I picked them up and held them to my eyes. I focused and pointed them away from the dome, seeing fields, blue mountains. I could make out the snow on top, like a white hat the peaks almost always wore. I turned and there was the neighbor's house. He had what looked like a weedy garden. And all over his property I saw words. Angry, scared words.

FOR THIS IS THE WORK OF THE FUTURE, read a sign against a shed. ALL HAS HAPPENED BEFORE AND WILL AGAIN, read another sign in a tree. This sign was so large and the tree so scrawny, the trunk seemed to sag, bearing it up.

I zoomed in on the signs. Though they did seem anxious and scattered—the large and childlike handwriting, the sloppy paint—the messages were written in a voice of both certainty and frustration. YOU MUST LISTEN. WHY DO YOU NOT HEAR?

I knew that kind of voice because I felt it and had felt it inside me my whole life. Something was different about me but my parents seemed not to notice or remember. Not enough to act, not to do anything.

Now the urgency I felt was everywhere, all around me in this valley with its dry wells and dead snakes and storms. It wasn't just a crisis for me.

YOU MUST LISTEN.

I zoomed in on the neighbor's house. Something had been written on the roof. Big block letters ran along both sides. He had turned his roof into a giant sign that read, THE BLACK BLIZZARD APPROACHES.

A man came out of the door. He was older, skinny with a gray beard. I quickly took my eyes away. Could he see me? I put the binoculars back on the shelf, untied the marker. I found my hand was shaking.

Garbage was strewn across the neighbor's property, encroaching into Gus's yard. It didn't seem like the neighbor had littered so much as left something somewhere one day and then forgot about it forever. I saw a hammer in the long weeds, like something Helen would paint. I saw a rusted bale of wire and a long bit of cardboard.

I looked behind me. Ray was coming out of the dome, two canned drinks in his hands. The neighbor had gone inside, but I felt certain he still watched from the windows. I uncapped the marker and grabbed the piece of cardboard from the ground.

I wrote I BELIEVE YOU and held up the sign.

13

In the truck, I fell asleep. It was the heat, the monotonous lull of the road that rocked me like a ship. I dreamed of an ocean of fields. Something was wrong with the fields, though. They were rising, rising up. I realized it wasn't the ground coming up at all.

It was the sky falling down.

But the sky was the wrong color in my dream. It was red.

I jerked awake.

Sam was talking, facing the road. "He keeps changing them, making new signs. Every time, there's _____. I don't know where he gets all the wood."

Some of the neighbor's signs were cardboard. But I knew, even still half asleep, where the wood came from. I had seen through the binoculars how the man's sheds looked threadbare, more splinter than building. He was breaking them apart, board by board, to write.

When we turned into the next winding driveway, I saw

a collection of trailers and pens. A line of people had been drawn by the dust and the sound. And I knew immediately why Sam had chosen this farm.

There were children here.

They ran up to the truck as soon as we stopped. I felt a sudden pang of missing my sister as a little girl and two boys clamored at the door. I tried to put my worry away and focus on them. They made it easy, shouting and reaching for my hand.

Sam went to talk to the relatives gathered at a distance. One of the children grabbed Ray. And then we were their prisoners, led around the homestead, shown dogs that were part husky, part wolf; a barn; a pet pig that snorted and galloped around us, black and fast as a lamb.

The boys were younger, but the girl was close to Amelia's age, I thought. I asked her—eight years old, I was right—and if she and her brothers were in school.

"My cousins," she corrected me.

We finished our tour at the barn and the boys scrambled happily up a ladder into the hayloft. The rest of us took the ladder more slowly. The girl's name was Patience, and she sat with Ray and me on the platform overlooking the barn, while the boys flung fistfuls of hay at each other. The loft had a huge window at one end open to the sky. The straw piled there felt so warm I looked at Ray in surprise.

"The sun," he said. "It heats it up."

There was no limit to the things I didn't know. I turned back to the girl, who was saying something.

"We go to school," she repeated herself.

"You do? Where?"

She pointed out the window. Not to a distant building, but at an RV right in the yard. "That's our school."

"Your teacher is your mom?"

She nodded.

"Did you ever go to a different school?"

This time she shook her head. "I want to, but . . ."

"You should meet my sister," I said.

"Does she like pigs?"

"Loves them."

I turned back to the hay. The boys were throwing it at Ray and they were all laughing loudly, dust spinning in the air. Patience and I kept stiller, not making a big mess or scene. As girls, we had been taught to do that, trained to make ourselves quiet and small. To make ourselves no one at all.

We ate lunch with the family. Their last name was Misty. The boys' parents had moved out to the valley first, then Patience's parents and grandfather followed. They were trying to grow vegetables, just like my dad, and made some money raising and selling the dogs. I felt bad taking their food, but I had learned the way of it, how kindness was passed on. Sam had helped them—to make some appointments, to figure out a letter from the bank—and now they would help us, feed us.

After we ate, Sam went to look at a broken fence with the men, and Ray and I took the chore of cleaning up away from the women. There was a big dumpster on the homestead. We collected the plastic plates and paper napkins, then pitched the food waste in the compost bin.

"I guess they don't recycle," Ray said, staring at the dumpster.

"If you talked to this family about climate change, do you think they would believe you?"

"Me?" Ray asked.

"If anyone did. Would they listen?"

"I don't know. Everyone's _____ about the weather. It's not like you can't notice."

I was thinking of my dad. "You'd have to be determined not to."

"Saying something isn't real won't make it go away. It's not like a monster in the closet."

"No." I pictured the dust cloud. I had seen storms strike our house, and a cloud on the road with Ray and Sam. Maybe I had seen a dust storm in my dream too. But the sky had been red then, not dusky brown. "It's not hiding," I said. "It's devouring, chasing. A monster that runs after you."

Ray moved his hands.

"Ray," I said. "When you do that—I don't know ASL. I never learned it. I can't follow."

We stood in silence, looking at each other. It wasn't a huge confession I had just made, merely a reminder. He knew I didn't go to school, and what my parents were like.

Hearing. Everyone I lived with was hearing. Abled, as Ray said. But still, saying it out loud, admitting it to him—where did I fit in, if not with my family and not with Ray? I couldn't understand everything when my parents spoke. I could understand hardly anything when Ray signed. Even with someone like me, I couldn't understand at all.

Suddenly, the sun felt too hot. The dumpster smelled too sour and sweetly rotten. I felt dizzy and wrong. I was always wrong, whatever I did, whatever I tried to say or how I tried and failed to fit in. I turned around, barely feeling the ground beneath my shoes. I walked back to the barn quickly, not really caring where I was going, only that I had to go. The hay smelled of dust, which was the smell of ruin to me now. Of things being left to fall apart.

By the door, an insect buzzed me and I flinched, thinking of the locusts, but it was only a bumblebee, drawn by the trash. It spun drunkenly toward some lavender. The fronds of the purple plant waved, one of the only streaks of color in this sun-bleached place.

Ray had followed me to the barn. I hadn't heard him.

"Do you want me to teach you?" he asked. "Teach you ASL? I'm not a teacher, but until those classes at the Grange start up, or you can find a real teacher?"

"I don't know if I'll ever be able to have a real teacher," I said.

"I can teach you what I know. Or, try to. Get you started."

"What if I'm too old to learn?"

"What?" he asked.

"What if I'm too old?"

"You're not."

"What if I'm bad at it?"

"Well, you probably will be, in the beginning," Ray said.

"I feel like I shouldn't be, like there's something wrong with me if I can't get it."

"Don't say that." Ray's voice was forceful. "There's nothing wrong with you. Nothing wrong or broken. And you listen, Thea. You pay attention."

I thought about Ray's words and I thought about the different ways of listening. Like the sky, how it had darkened before the dust clouds came and how the air felt still and wrong. I thought of Amelia's chickens shutting themselves up in their coop. I thought of the signs of Gus's neighbor, signs so loud they were screaming.

It came back to me then: my dream in the truck.

"Ray," I said. "I think something is happening. I think—"

I don't know what I was going to say, what I would have said. I had so many words and no words at all. Words that were mostly feelings, a terrible sense of dread. *A black blizzard. Black Sunday. Another Dust Bowl.* I had maybe seen those signs, I felt.

But I had not seen, not paid attention to what was right in front of me. The look in Ray's eyes: determined, steady, and full of bright hope. He leaned forward and kissed me.

It was a soft kiss. It was my first.

It ended when he said, "I'm sorry."

Had I heard him right? The lavender beyond his shoulder seemed especially bright. Bees were flittering all around us like stars. Had he *apologized*? "What?" I said.

"I should have asked you. I should have _____ permission. Can I?"

"Can you what?"

"Can I do what I just did?"

My chest felt like it was exploding. "Retroactively, yes."

"Can I do it again?"

"Yes," I said.

Beside the barn on the Mistys' farm, I had my second kiss. Longer than the first. I felt my chest detaching from my body, my lungs turning into fiery wings, fluttering away. There was so much lightness and trembling inside me. I was a golden sun, orange as the yolk of a good, rich egg, the kind of egg we had not yet gotten from our chickens in Colorado, but we would.

We kissed until we were interrupted. A child watched by the corner of the barn, one of the cousins.

Ray broke away first. "Hey," he said to the boy.

The child dashed off.

"Don't tell on us," I called after him.

"Oh, Sam won't care," Ray said. "He likes you. We've talked about you."

"My dad would care."

Ray looked at me and pushed his hair behind his ear. Just a moment ago, those lips had been on mine. Those hands had trembled around my sides, not touching me but close enough I felt electric.

Ray noticed when I didn't hear him. He repeated himself without changing his words, or revising what he said to me. He avoided walking or sitting on my deaf side, not wanting to be lost, not wanting *me* to be lost.

He still felt mysterious to me, with his rock collection, his school in the city. He traveled back and forth, from Denver to the valley, from deaf friends to the hearing, from speaking to signing. How did he do that? What was it like to try to be both, to survive both—and not pretend all the time like I did? His expression moved like light moved, blazing over a creek boldly, but in the next breath, hidden by a cloud.

I realized I was staring.

"My dad would like you though," I said quickly, "if he ever met you."

But I knew in my heart that wasn't true. My dad would be horrified; I would never be allowed off the farm again. He wouldn't wait around long enough to get to know Ray, to be introduced to him even.

Ray turned away from me, hearing someone coming that I did not. It was Sam, walking back from the pasture with the broken fence. "Time to head back, kids," he said.

The children ran to the truck as we were leaving. The goodbyes were longer than the hellos, promises to visit again, to bring family.

Patience pressed a small piece of paper into my hand. "For your sister."

Back in the truck, I sat on the end of the seat, close to the door. I was too nervous to look at Ray, and on my deaf side, it was easy not to. I felt sometimes like that part of the world didn't exist. If I couldn't hear it, I wouldn't know it was there.

Sam didn't seem to think our silence was strange. He probably thought we were exhausted from the hot day. I had nodded off once already, and had dreamed . . .

Ray reached for my hand.

Our fingers met, laced, squeezed together in the tiny bit of space between us on the seat. I forgot my dream, the hot red sky. Then Ray picked up our hands and set them on his knee where Sam could see perfectly.

> Dear Ellee,
> You won't believe what happened. I finally kissed someone.
> I like him and trust him and that seems like enough. It seems right.
>
> Dear Thea,
> Tell me everything.

Ray and I met at the library. We met at the café and Louisa gave us sandwiches and cold drinks to take out to the picnic table. We ate, then brushed the crumbs away and Ray started to teach me to sign.

He said he was beginning with the basic stuff. *My name is.* Two fingers of each of my hands knocking together like an *X*. Spelling: an alphabet that Ray said was easy but not used too much, not unless it was a name or a word you didn't know. *A*, my hand like a fist. *B*, my hand flat and straight, thumb tucked behind fingers. *C*, my hand cupped like a shell, cupped like my ear that didn't hear.

Ray was a patient teacher, but I felt so behind. "You can find some good videos on the internet," he told me, then realized his mistake.

My lack of a phone. The dead zone of the farm. Our dark house, which he had never seen and never *would* see if I had anything to do with it.

"At the library, I mean," he corrected himself. "You can look up videos for practice."

I didn't tell Ray that maybe *we* should practice more. I didn't ask what he was to me. What should I call him? My boyfriend? My friend—but friend I kissed? My secret? So much of my life was starting to be separate, things I couldn't tell my parents or even Amelia, in case she might accidentally spill. I wrote them to Ellee.

The best part of our lessons was when I felt frustrated or my hands grew too sloppy, or Louisa came to the back door of the café to call, "Let me know when you're done, honey. No rush." Which meant: *Time to come in*; I was needed and she just didn't want to be a bother.

I was learning that about Louisa. She would give all that she had, more than she had. She sent pastries off with me at the end of the day for my family, and food and coffee in the mornings I spent with Ray and Sam. But I had also watched her cross the road to the post office, big packages in her arms for those faraway nieces and nephews.

And it wasn't the best part because I got a break. Ending our lessons was the best because then Ray and I spent our last few moments together at the picnic table kissing.

I was learning two new languages, one with my hands and one with my heart. From the library, I was learning too, about history and science, filling in some of the gaps from my last few years without school. Things my mom never would have taught me because she didn't know. Like how storms developed. What greenhouse gases were and how they made the heat worse. And how the country had responded back in the year of the first black blizzards.

Not well.

After the first dust storms in the 1930s, there were movements to change how people farmed, to rotate crops, leaving more of the deep-rooting prairie grasses and clearing fewer pastures so the soil had something to hold on to, so it wouldn't blow away again.

But these movements never took off. No changes were made. It was too expensive, unprofitable. No government acted or helped, providing incentives for farmers to plant anything much other than money-making wheat. To do anything other than raze and plant, raze and plant, never switching crops, never giving the soil a break. The earth was tired and weak.

We hadn't learned much of anything.

The way people farmed now—the way my dad farmed—was very similar to the way it was then. He ripped up what was there, discarding the useless grasses. He planted crops that didn't seem to want to grow, not in the earth that was more dust than dirt. *Rip out your fences,* I had read in my library book that the Secretary of Agriculture once said, a rallying call to farmers. *Plant your fields edge to edge.*

And farmers listened, sowing crops in those feet of earth that before had been a divider, a place of native plants, wildflowers. There was no place for wildflowers anymore. And after World War I, there was a great hunger. A need, or perceived need. That land would hold crops now, as all of it should. Every bit of space held them more and more, replacing the prairies.

Our weather in the valley seemed familiar too, recalling what I was learning of history. Small dust storms every few days. The locusts. The heat was even more scorching than I had read about. But we had air conditioners now, factories, cars—and so our temperatures soared higher than in the past. Heat waves lasted for longer. The wells were drying up.

The snowpack, which Sam told me supplied the river, the melted snow pooling in the spring and summer and running into the valley like an IV—it was no longer steady. No more a full and strong flood rushing the foothills, to be captured by estuaries. It had dwindled, thinning out. It was strange that mild, snow-light winters made the summers worse, but they did.

Every day I read.

Every day I wrote to Ellee and she emailed back.

Almost every day I rode out with Ray and Sam, bouncing down driveways of dust and rocks. Dirt lined my fingernails and I was exhausted every night, but I no longer complained in the mornings. I couldn't wait to get in the truck with my mom, to reach the café.

She had given me some strange looks the first few times I had bounded into the passenger seat, more awake and excited than she had ever seen me so close to dawn.

But my mom was not one to question.

With Ray and Sam, I visited Elmer and Helen, the Mistys and Gus, and others. I observed Gus's neighbor from a distance. The nameless man. The man with the signs.

I didn't try to reach out to him again.

I started to notice things, small glimmers in the landscape, like a three-leaved shrub which Sam said was called sumac but also *lemonade* because of its sour drop berries. I saw sunflowers, smaller than the ones my family had planted by our house but just as bright, yellow pops against the dirt. I couldn't hear any songs from the mountain bluebird that perched on fenceposts and telephone poles, but Ray said it was a shy bird—and he couldn't hear it, either. I had just missed the sandhill cranes, which flooded through the valley in the spring. Ray said their bugle cries sounded like a marching band, and I would definitely observe them next year.

Next year? I thought.

We visited some families like the Mistys, but mostly we dropped in on loners, people making a go of it by themselves. Most of them were older than my parents. Some had lived forever in the valley, staying like Louisa after family members had moved away or died. Others had lived lives in the city, lives of commutes, crowds, and hustle. And now they were trying this other thing: alone in the desert but mostly, alone with themselves.

"Can you imagine that?" Ray asked me once.

We were in the truck, waiting for his great-uncle to finish up with someone. We had helped the man fix his internet and Sam had signed him up for an appointment. Now Sam was reminding the man that he could pick him up, go with him to see the doctor.

Ray and I took this moment for ourselves. His lips were on mine, his hand in my hair, reaching around the back of my neck as he pulled me into him. I felt like I was lifting off the old vinyl seat. Then Ray pulled away.

"Is Sam coming?" I glanced at the house.

"No." Ray had only pulled back to ask me a question, so I could see his lips. "It's just . . . can you imagine, living all alone like that? It makes me feel sad sometimes."

Cardboard covered some of the windows of the man's house. Black marks licked below the sills, as though the house had survived a fire. And trash dotted the landscape, old tires, cans, white plastic bags caught in the brush like a coating of snow.

I had never seen Ray's house where he lived with his great-uncle, his artist mother off leading tourists into the mountains, setting up her easel when she had a day off. Ray had shown me some of her smaller watercolors, colorful vistas of wildflower valleys and rocky streams. She ripped pages out of her sketchbook and sent them to him. He kept them pressed in a book.

Ray had told me he had his own room at Sam's house. It was a stucco house, clay with red roof tiles. The kitchen was painted yellow. Ray's room was yellow too, because his great-uncle had asked him what he wanted, was willing to paint it any color to make the room comfortable, to make a home for him—but Ray knew there was yellow paint left over already. He didn't want to ask for too much. His room was on the first floor and had French doors that opened out onto a patio ringed with aspens. The floors inside were cool tile, he said. Sam had bought a house in the shade. He knew what to do.

I hoped Ray would never see where I lived. If he did, he would know that I was poor. He would realize things about me, as sure as the dresses hanging out on the clothesline. They were symbols of a different kind of life. My fingers turned red washing those clothes. My skin was smudged by ash from leaning over the woodstove. I didn't have shelter like those covering aspens—not a clean, yellow room to myself, not a family who understood me.

In the front seat of the truck, I pulled away slightly too. "You can't picture living out here?"

"Not completely alone. This guy's internet and phones were even down."

My family had no internet, I could have reminded Ray. But I couldn't stop thinking about his *completely alone* remark. When you can't follow whole chunks of a conversation, you're not a part of it, even if your friends—like Ellee—try to include you. They don't notice your silence every time.

No one heard my every silence.

In a way, I thought, living alone might have been easier than my type of alone. At least living solo you might know what you were up against: loneliness rolling on like the highway. Being alone but surrounded by other people, I never knew when isolation might creep up on me, separate me from my family or friends, because I had replied wrong or laughed inappropriately or couldn't follow or smiled instead of answering, smiled when it wasn't right to smile. I never knew when I would be lonely, but loneliness was always with me.

"I'd rather live in a city," Ray was saying. "Like Denver, though Denver has a lot of problems. I still feel _____ it's easier for me."

"It's what you know. You grew up there."

"Yeah. But I also feel like there could be more people like me in a city."

"People . . . like you?" I asked.

"Like you and me. In a city, we could have dinners and go to concerts. Just be ourselves together."

It took me a moment to realize Ray was probably talking about doing those things with other deaf people in general, not just with me. I tried to shake the hopeful picture out of my mind: the two of us, hanging out in a city I had never been to. As if my parents would let me go to a concert with a boy, go anywhere with one. As if I could get to Denver.

"You don't feel like you can be yourself here?" I asked.

"Not always. People like Sam and Louisa, they try their best. Most of the people in my life do—I'm lucky like that. But they don't completely understand. I don't feel fully myself around them all the _____."

Am I fully myself? I wondered. How could I be sure when I didn't yet know who I was?

I thought of the black-and-white pictures from the library books: people not much older than me, living through so much. I did a lot, I reminded myself. Like those people from history, I could darn a sock, sew on buttons, whip butter into cream in a shaking jar—but that wasn't who I was.

My dad's dream had forced me into this role, but the role wasn't me. I didn't have my own dream. Not yet. My fingers traced the top of Ray's hand above his thumb. I hadn't even realized I was doing it until I looked down and saw myself. It felt natural to be together. And who I was felt like it was constantly changing, shifting as swiftly as Ray and I had moved from being strangers to friends to . . . something more. I felt as unfixed as our crops. I might struggle. I might grow. I would change, that was the only for sure thing.

Ray glanced behind me. "Sam's coming back." Then he said, "He wants to have you over for dinner."

I looked at him. *"What?"*

"You and your family."

"Well, that's not happening."

"Come on." Ray clutched my hands again. "I want to show you my room and all my rocks. Some of my mom's paintings are hanging up in the house. Big ones. We can walk to a creek _____, when it's running. And when it's not, you can find things in _____, quartz and granite."

"That sounds really nice."

"What?" he asked.

I repeated myself.

"It is nice. And Thea"—he squeezed my hand—"it's part of my life. I want you to know my life."

"I want that too. It's just . . ."

How could I explain it? My dad kept my interests restricted to home. We had so much work to do there; we couldn't keep space for anything else, not even allowing the possibility of it.

That Amelia and I might be different people than my parents, have different dreams—any dreams at all beyond family and farm—seemed impossible. Work took over everything.

I thought of Amelia and her love for animals, thought of Helen's still life. How had she learned to paint like that? How had she been allowed to? Maybe my mom could have done something else with her time if she didn't have to spend a whole day every week on laundry.

Sam had returned to the truck. "Ready to go, kids?" he asked.

14

I was hiding a lot of things. The prism from Helen, in Amelia's possession. The library book, which would come due soon. And the note from Patience Misty to my sister.

I could not figure out an easy way to give the note to Amelia. It wasn't the explaining that worried me so much—she knew about Helen and Ray and Sam already—it was expecting my sister to lie for me. Lie again. To sequester a secret, as she hid the prism in her pillowcase. Buried in darkness, the prism could never transmit light, as it was meant to do. Another secret would burn inside my sister the same way, eating her up like my secrets were threatening to consume me.

I wanted to talk with my mom about Ray; I wanted to ask her questions. How did you know for sure if you loved someone? When did you tell them? I wanted to know. I wanted to practice signing in the day, and share it with my family.

And I knew Amelia couldn't lie, either. Not like I had learned to. She was terrible at it, not having had much experience. She had never emailed in a library she was forbidden to even step foot in. She had never furtively met a guy, held his hand. Done more than held his hand.

I hadn't opened the note to her, which Patience had folded multiple times and squeezed tightly together in the way of little kids; it was less of a note and more of a brick. But I hadn't given it to my sister, either. I hid it myself.

And then she found it.

We were doing our weekend chores. The hot hours dragged by in sweeping, washing bedclothes. I cursed the homemade detergent that irritated my skin, lye stinging my eyes. I wrung the sopping sheets, hung them on the line outside. The heavy, wet fabric slapped against me as I fumbled for clothespins. The sheets would dry in no time. Everything did out here.

I turned to get another sheet from the basket. Behind me I noticed Amelia standing in the open doorway of the house, something white in her hand.

"What is PAT-IN-CE?" she asked. She was reading, trying to spell something out. My nine-year-old sister, who was not good at reading because we were not good at teaching her.

"Patience?" I guessed. I moved toward her, seeing she held a piece of paper.

It had been folded many times.

"What's _____?" My mom came around the other side of the house, her face still red from the heat of the stove. She had been baking bread, and had brought some to my dad while it was still warm.

I knew. In the moment my mom touched the paper, I knew.

The knowledge spread through me, sickening and hot. I

had hidden it under my mattress. But I had stripped the beds this morning to wash the sheets. My sister was remaking them with fresh linens, and she must have found it. The note.

"Amelia, did you draw this?" my mom asked.

I hurried to the door of the house, pushing aside the laundry on the line as it smacked against me. I felt like my steps were leaden and like they would float away, take me far from here. My mom shook out the note to examine it better.

Patience Misty had done a drawing of two girls. One was labeled *Patience,* the other: *Amelia*. In the foreground, she had drawn some buildings—maybe her family's trailers, maybe my family's house. The mountains in the distance watched. And in the far background: a dust cloud whirled. Even a child, in her drawing, her hopeful image of friendship, had drawn a terrible dust storm.

"Thea, you didn't...?" The end of my mom's sentence trembled in question, hanging over the yard like the sheets hung, heavy.

"I didn't write it," I said.

"Who did then?"

Amelia realized something was off. She had said the wrong thing, even though she didn't know what it was. "I'm sorry," she said quickly.

"Why are you apologizing?" My mom studied the paper. "It's Amelia with patience, having patience. Right, Amelia?"

"I don't know. I'm sorry."

"Thea?" My mom looked up at me.

Amelia seemed near tears. "It had my name on it. I thought it was for me," she said.

"Can someone explain this?"

I had to save my sister. "I met a family," I said. "Unschoolers, like us. They have a girl Amelia's age. Her name is Patience. I told her about you, Amelia. She said she'd like to be friends. I guess she drew you."

That brought a smile to Amelia's face, though her eyes looked glassy.

"How did you meet them? Did they come into the café?"

"Do you remember the rural outreach agent?" I asked. "I told you about him. Sam?"

My mom shook her head.

"The one I chopped wood with? He comes to the café a lot, actually. And his great-nephew. They're very kind, and they've been taking me . . . *out* with them, to meet people on farms and ranches, to help out."

My mom was stuck on my words. "What do you mean, out with them?"

"Sam does rounds, to check on people. I've been going too sometimes."

"More than the one _____, to chop wood? How have you been doing that?"

"Sometimes, at work, Louisa lets me—"

"You've been leaving work? More than once? With a stranger?"

"Sam isn't a stranger. He wants to meet you. And Dad. To have us all over for dinner." I was saying too much, I realized. The words were coming out of me in a rush, and I could see from my mom's face how jumbled and terrible it all sounded.

It was only the start of it, that was the thing. It was only part of what I had been doing, learning, in opposition to what my parents wanted. They were good secrets, good things happening to me, I felt: reading, studying, and making new friends. But I realized my mom maybe wouldn't see it that way. My dad definitely wouldn't.

He didn't want me and Amelia to know about the world. Unschooling wasn't about farming for him. It was about shielding us. And schools and libraries had technology like computers. Computers had internet. On the internet I had already learned information that stood in glaring contrast to my dad's truth: how other people farmed the land, how that land was changing.

All the newspapers, all the encyclopedias, all the science sites were in agreement about that. The planet was heating up, the seasons blurring together and distorting like paper burned in a fire: summers hotter, floods deeper, droughts drier, and winter storms more severe.

And dust coming.

My mom had taken the note from Amelia—the child's drawing looked so crude in her hand—and she asked my sister, "Where did you find this?"

Amelia seemed stricken.

"It's okay. Tell her," I said.

"Under Thea's bed."

Then it was over for me.

We went into the house. My mom, possessed by new energy, found the library book about the Dust Bowl under my mattress. She tore through the room, searching for more. She found the prism in the pillowcase. She held it away from her body as if it might sear her.

"Is this for witchcraft?" she asked.

"No, it's science," I said. "It makes rainbows when you put it in the sun."

She looked up at me and her expression held panic like I had not seen before. "Thea, your dad is not going to like this. It's almost *worse* that it's for science. We have to—"

"We have to what?"

My dad had entered the room.

His tone was flat but his eyes were white, his pupils small. He had looked like that since the day at the dry well. Haunted, as if even this next terrible thing wouldn't really surprise him.

It would only be more fuel for his fire.

"What's this?" He took the prism from my mom, and before either of us could answer—I saw my mom struggling to speak, but I couldn't find the right or any words—he asked a question which wasn't a question at all. "Have you been lying to us, Thea?" His eyes roved over the room. The library book, the opened note, the mattress shoved up so the slats of the bed were exposed.

Amelia turned and ran out of the room. I thought I could hear the beginnings of her sobs. I wasn't sure if she was crying over the friend that would never be, Patience, or the fact that she knew I was going to get in trouble.

My punishments were always about deprivation, which was especially hard because I felt my sister and I already had less compared to others. When I forgot to shut the latch on the chickens' coop and we had to chase them down, I wasn't allowed to eat eggs for a week. A better punishment, I had thought at the time, feeling my stomach rumble, would have been making me clean the coop.

But my dad and mom gave us everything, he liked to say, and he could and would take it away. *It could be worse,* he always said.

I never wanted to ask *how.*

As he sat me down at the kitchen table, I wondered if I was about to find out. It was serious enough that I had to be seated. He had to think about what he was going to say.

I had to think too.

"I don't understand what's going on with you," my dad said. He kept his voice low, which made it harder for me to hear. I could feel the straining headache beginning behind my eyes. "What started you down this path of lying, hiding _____ from us."

"I'm not doing anything bad," I said. "I'm meeting new people. I'm going to the library. Most parents would love it if their kids did that, if they were reading."

"We're not most parents. And you're not _____."

"Why aren't you most parents?"

My dad spoke with pandering in his voice, condescending, as if he was explaining to a much younger child. "We believe the way to raise you is a different, simpler way."

There wasn't anything simple about how we had to haul water to the house, or try to get the ancient, heavy cookstove to cooperate and bake food evenly, but instead I asked, "Do you think I'm in danger at the library?"

I snuck a glance at my mom and she made the slightest movement of her head and shoulders.

I thought about the small gains I believed I had made with her, how she never said anything about how dirty I was at the end of my days with Sam and Ray, how extra tired. I had been on the verge of explaining my interest in science, in the climate, to her when my dad had barged in the room—and I felt certain she would have understood. She would have listened anyway.

It was a silent warning from her now, that almost imperceptible head shake: I was going too far with my dad. But I had to go further.

"Why do you think I'm in danger?" I asked.

My dad's expression let me know this was the last thing on his mind. "We don't think you're in physical danger, Thea. We think you might be influenced by forces that we don't approve of, without you _____ aware of it."

"It's not we, it's *you*. It's not what you and Mom believe. It's always just what you think, and she has to go along. This is your fantasy, to be homesteaders. It doesn't have to be this hard. And it's a lot harder for us than it is for you." Words left me like light shooting out of the prism. I couldn't stop them. "And you never think about my deafness. You never think about me and what it's like for me. How I might be different from you."

"Everything we do is for you," my dad said.

"No. It's not. It's for you. Sir."

We sat in silence for a minute. I thought my dad would explode, but I was the one who had burst out in anger. My dad simply waited and simmered. What he was going to say next would be cool and detached, which made it worse somehow, his voice so low and soft. My head pounded with the pressure of trying to understand. "All right, Thea," he said. "Why don't you tell me?"

I glanced at my mom but her face gave me nothing.

"I don't understand," I said to my dad.

"I don't think about what it's like for you? Tell me what it's like then."

I paused and tried to listen through the silence, tried so hard my head throbbed.

I could not hear if Amelia was crying. I could not hear the dogs outside, if they were whining or scratching to get in. I *could* hear, in the near distance, motors on the highway, but I couldn't tell if they were trucks or motorcycles, if they were zooming away or coming close. I couldn't hear the clock ticking in the kitchen; I just knew it worked by the tremble of its hands. I couldn't hear if anyone breathed or whispered or sighed.

I said, "It's so lonely."

I guessed I expected him to listen; my dad had asked me, after all. But he hadn't asked seriously, I saw that right away. He didn't really want to know.

Instead, he rose from the table. The chair fell and struck the floor with a crash so sudden my mom and I both flinched. "If it's been so hard for you, if you're so lonely, you should spend more time with your sister." His comment was sopped in sarcasm.

My mom eyed the chair on the floor.

"I *was* lonely," I said. "But then I started going to the library and I started to help with Sam and I—"

"Whatever that is, it ends now."

"I think, if you just met Sam and Captain and all the people I've been meeting in town—"

"I'm not meeting anyone," my dad said. "And neither are you. Not in secret, or _____ you've been doing. Not anymore."

"Okay," I said. "I'll go to work and home, that's it."

"No. We tried that before. That was _____ to be the plan _____." My dad was shaking his head and he wasn't sitting back down. "You're done with your job."

I hoped I hadn't heard him. "What do you mean?"

"It's over. You're quitting."

"I can't. Don't we need the money?" I looked at my mom.

What was all that about Helen, and meeting nice people? Hadn't my mom wanted that? I saw it was a dream now, and only one my mom would share with me when we were alone, stuck together working in the kitchen. That was the time for sharing dreams. Not here in the harsh light with my dad, who would make sure they never came true.

There were no dreams but his.

"We need you home safe with your sister. That's what we need." My dad pushed away from the table. He had been leaning over it, his fists on the top, and now he shoved off.

"I can't just leave Louisa," I said. "She's counting on me."

"Your mom will tell her."

"But I should talk to her, on Monday—"

"Your Monday will be spent here. You're not going back _____. Not again."

"Dad—"

"I can't trust you. We have no idea where you are, what you're being exposed to, unless you're right here. So, you have to stay _____. You did this, Thea. You brought this down upon yourself." He turned his back. His last few words to me were a mumble, something about teaching Amelia, taking over for my mom.

I tried to make sense of it, my temples pulsing. "I'm not a teacher, Dad. I'm sixteen."

"Act like it."

Then he was gone, to the back of the house and outside. He slammed the screen door loud enough it boomed.

My mom leaned over to pick up the chair. "Thea—" she began.

But I was walking away.

In our room, Amelia was face down on her bed. She raised her head from the pillow when I entered the room and closed the door softly behind me. Her face looked swollen and pink. "Did I get you in trouble?" she asked.

"No." I sat on my bed across from her.

This was my prison now. This room, this house, this farm that my parents had promised would be so big, so wide—I had already reached the limits of it. I needed more space, more people, more time. More, more. I needed *something*. I thought of Ray and his rocks, Elmer and his books. What would be my thing? How would I ever discover it, trapped here?

I pulled my own pillow to my face and screamed.

"What's wrong with you?" Amelia said.

I let the pillow fall away. The magnitude of the loss was hitting me. I was being denied the outside world, my lessons with Ray, my new friends. "I messed up everything," I told her. "And there's no way for me to get it all back, to tell him."

"Tell who?"

"I messed up my job, my friends, Ray . . ."

"Who's Ray?" Immediately, Amelia was alert, sitting cross-legged on the bed, pillow pulled conspiratorially into her lap.

"The guy I met," I said. "He was teaching me things."

"What things?"

I was seized with contradictory feelings, that I had said too much already and also the urge to tell my secrets, to spill it all. Information burned inside of me, wanting to leap free and be shared. "Sign language, for one," I said.

Amelia didn't ask me why. She didn't say I heard just fine, I heard enough, and I spoke and used English, didn't I? She didn't do anything like that. I heard the questions and protests and accusations in my head that I imagined my sister might have said to me. They withered away into nothingness. Amelia understood.

She said, "Teach me."

"I don't know enough," I said.

"You know more than me."

"I was only just starting to learn."

"Okay." She resettled herself on the bed, as if getting comfortable for a long night. "We can learn together."

I had one more library book that my mom hadn't found. Hidden underneath the house, in a hollow pocket between the outside wall and the ground. Some of the dirt must have eroded away there, or maybe the foundation of the house was never solid to begin with. It made a small crevice, the house's framework forming a pocket protected from rain. Not that there was any rain.

I had thanked Cuthbert for his crappy construction work when I found the space and slid the second library book inside. An ASL dictionary.

Ray had said I couldn't learn everything from a book. I couldn't learn to sign except from a deaf person. Not a hearing person, he stressed, because they didn't know. *They haven't lived it. They aren't a part of the culture.*

Had I lived it? What culture? I had felt that I was living a half life. Not fully hearing, not fully deaf. I existed as if in a doorway. Ray had offered me a key, a way inside a room with him. But now Ray was gone and I was outside again.

I knew the book wasn't enough, but it was the only thing I had.

Monday dawned. It was hazy out, yellow. But the clouds in the sky didn't mean rain. They never did.

Amelia woke before me, dressed in the dimness of our room, and made her bed like a good girl. She brushed her hair solemnly twenty-five strokes, as if we had anywhere to go, as if anyone would see us. She shook me awake gently, not knowing I was only pretending to sleep, watching her through the dark brushes of my eyes.

"You don't want to miss breakfast," she said.

Her cheerfulness made me feel even more sour. I wanted to snap at her. *There will* be *no breakfast unless Mom and I make it.*

I groaned, getting out of bed. I pulled on clothes I didn't look at. I didn't look at my mom when I entered the kitchen. Numbly, I poked at the fire in the cookstove. I dumped oats in the big pot she had already filled with water. Precious water. I remembered when it was everywhere, when it had flooded our town. I remembered walking through the woods of Ohio, rain and dew droplets scattering from the trees as I brushed against them, my boots sticking in the spring mud. So many moments I didn't know I would miss. So much easy, available water.

My mom was busy with the coffee. I turned to get a wooden spoon. In the narrow, still shadowy kitchen I bumped into her.

I mumbled an apology, but she reached out and stilled my arm, bringing it down to my side and holding on to me.

"I'm sorry," she said.

I looked at her. Her eyes seemed tired, or maybe there was another reason they darted to the side, skating away from me. "Sorry about what?"

"I didn't know . . . that you had met so many people. That you had made friends. I'm sorry you can't be with them."

"Why can't I?"

"Thea." She dropped my hand. "Your dad needs you to listen. He needs to know you and your sister are safe at home."

"There are other places to be safe," I said. "Ma'am."

She must have heard that last word, the address I used only when I was fed up. She must have caught my tone; she could hear it. But she was already occupied with some other task. The farm was full of them. You could work forever rather than feeling.

That was what I did. I made breakfast, barely acknowledging my dad when he ate it. That was easy enough to do; he barely acknowledged me. I cleaned up. Once the table was clear again, my mom was gone and it was time to help Amelia with school.

"Teach me sign language now," she begged.

Our dad was in the fields. Our mom had left for work—what was she going to tell Louisa? What would Ray and Sam say when they came into the café to find me gone? No explanation or apology from me, no way to talk to them, to reach out and explain. For the hundredth time, I wished I had a phone.

"I don't know sign language," I told Amelia.

"You know a little."

"I'm supposed to be teaching you..." I checked the workbook my mom had left out for us. *"Adventures in Home Education!"* There was an exclamation mark in the title, as if anyone would be excited about learning from this thin and gray, faded volume. Then I checked the copyright date. 1992.

I had stuck my letters to friends in workbooks like these, knowing they would never be mailed, unheard missives I was mostly writing to myself. When Ellee had started emailing, I had stopped writing them. But there was no way for me to answer her now.

"Teach me something I can use," Amelia said.

"You can use fractions," I said. "In cooking. You can't use ASL."

"Yes, I can."

"With me?"

"With you, for one thing."

It was still morning. My mom would be gone all day, and my dad would be outside for at least another hour. I fetched the book from beneath the house.

Signs that were important to me: *love, boyfriend, friend, sister.*

Signs that were important to Amelia: *dog, sister, candy, chicken.*

"I don't know why Mom and Dad kept this from you," Amelia said when I had convinced her to shut the book and we had hidden it under the house again.

"I'm not sure. Maybe"—I stepped back, examining the outside of the house to make sure you couldn't see any part of the book peeking out—"they didn't know what they were doing. They thought it was the right thing, to make me listen hard and read lips and try to be like everybody else."

"But you're not like everybody else."

On the school bus, I had sometimes heard my name hissed loudly, followed by laughter. Even before Emily and Frankie, June and Isabel dropped me, I was never picked by teachers to read aloud in class, and was chosen last for groups and teams. I was aware, even if I couldn't make it out exactly, of noise as I passed by in the hall. Someone behind me imitating my confusion or voice, the way I said *What?* constantly. I wasn't sure what Amelia remembered about that time. She had been so young.

"People at school weren't very nice," I said.

"Kids suck," said Amelia, who was a kid.

I smiled at her. "What's it time for now? Math?"

"I think a break."

I was trying not to let the frustration of being stuck at home show, not to her. I was trying not to make my sister feel bad, trying to make a game of it all. But I felt disappointment through my bones. It made all my movements slow, like I was pretending, just going through the motions with her. In my head, I was far away with Ray, bumping down a dirt road, his hand laced through mine. I was talking with Helen about light, or Gus about the weather. I was eating a sandwich on the bed of a truck.

I had to be here, to manufacture joy and energy for Amelia as she bounded around the farm, intent on showing me what was new with the chickens. But I felt every moment tinged with absence. Sam would have been out on his rounds by now. Was Elmer asleep at the library, or had he finished writing another chapter? How would Louisa feel, knowing I couldn't come back to help? I thought of her alone in the empty café, rattling around like a ghost. Her family had left her. Now I had too.

It was my own fault, I thought. I had gotten sloppy, going out with Ray and Sam almost every day, hiding too many secrets and expecting them never to be found.

I feigned interest in the small improvements Amelia had made to the coop: the ramps and a more secure, fenced area to protect the birds from hawks. But my sister looked at me and I could see the frustration on her face. Her thin lips almost vanished they were pressed together so tightly. I forced myself to listen.

I hoped Louisa was all right, not working too hard. I hoped Captain didn't feel betrayed by how I had disappeared. He had never said much about the library's new books, not after that first week. I wondered if there really *were* new books, or if it had all been an excuse to get me to the library, to help me make a friend.

Amelia was demonstrating how to open the door of the coop so the chickens could go in and out of the fenced area freely. She worked the flap back and forth, then stopped. She gave a small sigh.

I thought she was mad at me again for drifting. I was prepared to say something supportive, that I was proud of her work, when she said, "Dad always thinks things are right to do."

"What?" I asked.

She straightened up from the coop. All around her, the birds flocked, ankle-high clouds. "You said he thought it was the right _____ to make you read lips, not sign? He's always doing things like that. He thought taking us out of school was the right thing. He thought moving here was right." One of the chickens had wandered close to Amelia, and she scooped it up, held it to her chest. Its clucking subsided and it seemed to relax in her arms. "What if nothing's right?"

It had been a long time since I had talked to my sister like this, just the two of us, uninterrupted by our parents or chores. Amelia was more thoughtful than I had realized. Or, maybe she had changed. In the time I had been away, that I had been busying myself with my own life, my sister had grown up.

"Dad is obsessed with doing the right thing," Amelia said. "Maybe it was the right thing to move out here, maybe not. Right for _____? For us? Or for him? How do we know it was right? We won't till it's over."

How will we know?

I followed Amelia's gaze. She was looking out at nothing, just the fields and beyond them: the road. It was a look she had learned from our mom.

"Maybe the trick," I said, holding the little wire door open for Amelia so she could duck out of the enclosure, a chicken still in her arms, "is adapting. So, it didn't work out like we planned, moving out here. What do we try next?"

"Yeah, I don't think Mom and Dad are so good at that."

"No," I said, watching as Amelia let the chicken go and it fluttered off.

I wondered, *Am I?*

Loneliness pressed down on me like a sunburn. I tried to be there for Amelia. I spoke politely to my dad. Made him lunch when he returned from the fields, cleaned up his lunch when he was finished. He dipped in and out of the house like a dragonfly. He didn't want to be around us, either. And he didn't want to talk to me, the girl who missed whole chunks of his sentences.

When my mom came home in the late afternoon, the grief broke open inside of me. That should have been *me* in the truck. Was this what Amelia had felt, all this time, when I had been gone every day at the café?

My mom parked the truck, smiled to see us both and all the dogs. Then she reached into the back seat and brought out pastries and cookies. "From Louisa."

"Did she say anything?" I asked. "About me being gone?"

My mom shook her head, but her face looked strange. "She understood. She'll miss you, but she _____. Family comes first."

If family came first, didn't that mean *everyone* in the family sometimes, including me?

When I had been pulled from school in Ohio, I had felt cut off. But we soon had the homeschool group, Ellee and Angie and friends for my sister. It was a short trip into town then, a village so small that we couldn't go anywhere without running into a person we knew. My mom used to joke that she had to get dressed up every time we left the house. Because we never knew who we might encounter, but it would be someone.

In Colorado, the drive into town—just the stretch with the library, Louisa's, Second Chance, and the post office—was so much longer. Time spread as slow as water through creek beds, like the one behind Ray's house. Dry now, he had told me. Baked, its earthen sides cracking.

There would be no coincidental run-ins in the valley. No reason to dress up. No one even had my dad's phone number.

And I didn't have Ray's.

I carried the basket from Louisa into the house, leaving my mom at the truck. Amelia was telling her about our day. I knew my sister would leave out our signing practice. She was learning to hide better, just as I had, to anticipate what might anger our parents, especially our dad, what would cause trouble.

But her voice sounded excited, and for some reason, that made me even more sad. Of course Amelia was happy; she had me home at last. She was the only one who won in this situation.

I went into the kitchen and unpacked the basket. Chocolate chip muffins, blueberry scones, some snickerdoodle cookies that looked large and soft and smelled of cinnamon. I wondered if Louisa had baked them especially for Amelia. Or, in a hope that I knew was wishful thinking, if Elmer had.

In the bottom of the basket, my fingers grazed something else.

A small scroll.

It was a piece of paper, rolled up like a treasure map. It could have been a bit of receipt accidentally left in the basket, curling at the end of the cash register's paper roll. But it wasn't. I knew it wasn't.

I could hear my mom and Amelia talking in the yard, just a faint, wordless murmur to me, like how I imagined the ocean might sound. Standing over the kitchen sink, I unwrapped the scroll.

I saw Louisa's handwriting, which I had glimpsed so often on the labels of sandwiches in the café. *Chicken Salad. Turkey Swiss.* I had read it scrawled on the sleeves slipped over the to-go cups, misspelling various names—including my own name at first. *Thea*. Short for Amalthea.

As a child, I had had trouble distinguishing my name from Amelia's, once my sister came along. *Amalthea, Amelia.* I couldn't hear the difference. Couldn't tell who my parents were calling. So, *I* had to change; I had to accommodate. I had to go by a new name.

I saw my boss's handwriting in a message, written on the scroll. There was no name on it, but I knew it was for me.

Don't give up, Louisa had written.

15

In the morning, my mom acted strange. I hadn't slept well myself. I had had the dream again, the one I had in the truck with Ray and Sam. The one with the rising dust and the red sky.

Of course I kept dreaming of dust in this place, I thought as Amelia coughed, brushing her hair in our room. She set the brush down when a particularly intense spasm rippled through her. I looked away. Thinking about Ray and Sam had made me sad, and I couldn't listen to my sister struggle to breathe. It made me feel helpless.

In the kitchen, my mom waited for me, a smile on her face. She wasn't her usual, stressed-out self, hurrying through the motions of making coffee.

"What's going on?" I asked.

"Is your sister awake?"

"She's coming."

My mom couldn't wait. "I have the day off," she said, "so I'm taking you girls on a field trip."

The library. My heart gave a jag straight to my throat. In our old life, before my dad decided computers were unnecessary and a gateway to worse, a field trip often meant the library. We would spend a whole morning or afternoon there, leafing through books, Amelia playing in the kids' section. We might do a craft or sit through a lecture, or meet other homeschoolers.

Surely, my mom didn't mean the library now. Surely, she wouldn't take us back there.

"Where are we going?" I tried to say it casually as I dumped oats into the big pot on the stove.

"It's a surprise."

I wouldn't allow myself to feel hopeful. "Mom, that book you found—"

"One of the things you hid?"

I ignored that. "The history book? It's a library book and it's due soon."

"I've taken care of it. I've already taken it back."

Hope dropped like a weight from a great height. Leaving me.

"You know, we would have checked out a book for you," my mom said. "You didn't have to sneak _____."

"But you wouldn't have."

"If you're interested in history, what about *Heroes of Freedom*?" She named an ancient homeschooling book, one as skewed as it was outdated.

I thought about the workbooks from which I was supposed to teach Amelia, their musty, cartoon covers and obsolete facts. Everything we had was so old, from the cookstove to our learning materials. The stove worked, at least—most of the time. But the textbooks didn't. I couldn't teach Amelia antiquated ideas, theories that had been proven false. Those books skipped over or ignored so much: the lives of women, of disabled people like me, the changing climate.

"It's not just history I'm worried about," I said. "It's what's happening right now."

"And what's that?"

"The heat. The dust clouds. It's—"

Amelia bounded into the kitchen, interrupting me. She could barely contain herself. "I heard something about a field trip?"

The easy ways of the hearing, and how they could just *know*, hear enough to anticipate and guess. Enough not to feel left out. Every conversation always included them, even the ones that didn't. They were spies, hearing people, lurking around corners, always figuring things out.

Any progress I might have made with my mom receded as she turned her attention to Amelia. My mom said brightly, "You heard correct."

"Where are we going? The library?"

My mom's smile wavered a bit. I saw the strain cross her face. But she was not going to lose control; she would not have an argument with us in the kitchen, the oats not even cooked yet and the sun not fully up. The dogs needed feeding. My dad would want his breakfast. If I could hear like my mom and sister, maybe I would have heard him stirring in the bedroom, the squealing of the mattress springs, the heavy thunk as he pulled on his boots. Maybe he was waking and that was why my mom hurried.

Maybe she hadn't told him we were leaving the house today.

Her voice sounded rushed and I strained to catch the words. "I know you girls are interested in weather, how it's different out here in the valley. Your dad and I want to encourage _____, and we want you to explore. That's one of the reasons we're teaching you the way _____. So you can feel free to pursue what inspires you."

Feel free to pursue what inspires you and Dad, I thought. Cooking, farming, and free labor.

"I'm inspired by animals," Amelia said.

"I know you are, honey, but today we're going to do something your sister likes too. Today . . ." She looked at me, drawing it out. I could see the anticipation and hope in her eyes, and I hated her for it. She was trying to make me forget what had been taken from me, make me forgive—and I couldn't, not so easily. I looked away. She turned her hope to Amelia, and her bright voice. "We're going to a tower!"

It was the big reveal, but Amelia looked confused. I was too.

"A tower?"

"What tower?" I asked.

"Well," my mom said. "This is going to sound strange, but I heard about a tower right off the highway. It's _____."

"What kind of a museum?" Amelia asked.

"Things have been left there and preserved by the owner. So, a homemade museum, I guess."

"What kind of things?"

I thought I knew. "It's the Alien Watchtower," I said. "Isn't it?"

Ever since we had moved to Colorado, we had driven by the exit. The sign was wooden, a green shade faded by dust and sun to gray, in the form of a figure with a great round head and large insect eyes. The alien sign pointed with a long, knobby finger toward a turnoff we had never taken.

"Why are you letting us go there?" I asked.

"Well, you're supposed to be able to see for miles. I thought you'd like that, Thea."

I could tell my sister and I were perched on the threshold of asking too many questions. It was a risk my mom was taking, bringing us to the watchtower, even bringing it up. And I wanted to go. It was out of the house, at least.

I said quickly, "It sounds great, Mom."

Amelia fell in line. "Thanks for taking us."

I felt steam and turned to see the oatmeal churning in the pot. Amelia pulled on her shoes to feed the dogs. "Girls," my mom said before Amelia left the house. "Don't tell your dad about this, all _____? It's just the *name* of the tower. It sounds so strange, I don't want him to worry."

"Of course not," I said.

"Sure, Mom." Amelia went outside.

I stirred the oats, feeling the curls of steam wrap around my face. "What made you think of the tower for today?"

"Oh, I don't know," she said. "We always drive past it."

"I remember the sign."

"Louisa suggested it, actually. She thought it might cheer you up."

I had to look down at the oatmeal. I didn't want my mom to see my grin.

We piled into the truck like old times. It had been days since Amelia had left the farm, the weekend we had tried to get water. I knew that wasn't good for my sister, this isolation. I knew it wasn't right. Kids needed light and energy, just like plants did.

Amelia sat in the small back seat but didn't seem to mind

how squished she was, leaning up into the front. She smiled in the wind that roared through the windows, pushing back her hair.

Well before the café, we turned off the highway. The alien pointed the way. The turnoff was rocky, a pitted gravel road.

Soon, the Alien Watchtower took shape in the distance: a small, one-story building with a giant raised deck. It wasn't so much a tower as it was a high balcony. Junk covered the ground. I noticed old tires, some papers fluttering in the wind. No one else was around.

"Cool," Amelia said when my mom parked. She ran right up the deck stairs.

My mom took her time at the entrance of the building. There was a little guest book to sign, and a glass jar labeled *tips*. She put a folded five-dollar bill into the jar. That was a lot of money for us. That was a new packet of underwear or two pounds of dried beans. That was water.

My mom looked away from the jar quickly, as if turning before she could change her mind, and went after Amelia. She hadn't signed or even glanced at the guest book. I picked up the pen attached with a chain and wrote *Caroline, Thea, Amelia*. I glanced at the names of those before.

A few rows above our names: *Ray*.

He had been here. He had visited. Recently.

As I climbed to the deck to join my mom and sister, his name sang through me, infusing everything. You really *could* see forever from the deck. And forever was flat, brown on the bottom, blue on top, but the mountains still glowed in the distance, hazy like a promise. Why had Ray come? Had he known I would visit—had he and Louisa tried to coordinate a meeting? The wind whipped across the flat space, and yes, the wind stung with dust, but the hot breeze lifted the notes and other items that had been left around the tower—the fake and dried flowers, the crosses and wreaths—and made them dance, animating their forms.

"What is all that?" Amelia asked.

"People offer things for the aliens." My mom had gotten a pamphlet from the entrance and was reading from it. "The owner just leaves them out for a while, because they seem personal."

"What would you leave for an alien?"

"I don't know," my mom said. "A note?"

"Asking what?"

"Maybe for help?"

There were viewing scopes posted along the deck. But those took quarters, and I didn't want to ask my mom if she had any money left. Below the deck, someone had arranged stones on the ground in deliberate formations. They looked like spirals, paths leading around the tower.

Amelia swung on the deck railing. She stood on the middle rail and balanced her body, the railing pressed against her stomach. "There's the gas station and Louisa's café." She pointed from her perch. "There's the library. There's the post office. There's a truck. And there's . . ." She stopped, trailed off.

I thought I hadn't heard her. "There's what?"

She hopped off the railing. "Never mind." She rushed past me to grab our mom's hand. "Do you believe in aliens, Mom?"

"I'm not sure."

"What does the brochure say?" Amelia was steering her away from the deck, and making a face at me as she did so. Subtlety wasn't my sister's strength. She was leading our mom off for a reason, trying to prevent her from seeing something, something I had to see.

"Thea?" my mom called.

"I'm just going to look for the café. See what it looks like from here."

"I want to go inside," Amelia said.

I walked to one of the viewing scopes, spinning the handles until my mom and Amelia left. I had reached the part of the railing where my sister had stood and pointed. In the distance I could see the buildings perched along the road. But close up, below the deck, were the items people had left on the ground. Shells and concrete figurines and beads. And stones, more stones. These looked deliberate, even more purposeful.

Spelled out in the stones was a word.

Thea.

Someone had written my name.

When I climbed down from the deck, Amelia and my mom had gone inside. I followed them into the building. The museum held model displays of aliens, like the dioramas I had made in school ages ago. There was a life-sized—or, human-sized—plastic figure of an alien, green like the sign to the tower had once been. There were newspaper articles in frames, headlines about sightings, vortexes. There were T-shirts for sale.

Mom was talking to a woman. She introduced me. "This is Stevie. She runs this place."

Stevie had shoulder-length hair which had frizzled to gray,

and bright green eyes. Her eyes, which flashed with light, made her appear younger than she probably was. So did the rainbow socks she wore in wide-striped sandals. She was excited to show us everything, especially Amelia, pointing out the toys in the educational area, action figure aliens and green dolls.

"We have stargazing programs," she said. "An astronomer comes in _____. Other homeschooling families attend. Have you met those families yet?"

Amelia looked up from the doll she was making dance against a countertop. "We haven't met anyone."

"Oh." I could see the emotions cycling through Stevie's face. She didn't think it was right, either, a little kid like Amelia being all alone. But just like my mom, she wasn't going to say anything. "Well, I bet you would if you came to stargazing night."

"We've been so busy," my mom said. "With the farm. Trying to get it going."

"Oh, I bet. It's hard for a farmer."

"Especially the way *we're* farming," Amelia said.

My mom pretended she hadn't heard my sister. The hearing could do that, choose whether or not they wanted to respond, but I could tell from the way my mom lifted her chin, she was ignoring Amelia.

"What else can you see from the tower?" I asked Stevie. "Other than stars, I mean. Do you see the weather coming in?"

"Oh definitely," Stevie said. "We can see storms rolling in from miles out."

"Did you see the locusts?"

"I did. It was awful."

"They ate our potatoes," Amelia said morosely.

"I'm sorry to hear that, sweetie."

"Did you see the dust?" I asked.

"I did," Stevie said. "Like a great blanket. I didn't know the storms were coming _____, thought there was something wrong with my telescopes. Dust just enveloped everything."

"Did you know dust once covered the Statue of Liberty?"

My mom looked at me.

"I read about it."

"I believe it," Stevie said. "I was worried it might swallow me."

"Do you think it might come back?"

"All right, girls," my mom said. "I think we've bothered this nice woman long enough."

"Oh, it's no bother," Stevie said. "You're welcome anytime. It gets lonely out here, looking for aliens," she said as my mom ushered us outside.

On the drive home, Amelia dozed in the heat. My mom waited until my sister's eyelids fluttered closed and she didn't brush away the hair in her face, until she was really asleep. Then my mom asked me, "What was all that about the Statue of Liberty?"

"It was in a book I read."

"Why are you so interested in dust all of a _____?"

"It's not that I'm interested, Mom. I'm just worried. It's so different here."

"How is it different?"

"How can you say that?"

"All right," my mom acknowledged. "It's hot and dry."

"Too hot. Too dry. I think it's building to something."

"Like what?" my mom asked.

"Another storm. Another Statue of Liberty storm."

"Thea," my mom said. "I'm glad you're _____ an interest in this place. I'm glad you're finally starting to think of it as your home—"

"I didn't say that."

"But you have to stop it with this storm _____. You're scaring your sister."

I looked back at Amelia. She smiled in her sleep. She had rested her chin in her hands. "I don't think Amelia's scared. I don't think you give her enough credit. Or me."

"Well, you're going to upset your father, talking about storms and drought and _____ all the time. He's worried enough. He doesn't need this."

Just because you didn't need something didn't mean it wasn't on its way, I thought. I could have listed all the things I didn't need: the extra work of running the farm the "simple" way, of being a pawn in my dad's dreams. I didn't need doing laundry by hand or grinding grain instead of going to school.

I stared out the window and said nothing. I didn't want to fight with my mom. I didn't want to fight with anyone. I just didn't want to be disbelieved. I tried to hold on to the image of my name written in stones.

16

Louisa's scrolled note and Ray's in the rocks gave me energy that carried me through for a while. I thought of them when I rose early and when I went to bed, so soon after the sun dropped. I thought of them when I couldn't sleep, imagining the reunion we might have. My friends hadn't forgotten me. But how long until they did?

One morning I went to water the sunflowers in the patch along the house and found that they were gone, withered away. They had been fine just the day before. One single day had killed them.

It had been a day of unrelenting heat. A day of dryness, aching pressure from the sky. Under the stress, the sunflowers had shriveled, their leaves curling in. They looked as brittle as old paper now, like the sun-bleached notes weighted down by rocks at the Alien Watchtower. The sunflower stalks were husks. But worst of all were the sunflower heads.

Their petals, pale and shrunken, closed in on themselves like a trap.

Sunflowers would turn their massive heads down when it was time for the seeds to be collected. It was a way to protect themselves, to keep the seeds safe from birds. The plants hadn't adapted a way to keep their seeds safe from us humans, the most severe predators. We were ruthless. We took everything. We spread the seeds though, too. We replanted them and allowed them to grow.

Not this time. The flowers along our house had died before their seeds were ready. Their centers looked hard and black. They had been burned by the sun and the heat. Fried.

I set the heavy bucket of water down. We'd had to drive to a different well for it. I went around the house to find my dad. He was weeding what remained of the herb garden.

"We lost the sunflowers," I said flatly.

His hands froze. "Any salvageable?"

"I don't think so."

"It was just an extra _____."

I knew this. It was a small, easy thing to try and grow them. They looked nice. They made my mom and sister happy, the rows of them bobbing against the house. Amelia said they seemed like girls waving with their faces in yellow bonnets. We could also make butter with the seeds and sell it, or roast and salt the seeds and sell them. My mom would bake the seeds into bread, a loaf she called "birdseed bread," which Amelia and I secretly hated because it was so dense.

My dad wasn't counting on the sunflowers to make a lot of money. But the crops my parents *were* counting on weren't faring much better. In their rows behind my dad, they seemed too small, thin stalks tipping over as if they were fainting. The locusts had eaten whole chunks out of the fields, like sweaters chewed by moths.

It was only late morning, but already sweat snaked down my back and my head hurt. None of us were drinking enough water; we couldn't afford to. Maybe it was the heat. Something made me blurt out, "At what point do you just give up?"

My dad had gone back to weeding, but now he stopped. "What are you saying, Thea?"

"When do you and Mom say, *Enough*. And move to plan B?"

My dad was silent for a moment. He had been on his knees, pulling the weeds. They lay in a pile beside him, already wilting.

I knew Colorado would change us. Any place made a mark on you, maybe imperceptibly until you were gone, on to your next move. Only then could you see what you had left, and what it had left on you. Living here had changed Amelia the fastest and the most obviously: the new rattle in her lungs. At night, her cough punctuated my dreams. During the day, I could hear her coming down the hall.

But the series of disappointments—the dry well, the locusts, the storms—they seemed to be changing my dad too. He had been quieter since the day he had yelled at me at the kitchen table, the day my mom had found the note. Sometimes I would catch glimpses of him out the windows. Pacing the fields, shaking his head. When he came into the house for meals—only for meals and to sleep—he would stare at the floor, looking anywhere but at me, my mom, and sister, like he couldn't bear to meet our eyes. His own eyes had grown small.

Faintly, I could hear the goats bleating. I knew we would sell them first before the chickens. The goats provided milk. The chickens: eggs. But you could live without milk, I thought.

My dad sat back on his heels. "Thea," he said. "This *is* plan B."

I squinted in the sun. "I don't understand."

"Leaving Ohio. Getting a farm in Colorado. This is our plan B."

"Ohio was plan A? What was wrong with it?"

"It wasn't working. We didn't have anything of our own, for our own family. We weren't working toward anything. One _____ big flood could have swept us all away, and we wouldn't have had any place to go, any claim to anything. We didn't even own land."

I gestured at the dead sunflowers, the rows of weak and patchy plants. "Who cares if you own land?"

"I care. Your mom does. We want to feel like we're building something, working toward _____. Keeping you safe, no matter what the world does. We want to have something to leave you girls."

"So, you're leaving us dust?"

"That life back there, the life we had before, going to work, going to school—it wasn't a good life, not a real one. I was tired of the rat race and so was your mom. In my dream, I saw us happy and safe here."

I had had a dream too. A dream at least twice now, that I remembered.

A dream of a red sky.

What made his dreams more important than mine? We had all listened, packed up our lives and moved away because of something that had come to him. Could something ever come to me? Would he even consider that?

The wind swirled. A great brown cloud had risen from the road and was traveling up the driveway. I felt the stirring of the dogs from their places all around the farm: napping in the shade of the house, keeping watch over the chickens. A couple of the dogs began to growl, low sounds I felt in my chest.

Someone was coming up the driveway. A truck.

This had never happened before. We had never had a visitor.

"Dad," I said.

He was already standing, brushing off his hands. His jeans were still dirty, the knees of them caked with orange. There was no time to prepare ourselves for strangers, to brush my hair or to straighten up. On the unfinished side of the house, plastic flapped in the breeze. I didn't even have time to gather the dogs so they wouldn't run to the truck, or to warn my sister: *Pretend to be studying.*

"What's going on?" My mom stood in the doorway of the house.

"I don't know," my dad said.

Any truck coming down our driveway would have been out of the ordinary. It was too far for a vehicle to just turn around. Our driveway was too long, too rough with potholes and prairie dog holes. This wouldn't be a casual visitor.

And it was a truck I knew.

17

In Ohio, a stream ran through the woods, along the gravel driveway that led to our place. In winter, my sister and I would skate, our boots slipping along the frozen white surface (we had no actual ice skates). In the spring, the creek became a breeding ground for tadpoles, the skittering of boaters and dragonflies zooming in for a drink.

And in the summer, the water was everything. We waded up to our calves. Sometimes, if it had been raining, even higher. We pulled up rocks from their sucking places, the mud swirling about our ankles in tiny private storms. Holding the rocks aloft and streaming, we damned parts of the creek. We would watch the water building for a few days, swelling like an insect bite, then we would tear the dam down again, restore all the rocks, and let the water flow free.

We found watercress, which my mom served for dinner in a salad. We watched the small, translucent fish we never could seem to catch, no matter what pole or net we constructed, and the fat frogs we always let go. Amelia screamed every time she touched an amphibian, and yet she would let hairy wolf spiders crawl up her arms.

Ellee was often with us at these times. Her mom would drop her off with a lunch box and a sweater. Sometimes, our mom would do the same at her house, or at Angie's. But both Ellee and Angie lived in town. And Amelia and I had the stream. We had what felt like miles and miles of wild space: water and woods and rocks and the hill our house sat upon, looking down upon more rolling hills and valleys. It was only a few acres. I didn't know space, not really, until we moved to Colorado.

At Ellee's or Angie's, we sat in the kitchen and made cookies with their moms. Or Amelia and I rode borrowed bikes, racing after our friends to the school. We would coast in circles on the blacktop of a playground we could never play at during school hours.

Not then and not ever again.

It felt like a ghost playground—ours alone—and that was fun as long as we didn't stop to think about it. We had to take turns pushing one another on the swings. We didn't have enough people for tag, or even for the merry-go-round if we wanted to go fast. Always, the school building loomed behind us, echoing and watchful and sad. Regarding us as we dashed through the playground, never entering through its doors.

The creek was better. Better to be far away from any memories of school, any feelings of loss. Better to make new memories.

We passed a whole summer that way. We took our lunches at the stream: bread, cheese, and apples. Milk in a silver thermos would stay cold if we propped it in the shade.

It was inevitable that we would fall in the water. We did many times. But it had always been just my mom supervising us during the day. My dad was off in his garden or woodshop, or working his job at the hardware store. Off dealing with the men in town, off *being* a man in town, getting to leave and go about the world. When we fell in, it was my mom who would laugh as we came straggling and dripping out of the trees. She would send us in to change, wring out our wet old clothes, and that would be the end of it.

Not so my dad. For him, even an accident meant a punishment.

The last time we fell, Amelia fell in first.

With her, you could never tell if she did things like that on purpose. She wanted so much to be up close with the fish, and she wanted attention. She also wanted to drag us in.

After she fell, splashing around, Ellee innocently tried to give her a hand back up to the bank. She was pulled in too by my sister. Then I only pretended to help them out of the water. I knew they would pull me in, and they did, laughing.

It was a wide portion of the stream, a little pool we had dammed to make deeper. I plunged in to my knees, my feet stuck in mud. The water felt shockingly cold, like washing my face in the morning, as bright as the first cool rain of spring. In only a moment, I got used to it.

We splashed for a while. We didn't have enough room to really float so we just stood around. And when we got bored, we scrambled up the bank. A truck was coming up the driveway.

We waved and the truck slowed. My dad rolled down the window. We approached the truck, so soaked our long dresses clung to our legs like pants. Ellee and Amelia held on to each other for support, they were giggling so hard.

"What's this about, then?" my dad asked.

I reached the driver's side window first and leaned inside. Only then did I realize a second person was in the truck, a man I had never seen before.

"We fell in the creek," I said.

"I would expect you to be more careful," my dad said.

"It's just fun."

"Hello, Mr. Taylor," Ellee said.

"I expect more from you, Thea," my dad said again. "And with company _____. What kind of example are you setting for your sister?"

Amelia was the one who had started it. But I only mumbled, "Yes, sir."

I knew not to argue in front of a stranger.

The man in the front seat was a neighbor, come to look at an extra truck shell my dad was selling. But it didn't really matter who he was. I had embarrassed myself and by extension, my family, my dad told me later. He told me before dinner, which I had to have alone in my room. At least I got to eat that night.

"But why me?" I asked when he doled out the punishment.

"You're the oldest, you know that."

It wasn't just that, and I knew it.

"You have to make a better first impression," he said. "People are always going to be looking at you to fail, to mess up. You have to be better than they _____ you to be."

"Why?" I asked him. I wanted him to say it.

But he wouldn't. "You know."

My dad couldn't bring himself to say the word—to say any of the words. *Hard of hearing. Deaf.* Why couldn't he just say *disabled,* just call me what I was? My parents always had to dance around it. It made me feel there was something shameful about my body.

Why did I have to be *better*?

"You're too old to be playing in that creek, anyway," my dad said.

And after that, I wasn't allowed to.

What I could do was slowly taken away—playing in the creek, riding bikes to the playground, playing at all—replaced by work, learning the chores that weighed my mom down, heavy as another child strapped to her back. It was slow at first, so slow I might not have even noticed, day to day, how the restrictions built.

First the creek was off limits. Then the next week or the week after that, I couldn't wear jeans anymore at all, not even to work in the yard or woods. Something my dad had read in the pamphlets or books had resonated with him, lodging deeper and deeper like a seed. He thought my sister, my mom, and I should always wear dresses or skirts. It was more respectable. It was the way the pioneers had done it.

Those books were all about going back to the land—but for him, they seemed to be about going further. Back in history, back in time to when women and girls were allowed nothing, especially not freedom.

All our time was spent in work. My dad worked too, but it was different for him. He didn't serve meals. He didn't make or clean them up, or clean up anything. Self-sufficiency was related to women's suffering, I would learn. Days of drudgery, grinding the wheat berries, making candles from tallow—chores that didn't have to take as long as they did, but we were doing them the way our ancestors had.

And slowly but surely my dad morphed into a different person, one I recognized less and less. His rules organizing my life were much stricter than the whiteboard school schedule we never followed. That could be erased. The changes in my dad seemed permanent. And they deepened.

After the stream incident, Amelia and I were barely allowed off the farm in Ohio. At the same time, my dad started accumulating more things for the house. These items were going to fuel our new life, shown to him in a dream, but he hadn't shared that with Amelia and me yet.

Every time he came back from town it seemed he had something else in the truck. Another pallet of canned goods, or a water purifier, silver and huge. My parents stored the food in the basement, but the shelves along the walls soon filled up. Some of the cans were too heavy to rest on a shelf and those had to sit on the floor. I didn't know they sold baked beans in containers that big, wide enough Amelia could barely get her arms around one. I didn't know how long it would take us to eat it all.

But my dad said the food in the basement was for emergencies only. Off limits.

Other parts of the basement were soon too. That was fine with me. The basement felt damp and smelled like a graveyard, and both Amelia and I thought it was too dark. As much as she was fine with spiders, some of the spiders of Ohio, like brown recluses, who liked to hide in firewood, *bit*.

My dad stored vats of canned tomatoes, big as barrels. My mom dried cookie sheets of corn, the yellow kernels shrinking and rattling, and sealed them in Mason jars.

"I don't even like corn," Amelia said.

We watched my dad unload canisters of propane from the truck. We got excited for a moment, thinking that we might be going camping, but we never did. He unloaded jugs of water. When he carried these over his shoulder to the basement, he looked like Santa Claus hoisting a sack of toys.

I would think of that image later, after we used the emergency water, jug by jug, in Colorado. We ate all the food. The big barrels were the worst because we had to use up the food inside pretty quickly, so it was a week or more of tomato dishes or sickly sweet baked beans. We lit the emergency candles and burned them down to puddles. Then we made more of our own.

I was curious about what my dad was doing down there in the basement, what else he kept hidden in the dark. One morning before breakfast, when my mom ran out of jam for a roll she was baking, I offered to go downstairs.

No light came through the tiny, half windows that ran at ground level along the top. A single bulb lit the basement, hanging at the bottom of the steps. You had to race down in darkness and reach up in the webby ceiling beams to pull on the chain to the bulb. And you couldn't actually run because the steps were rickety. They had different spacing. They creaked and more than one felt loose.

A lot of things in the house creaked. It was an older farmhouse, set in a clearing between trees and at the crest of a hill. In winter, it was drafty and my parents sealed plastic around the worst windows. When the winter wind blew, the plastic puffed up with air, tight as a bouncy castle. Those windows without plastic, rattled. The winter wind sounded sad, like a person in pain, so different from the hot, summer wind in Colorado that resembled, I would grow to learn, a hunter. A predator, coming close.

My mom didn't seem to suspect anything when I volunteered to go into the basement in Ohio. My dad had brought all sorts of things down there: a small silver mill with a hand crank, a glass lamp that looked like it would break. It was hard to add them together into anything that made sense, and I knew we didn't have a lot of extra money. My mom wasn't working then and my dad worked only at the hardware store. On weekends, we sold vegetables, jam, and salves at the farmers' market, but that didn't bring in a lot, especially in cold weather.

And yet he had bought seeds and bags of grain.

In the basement, I reached the bulb and yanked. A cone-shaped area lit up like a spotlight. The rest of the basement still shadowy, I went to the shelf closest to the stairs, the one with the food we were allowed to use, and found the jam. My mom, my sister, and I had canned it last summer from blackberries we had picked in the woods. Then I stepped away from the cone of light, into the dimness. Beyond the shelves, my dad kept his mysterious purchases.

In the shadows, I saw tarps. I saw a large square with buttons and knobs. It rested on two wheels so it could be carted around. It was a generator, I would learn later. In Colorado, I would grow to know it well, learn its quirks and frustrating stutters. Amelia and I would even name it: *Genny*. It made us feel better, I thought, to complain about the fickle machine responsible for our lights being on or off as if it were a person.

Annoying Genny.

Genny's being a prima donna again.

Other purchases my dad made during his slow fall into worry and preparation, I would never become familiar with.

Like the guns.

Behind the generator, something leaned against the wall, covered with a tarp. The thing was tall. I wondered if it might be fishing poles for me and Amelia. My dad kept promising to buy us real ones. Like most of his promises, they never materialized.

And when I lifted a corner of the tarp away, two long guns stood in the corner.

Even silent, they seemed to pulse with danger. Their barrels looked like the snouts of wild creatures. What were they doing here, unprotected, out in the open? Amelia was even more curious than I was—what if it had been her who had discovered them? What if she knocked into a gun, or what if her curiosity didn't stop with just looking?

I couldn't think it. My hand trembled and I almost dropped the jam. I set the jar on the ground, then covered the long guns back up. I tried to make the tarp look as it had before but I couldn't remember, and I didn't want to spend any more time down in the basement, near them. I picked up the jam, pulled the light off, and pounded up the stairs.

We hadn't hunted in Ohio. We grew some of what we ate—vegetables, potatoes, garlic—but only to supplement the food we had to buy; we couldn't live off it. We gathered berries in the summer, and apples in the fall. We harvested nettles for tea and soup. My mom made a sweet drink from honeysuckle. We picked calendula and lavender and grew aloe to use in the salves and lotions we put into jars and sold at the market.

But we rarely ate meat. It was too expensive. My parents said it was full of antibiotics and hormones. I had been taught that antibiotics were a bad thing. Bad medicines, my dad called them, as more and more became bad in his mind.

We had had electricity in Ohio. We paid the bill, every month higher and higher—and that became a bad thing too, giving money to *the man*, funding the dark wheels of this industry that just kept churning, my dad said.

As a boy his idea, he told us, had been to leave school. To be free, roaming the hills or taking off into the woods alone to pursue whatever notion had gotten into his head that day: mushroom-picking, whittling, gathering tadpoles to watch them hatch in an aquarium in his room. But then, like most people, he had settled down and graduated high school. He had gone to college for a little while, before dropping out and getting a job. School was too expensive, he said, but if he wasn't in college, he had to be working. That was expected.

But what if he dropped out again—out of the rat race, out of this exhausting, futile life, a life that only seemed to be getting worse? What if he brought his family along?

I wasn't my dad and neither was Amelia. I didn't want to spend my days whittling, and I didn't want to spend them alone. Amelia was little, though, little enough that she believed my dad.

And my mom believed him too.

I asked her about the guns.

It took me days to work up the courage. One morning at the farmers' market when the rain meant business was slow, my mom rearranged the jars for sale, and I told her, "I saw what dad's keeping in the basement."

Her hand stilled on the jar, a blackberry jam not unlike the one I had retrieved that day. "The generator?"

"The guns."

She turned to me. Amelia was splashing in puddles by the truck. People milled about, browsing, greeting one another. The market had been closed for so long, since the pandemic. People hadn't wanted to come back for a while.

And now the farmers were finally starting to return, and the weather had been so terrible all spring. The rain fell on only a handful of booths, their tarps bright as mushrooms. We had fruit jam and jars of lavender-scented hand cream and burn salve for sale, eight or so dollars each, the money like the drizzle that pooled on the tarp above our heads—but slower. Never enough. Nothing ever seemed to be enough.

My dad wasn't around. He never came to the market with us, never did the work of making or selling.

"Is Dad turning into a hunter now?" I asked.

"Those are for protection," my mom said.

"Protection from what?"

"You have to ask your father."

But I couldn't find the words.

In the days to come, the rain would increase. It just kept coming, gaining in volume, heavier and harder each night until the river overran its banks. The water rushed through town: sand filling an hourglass. And it was only afterward, after the flood, that my dad told Amelia and me he had seen it coming, had had a premonition. That was why he had stocked up, started preparing.

My mom told me he felt guilty that he hadn't warned people. But who would believe a dream? People had dreams all the time.

It grew to anger me, the way she just followed him, accepted his instructions even if they felt wrong. That she was supposed to cook and clean up. She alone was responsible for teaching us, watching us. She never rested. After dinner when the dishes had finally been washed and the table cleared, she would work on clothes that needed mending while my dad would read his newsletters.

It was on one of these nights that he turned to the classified section in the back. It listed chickens and tractors for sale, auctions, and situations: renters or house sitters wanted, people to go in on a homestead together, all over the country. He folded the page and an ad caught his eye.

A farm in Colorado. Cheap.

18

The truck barreled toward the house. Coming fast, purposeful. The yellow sides were dented from days on the road. Brown hands gripped the wheel below the shade of a cowboy hat, and the passenger side window was down. Straight dark hair streamed through it.

I had hoped for just this. To be reunited with my friends again, to be returned to the life I had only barely made. But in my daydreams, I hadn't imagined myself sweaty and frazzled. Hair stuck to my face. My parents stood right behind me, and I was wearing what my mom called a *work dress*, faded denim, heavy in the heat. It had once been hers.

The truck stopped in front of the house. It took a beat longer for the dust to settle down, the dogs fanning around the truck. I struggled to see through the mist of dust. Doors were opening and closing.

Sam and Ray were laughing—a joyous sight that made my

stomach hurt. They tried to pet the dogs as they crowded all around them.

"Whoa, whoa." Sam came around the side of the truck. "Your watchdogs need some work." He was smiling.

My parents were not.

"Can I help you?" my dad asked.

"I'm Sam. Thea's _____ you about me? I'm an outreach agent for _____."

"She hasn't said much about you, no."

Ray stood by the passenger side of the truck, pinned by the dogs and their excited shaking.

"You can just push them away," I called.

But maybe he didn't hear me. He wasn't looking at me. And I didn't know the signs.

I didn't know how to sign.

I *couldn't* sign in front of my parents.

They were looking at me for answers, for some kind of explanation as to the strangers in our yard. I had two worlds, I saw now. One was smaller than the other. But as tiny as my home life was, it threatened to swallow my other, better world: the one where I felt I mattered, where I felt safe and belonged, where I had been helping others.

How could I explain to my parents what Sam did? What I had tried to do on some small level? To reach out to other people, to make a connection. It mattered so much that I had snuck out to do it; I had left work; I had lied. It wasn't just about my heart.

Though that was part of it, I thought, as Ray reached down and patted Wednesday, gently pushed the muzzle away of Sunday (he nipped). I felt so much looking at Ray, a rising bubble of hope inside me. Someone who would speak with me openly. Someone who wouldn't judge me. Someone with dark hair sliced across his chin like a knife.

Sam was saying to my parents, "My job is to drive out and check on homesteaders like you. I'm sorry I haven't _____ before. The locusts and dust storms _____ behind."

"No apologies necessary," my dad said. "And no help needed."

"This is my great-nephew." Sam gestured to Ray and now he came forward, walking into the uncomfortable circle made by me, my parents, and Sam.

Ray's eyes flickered to mine then darted away quickly, as if just by making eye contact we would reveal ourselves to my parents. He was nervous. He waved awkwardly, then seemed not to know where to put his arms, or how to stand. He would have shaken my dad's hand, probably.

But my dad did not extend his hand.

"It doesn't cost anything," Sam said. "It's a service the county offers."

"What service?" my dad asked.

"Ray here and I can chop firewood, help with home repairs. Phone lines are sometimes an issue. I hear you don't have internet, so we can get that set up for you, if you want it."

"We don't want it."

"Making appointments, then. So many of them are online _____. We can get doctor or dentist appointments for the girls."

"That won't be necessary."

I waited for my dad to notice that Sam had said *girls*. Sam had been told things about my family, my life. He knew I had a sister. It was obvious he and I knew each other well. Soon my dad would discover that I was familiar with Ray too, very familiar.

I could hardly bear to look at Ray, though I felt his presence vibrating at my side. I swore I felt heat, even more than the sun striking my back, and I was conscious of every motion he made: when he shifted his weight, when he brushed his hair back from his eyes. I wasn't sure if I wanted him to look at me, to meet my glance for longer than a second. Would that tip off my parents? We had kissed in the truck, by the barn, at the picnic table.

"I know who you are," my dad said. "I don't appreciate you distracting my daughter." My dad was cold to all strangers. He would have acted this way to anyone who drove up our driveway unannounced, but this unfriendliness ran deeper. It was bordering on hostile. "The way we're farming _____, it's different than you're used to. We want a simpler life. Just want to be left alone."

Sam didn't appear rattled, or he hid it well. I knew he had faced a man with a shotgun. Ray said once another man had answered his farmhouse door completely naked. Sam dealt with a lot, and in the face of my dad's anger, he stayed calm.

He talked lightly, casually, as if my dad was already a friend. "Your daughter is such an asset to this community. I know Louisa appreciates her, but so does Captain at _____. And she's been a good friend to Ray."

No one had ever called me an asset before. I glanced at Ray—I couldn't help it—and he met my eyes. We finally shared a look, warm and long. Too long. His eyes were friendly, the same canyons. They lit up as his smile beamed. But then he did the worst possible thing in front of my parents.

He signed.

Two letters, finger-spelling.

OK?

It was a quick, easy sign. I knew it. But Ray didn't know Amelia and I had been practicing in secret, on our own. He signed it slowly so that I could clearly follow, see plainly the movements of his hand.

But my parents saw too.

Would they even know what it was? They would know Ray and I had a way to communicate that didn't include them, that was for certain.

My dad raised his brows and his forehead erupted in lines. His pupils narrowed even more. "What's this _____?" he asked, to none of us or all of us. "We knew Thea was leaving the _____. Was it to meet a boy?"

"No, it's not like that, sir," I said.

Amelia came running around the side of the house.

My dad addressed his next comments to Sam. It was like I didn't even exist in the presence of another grown man. Maybe I didn't. "Why exactly are you here?" he asked him.

"Honestly, I'm here on behalf of Louisa," Sam said, "to ask if Thea might return to work. Louisa needs her in the café. And we need Thea in town."

My dad scoffed, "There's no town. That's part of the reason we moved all the way out here. To be alone."

"You don't have to be alone."

"You're not understanding. And I think it's time for you to leave."

"You don't have to accept help, that's fine," Sam said. "But please, think of your daughter. Think of both your daughters."

Amelia leaned on the house. Unused to strangers, unsure of herself, she looked at once like a much smaller child. She had pulled a strand of hair into her mouth and sucked on the end of it.

I thought of the pictures in the library book about the Dust Bowl, the survivors from almost a century ago. If I took a picture of Amelia now, would a girl see it in a hundred years and find her own sister there?

"I need to get back to work," my dad said. "*Both* my daughters do. And you need to get back in your truck _____ go."

"All right then." Sam turned.

That was it? He was just giving up? He didn't even look at me, head down, his hand on his hat to keep it from tumbling off.

Ray didn't budge. "Thea," he said.

"Ray. Time to go, kid." Sam had parting words for my dad: "Both of your daughters will be enrolling in the valley school in the fall, I _____?"

Did Sam know, did he have any idea how those words would enrage my dad?

"We do our own thing," my dad said. "I would expect you to respect that."

Sam and Ray couldn't just go, they couldn't. They couldn't just leave me here.

Everything felt slow and sped up at the same time, like when I had fallen off a ladder in the barn back in Ohio. I had felt the ground flash up to meet me, but it had also seemed like the longest journey to the hard earth, scattered with straw. I had broken my wrist, though we didn't know it for days because my dad had not wanted to take me to the hospital, not wanting any questions (*what was I doing on a ladder and not in school?*).

I felt that old ache in my bone, healed wrong, healed just a little differently when Ray reached for my hand. It was the memory of pain—and now, new pain.

"Thea," my mom warned.

"This is how to reach me," Ray said. He squeezed my hand tight.

Sam called Ray's name again. Casting one last look at me, Ray dropped my hand and returned to the truck. The doors closed with final slams. The dogs resumed barking as Sam started the engine up and backed away. He turned the truck and they retreated. If Ray waved goodbye to me, I didn't see it. The windows were rolled up and dirty. I couldn't see anything in the dust.

Or through my tears. I was crying, and I didn't even realize it until I felt small fingers pulling at my side. Amelia slipped her hand into mine. I felt the sting of the tears on my face then, slicking the dirt from my cheeks. My sister struggled to hold my hand and we both looked down and saw why.

Ray had pressed a tiny piece of paper into my palm.

Amelia looked up at me. My mom hadn't seen. My dad hadn't, either. They were too far away, back by the house. My sister used her hand to cover up the paper, to keep it hidden. For some reason, this gesture, her attempt to help, made me cry even harder.

She held my hand as our parents went inside, to argue or decide my punishment. As if I were responsible for Sam and Ray driving out here. As if I had brought everything bad down upon us: the drought, the locusts, and now the judgment of locals. We had only just moved here and already people were aware of what we were: strange homesteaders, back-to-the-landers, unfriendly, backwards, and weird. My dad's anger stuck to us, like dirt that would never wash off.

Once we were alone, Amelia removed her hand from mine. The note lay in the middle of my palm, tiny and white like the boats we used to fold out of paper and send on doomed trips down the stream. I felt stuck, rooted with dread and anticipation both. When I didn't move, Amelia unfolded the note for me.

Written on the paper was a phone number.

19

I brought the water down the line. The potato fields had trenches where my dad had planted the seeds. He had tilled when we had first arrived in the Bloodless Valley, using rented equipment. The equipment kept breaking and it took longer than he had planned for the clearing of the earth.

Everything had taken longer and been harder.

Amelia and I had walked the rows to help prepare them for planting, picking up and tossing rocks and breaking up big clods of dirt with our hands. Back in Ohio, we would pick up rocks from the stream. But in Colorado, the rocks felt dusty and dry. They had not seen water for a long time.

This wasn't the best way to do this, I thought as I went down the row carefully with the heavy water, trying not to spill as I bent to each crop and gave it a drink.

Not enough of a drink, I knew.

This wasn't the best way to do a lot of the work on the farm. It wasn't the fastest and it certainly wasn't the easiest. All the sweeping we did with brooms. Then again in the morning, it started all over again: dust re-emerging in the night. Instead of elves leaving us shoes or Rumpelstiltskin turning straw into anything, dust appeared like magic, the greatest resource of this place.

Potato plants grew above the ground in leafy, long stalks. Each plant would only produce one potato, under the earth. It seemed like a lot of leaves for not a lot of starch, I thought. But I did as my dad told me. I watered, then moved on.

As I worked, I repeated numbers in my head, the phone number on the paper Ray had passed to me. It had to be his number or maybe Sam's.

I had tried dialing it. One morning, my mom had driven off in the truck and my dad had finished his coffee, leaving the mug in a dirty ring on the counter. I waited for Amelia to head outside to feed the animals. I listened for the ringing slam of the back door, then I ran through the house, into my parents' bedroom.

I never came in here. The bed looked neatly smooth with quilts. My mom had made it perfectly before she left for work. The drapes were still drawn, which made the room pool with shadows. I didn't see what I was looking for on the nightstand, which held my dad's farming books and a kerosene lamp.

I went to the chest of drawers, a high antique of pale oak wood. Over its top, my mom had draped a linen table runner, scalloped on the edges and embroidered with flowers. There was a framed picture of me and Amelia from a few years ago. We stood in front of the stream in Ohio, laughing, happy, with no idea how our world would change. On top of the chest of drawers was my dad's pocket watch, chain curled around it like a dragon's tail. If he left that behind when he went to the fields, he would have left what I was looking for too.

But I couldn't find it. I checked behind the picture, felt around behind the mirror propped on the chest's surface. Nothing.

I opened the first drawer of the chest. It stuck, squealed. I looked back at the doorway. Still empty, Amelia and my dad both gone. I would have my back to the door as I riffled through all the drawers but I had to check. This drawer held rows of socks, darned by my mom. I was ready to move on to the next one when I felt something hard at the back. It was palm-sized, cool to the touch.

My dad's phone, shoved under the socks in the drawer like something forbidden.

I pulled it out. I had Ray's number memorized. But I hadn't given any thought to what I would say. It didn't matter. I just had to reach out, just had to reach him. Just had to dial.

I turned the phone on.

It stayed black.

I pushed the power button again, waited. Pushed it hard.

The phone wasn't turning on. It was dark. Dead. I felt around in the back of the drawer one more time but there was no charger. If I found it, I would have to find a way to plug it in secretly when my dad started the generator up. I looked away from the chest of drawers and scanned the room. A rocking chair with my dad's clothes slung over the back. The closet door, which hung slightly ajar, revealing my mom's row of long dresses. A charger would stand out, like a bolt of lightning from the modern world. I couldn't see a cord anywhere.

"Thea?"

A door slam and Amelia's voice came from somewhere. I didn't know where.

I threw the phone in the drawer—useless—and shoved it shut.

Other times as I worked, I thought about signing. Since Ray and his great-uncle's visit to the farm, I had not taken the ASL book out with Amelia, even when we were alone after my mom went to work. I felt like I was being watched, always. Like somehow my dad would know. I couldn't sign with Amelia, with anyone.

But I remembered signs in my head. When I set the water jug down, my fingers moved, silently practicing. At night, I would practice in the dark. I was always so tired from helping my sister all morning and helping my dad with the farm all afternoon, long hours which stretched into the evenings. I fell asleep quickly and morning came far too soon. Every sunrise woke me like a bad dream.

But I wondered what the sign for *wheat* was, the sign for *cloud*. I knew the sign for *water*: a *W* pressed to my mouth.

My dad rose from his row. "What's that now?"

For an instant, panic flashed through me. Had he seen my fingers move? But he was not speaking or even looking at me. He was looking at the road.

Another dust cloud. Moving quickly, which meant a vehicle. My dad glanced at me, and in his eyes flared annoyance.

"I don't know who it is," I said.

"Your friend, come back?"

I felt my heart beating fast. I tried to speak without giving away the spark of hope inside me. "I don't know why he would.

I haven't said anything to him. It's not like I can talk to him. Or anyone," I added for good measure, though my dad had already turned and was headed toward the driveway.

I followed him. By the time my dad and I exited the field, a car had stopped. The dust fell around it like glitter. I didn't recognize the car. It *was* a car, a dirty minivan, and not a truck with four-wheel drive. Not the best for traveling on these rough, rural roads.

Then the back door opened, and a girl got out.

"Ellee!" I shouted. I ran down the driveway, my dad forgotten.

We embraced by the minivan door. She was taller than I remembered.

"I'm sorry, I'm covered in dust," she said.

"So am I. So is everything. What are you doing here?"

"Family vacation." A man had gotten out from the driver's side and was extending his hand to my dad. It was Ellee's dad in a flannel shirt too heavy for the summer and a black beard that had only gotten thicker and darker while my dad's had thinned and paled to gray. Our dads shook hands.

"This is a surprise," my dad said.

"Family trip out to Moab."

"In this ride?"

"It's an adventure," Ellee's dad said.

Ellee's mom was getting out. She looked barely taller than Ellee now, and was patting the ends of her hair. It didn't matter that she had fixed it. It would only flatten, go limp and dry in the arid heat. "Is it always this hot? I thought the van was going to overheat, back in that little town. What's it called?" She looked to her husband, but he was no help. "Luckily, an older man helped us at the gas _____. They have the cutest little café. Have you been there?"

My head was trying to follow her quick and low words, but my heart was dancing in my throat. Had Ellee's family met Sam? The café had to have been my café, the place I now thought of as my own. I was bursting with questions.

But my dad only said, "Caroline works _____ store."

"Caroline is working now?" Ellee's dad asked.

My dad put his hand on the other man's back and steered him toward the fields. He would not tell Ellee's family about *me* working, I knew, about how we were intimately familiar with that café. It must have been shocking enough that my dad's wife was working outside the home, let alone his daughter. We had come out here to get away from all that, after all, as Ellee's parents well knew, to escape the grind of capitalism, according to my dad. And here we were, contributing to it.

"She'll be back this afternoon," my dad said. "She would have greeted you but we didn't know you were coming."

"We tried calling," Ellee's mom said.

"It just rang and rang. You changed your number?"

I looked sharply at my dad.

"That thing hasn't worked for a while," he said. "You know technology."

"Can't live with it, can't live without _____," Ellee's dad said.

"Well, they're trying to, hon," Ellee's mom said.

Hasn't worked? My dad wasn't making eye contact with me. How long had his phone been broken? We had no landline, no internet, and only the one truck. The phone had been our lifeline, our only way to contact anyone if there was an emergency, to get help. No wonder I hadn't been able to get it to turn on. It hadn't simply been out of charge. It had been dead.

"Let me show you the farm," my dad was saying. "Thea, you girls go get some lemonade _____ everyone."

Did we even have lemons? It was just like my dad not to know what food we had in the pantry. He wasn't responsible for it, having to be thrifty, having to prepare. He wasn't cooking it.

I took Ellee's arm, still reeling from the phone news. Her mom headed with the men toward the crops. My dad didn't have much to show off, not anymore, but you couldn't tell that from his face. He was beaming with pride.

Or maybe that was the heat, sweat making a sheen on his skin. *Had his shoulders always slumped so much?* I watched the adults walk off. Next to Ellee's dad, my dad seemed smaller. Shrunken.

"Tell me everything," Ellee said.

"What was the last email I sent you?"

"It was a while ago. I wrote back to _____ we were coming, but you never responded."

"Well, I haven't been able to go to the library. I got in trouble."

She seized my hand. "You did?"

"My dad found out I've been spending time with Ray."

"That guy?" Her fingers tightened around mine.

"Yes, but it's not what you think."

"Oh, I think it *is* what I think."

"Tell me everything about home," I said. "I really miss it."

"No, you first."

So, before Amelia came running from the goat pen, where

she had been tending the animals, I told Ellee everything about Ray. Or, most things. I found myself growing shy telling her about one thing.

"Ray is like me," I tried to explain.

She didn't understand. "Homeschooled?"

"No, his hearing. He's hard of hearing like me," I said simply.

Her face took it in. She knew what this meant. "Oh, wow. Have you ever met anyone like you before?"

"No. And he's not exactly like me. He knows sign language and he has this supportive school and community."

By now Amelia had run down the driveway. She threw herself into Ellee's arms, a tumbleweed of braids and a faded, flowered dress. The dogs followed and surrounded her, barking, their tails lashing. It overwhelmed my friend and we moved on from my admission about Ray.

"You have so many pets!" she said to Amelia, distracted. "Is this your dream?"

We weren't going to talk about what I had just said, and I tried not to be sad about it, not to feel the quick flash of annoyance at my sister, how she cut in. This wasn't the time for my words, my feelings. I was used to it, I told myself. The conversation moved on, and I couldn't hear what they talked about, anyway.

We made our way inside; my dad would be expecting lemonade. I felt embarrassed for Ellee to see the house. So dim, dust coating the floorboards and countertops like chalk. No matter how many times we cleaned and swept, the dust was always there.

Where do you think the dust comes from? Amelia had asked me during one of our long mornings together when the schoolwork became unbearable: our assignments, never checked by any parents. Our workbooks were so old, the math beyond my understanding, and the history facts fuzzy.

Amelia would get a hazy look in her eyes when she asked questions like these, as if she could see into the future, *our* future, past the long driveway and the longer highway.

I don't know, I had said.

I think it comes from far away. That the wind brings it here. Like you said the wind brought our dust to New York?

Maybe. That was a long time ago, though.

I didn't say it might be happening again. It all felt familiar, everything I read and everything I saw out the window of the farmhouse, as if the world were a roll in a player piano, winding and replaying again. There was never a new song. I thought of my dream, which I hadn't told Amelia—or anyone—about.

The red sky.

Did you know the calcium in our bones comes from stars? Amelia said. *Mom and I read that. It comes from stars exploding.*

Supernovas?

That's the word. Supernovas. Amelia repeated it to herself, liking the sound of the word on her tongue and against her teeth, her teeth that came from stars. *So, our dust might come from Mexico now. Or Washington.*

Maybe they should take it back, I joked.

But I've never been to Mexico. Or Washington. I only know their dirt.

I couldn't stop thinking about that. My sister's words echoed through my head as I showed Ellee around the house. Amelia would only know the dirt of other places, never get to travel there herself. Not if our parents had a say.

The house was dark and crowded. But Ellee wouldn't bring up anything negative about it. She wasn't like that. She didn't even make a face when she saw the ceiling tiles stained with mushrooming water damage, a leak from before our time. The fake wood panels of the living room were each a shade of dull brown. They still didn't match; they must have been whatever was once on sale.

That was Cuthbert, I thought.

"The house is a work in progress," I tried to explain to Ellee. "But my dad doesn't have much time to work on it."

"Show me your room."

It was a normal, cheerful thing for a friend to say. Supportive. But I noticed her face fell, just a little, when I led her down the narrow hall to the space I shared with Amelia. My sister plopped onto her bed. We had each had our own rooms in Ohio.

"You two have to share?" Ellee asked.

"It's not so bad."

My sister rolled her eyes. "Well, you snore."

"I do not."

"Maybe it's one of the dogs you sneak in here," Ellee said.

"How did you know?" Amelia asked.

"I know you." She threw a pillow at my sister and Amelia threw it back.

It was like old times. Then Ellee asked for the names and personalities of the dogs. That kept my sister busy, listing them all, and distracted us from commenting on the depressing room.

The single window, the corners gray with grime. It was not like I hadn't seen the house before, not like I didn't know. But viewing it as I imagined Ellee must have, it made me feel sad all over again. We could have done things to make the house seem lighter. Paint, like Ray and Sam's yellow walls. Hang up pictures, like in Helen's house. But we never seemed to have time.

In the kitchen, the three of us made lemonade from fruit too old and dry to squeeze out much juice. The drink was really more sugar water. *Sugar* we had plenty of; it was the water that was the problem.

My dad and Ellee's parents pulled chairs into the yard, and they sat around, drinking the lemonade in glasses that sweated in the heat. Ellee, Amelia, and I chased the dogs. A memory of fireflies came back to me, running after their blinking lights in Ohio. How had I forgotten them? But I had. There were no fireflies in Colorado. No mosquitos, either, my dad liked to say. It was too hot for them.

But there were birds: the large, long-tailed magpies that looked like spinning white and blue pinwheels when they flew, chattering birds that resembled blue crows, and the brighter, smaller bluebirds I had seen perched on fenceposts. Louisa had hummingbirds that buzzed the red feeders at her house. If I looked long enough, sat still enough at the picnic table where I ate my lunch, I would always see them.

That time was over, I reminded myself. The café was no longer mine.

Amelia grew tired of chasing the dogs. "I dare you to run through the goat pen," she said.

"No," I said to Ellee. "That's a trap. They bite."

"Even the curly white goat?" she asked me.

"Especially the curly white one."

The wind blew up then, a thick gust. It carried debris, dirt and sand grains large enough to hurt. We closed our eyes and turned our faces from the pebbly spray. It was too intense to talk. When the gust died down, I opened my eyes and Amelia shook the grit from her hair.

"Wow, Abraham," Ellee's dad said. "The wind is strong out here. You should get yourself some wind energy. And solar panels."

"I don't know," my dad said. "I don't go in for all _____."

"They say it's good for the Earth," Ellee's mom said.

"It's expensive technology. And that's not the way we're trying to farm."

"But it can't hurt," Ellee's dad said. "To harness some of that power _____ give the electric grid a little break?"

"We're off the grid," my dad said proudly. "_____ independent here."

Ellee's parents murmured approval and interest. Her dad said something I couldn't catch. I heard enough to know they were moving off the topic, almost as soon as they had landed upon it. My dad didn't want to keep talking about it.

It didn't make sense. How could you move your family to a wild, rural place—and not want to take care of it? Not want to preserve the very thing you depended on? Solar panels were too much technology for him, hydroponic too much of an expense. It didn't fit with my dad's plan.

I had believed it was about self-sufficiency for him. He could do it all alone. He knew how or could teach himself through books and newsletters. He didn't need anyone's help or advice. Maybe it was worse than that, though. Maybe he thought he had earned it. He deserved it, what the land had to offer. It was his right to take from the dirt and from the sky, to take everything in the forest.

Soon after I had found the long guns in the basement in Ohio, my dad started going out with them. He would disappear into the trees and return with very little: only his anger, empty as his hands. Sometimes he brought home squirrels or rabbits. He never was able to shoot a deer. But my mom learned to skin and fry the small animals he killed, and my sister and I learned to pretend to like them.

I became almost used to the jarring, popcorn sounds coming from the woods as my dad roamed. It was his land, he said. He could take from it. We all needed to learn to live off it.

I hated never knowing when I would hear the guns. I couldn't tell where noise came from: if he was shooting close to the house where my mom and sister and I were, or far-off on some ridge. I felt like I couldn't go outside when he did. I never knew where his bullets would be.

My mom, when I had confronted her at the farmers' market, had said the guns were for protection. But what did we need protection from here?

One afternoon when my dad was gone in town, buying supplies or working at the hardware store, Amelia and I went looking for mushrooms, bright orange chicken of the woods, which bloomed from dead trees. They tasted savory and salty, and were easy enough to spot, even Amelia could locate them.

In a clearing, we stumbled upon the big felled log. Bottles and cans lined up across its flaking, lichen-thick surface. More cans lay in the grass, twisted and contorted by holes. Bullet holes. I stumbled into a nest of broken glass, which crunched under my shoes, and I warned Amelia not to go farther.

What happened here? I remembered her asking.

I must have said it was just Dad practicing. I must have told her not to worry.

Practicing for what? she had asked.

It was a question I could not forget.

Or answer. I felt like our basement in Ohio with its emergency food, jugs of water, and long guns was all a big rehearsal for something. But what? What was my dad expecting?

I waited for my parents to tell me. For months, I worried and dreaded the day they would finally let it slip, or at last decide Amelia and I were responsible enough to know. Another pandemic was coming and we had to stock up. Or war had broken out and we were on our own. A nuclear bomb had been detonated in a city close by. A second flood was imminent.

The world was full of emergencies, more and more every day. It was incredible we were expected to go on living in it, to act like the laundry mattered when any moment the river could rise. My sister and I were out of school by then. We had little access to real news—or to the outside world: only what was filtered through our parents. I braced myself for it, for the worst possible thing.

And when it finally came, it came in the form of our parents asking us to come back to the kitchen table one night after the dinner dishes had been cleared away. My sister was getting ready for bed. She had already changed into her nightgown.

I knew something was coming, the news I had been dreading. I felt the anxious drop of my stomach—but Amelia didn't have any idea. I had shielded her as best as I could from ... whatever it was going to be. Sickness. War. Something, something bad.

It was land.

Land, cheap.

My dad had seen an ad in one of his newsletters. A farmhouse offered for sale by the bank. Colorado needed farmers, he claimed. The country needed more food; it always needed it, acres upon acres of grain. And Ohio was trying to drive us out, to drown us. He had had another dream, like his dream about the flood—but it was more than that, he explained. It was a premonition.

He had seen a house in a wide yellow field surrounded by crops, blue mountains in the distance. It was quiet, serene. And dry. So different than his dream about the flood, and that had come true, after all. Maybe this dream would too.

"I felt happy when I woke up," he said. "Content. I haven't felt that in a long time. I know we'll be safe out west."

My parents had not renewed the lease on our rented farmhouse. We were going to lose the woods, the creek. Our separate bedrooms. Our friends. We were losing Ohio, leaving it. Moving across the country.

I remember being so confused. "This is why you've been hoarding supplies?"

My parents had looked at each other, but my mom answered, her voice trembling only a little. "We just want our own place. We want to truly live off the land."

"We're tired of being bothered," my dad said.

"No one's bothering you," I said.

But someone was. Someone had complained about the shooting at all hours, the target practice in the woods where anyone could walk by. That land with the felled log wasn't even ours. It was over the property line. The landlord hadn't liked it, my mom told me later.

I hadn't liked it, either, but I didn't have a say.

Questions led to other questions. Poking around led to discoveries. The landlord was asking why Amelia and I weren't in school. He must have not liked my dad's answer: that it wasn't any of his business. The landlord raised the rent to get us out, my dad said.

It was working.

"We want a simple life," my dad said. "A return to the way life used to be."

Life had never been for us what it would be in Colorado: no running water, no power except for what the genny could muster. It had barely been like that for my great-grandparents when they were young. This wouldn't be a return. It would be a revision.

"In my dream," my dad said, "it all works out."

But I never dreamed that dream.

I dreamed of a bloodred sky.

20

I started to wonder if I should tell someone about my dream, if it might be more than just a nightmare, a strange image imprinted on my eyelids and the feeling I had woken up with each time of something coming, of being hunted.

But I didn't get a chance alone with Ellee.

When my mom came home from work, my dad insisted everyone stay for dinner. I could see my mom's eyes widen and her face go white and I tried to keep my own face emotionless. I knew what she knew. We might not have enough food.

I relaxed only when Ellee's dad demurred. "Thanks for the offer, but we better get to our campsite before dark."

"You're camping?" Amelia asked, unable to disguise the interest in her voice.

"Isn't it a little hot?" my dad said.

"We've got a shady spot. At the campground down by the river. But we were _____ if the girls would like to show Ellee around tomorrow, see the town."

"There isn't much here."

"Whatever you want to show me, I'd like," Ellee said.

I knew it was true. "There's the tower," I said.

Instantly I realized what I had let slip.

"What tower?" my dad asked.

My mom broke in. I was surprised how calm she sounded. She covered for me smoothly, as if she had done it before. "We've driven past it a hundred times. There's an observation deck right off the highway. A tourist trap, maybe, but something _____. You can see _____."

"Sounds fun," Ellee's mom said.

I hugged my friend as the adults made plans. Without a phone, they had to decide on a meeting time and place. I heard the word *café* mentioned and tried not to feel hopeful.

It was hard to watch Ellee drive away. It reminded me of Ray, and it reminded me of losing my home. After her family's trip, Ellee was headed back there, returning to Ohio. To Angie, to the woods and small-town streets and creeks I knew so well. I felt I would never see it again.

I turned away from the driveway, waving off the dust clouds that drifted, stirred up by the minivan. They spread through the fields like pesticide. I would see Ellee tomorrow, I told myself. Maybe I could tell her about my dream then.

But the night was rough. So hot, not a single breeze stirred the curtain in our room that hung at the open window, slack as a rag doll. Burning hot even after the sun came down with a stillness that felt wrong. Final somehow, like a slamming door.

Amelia and I were already in bed when the wind came. I was not asleep; it was too stifling for that. I turned on top of the sheet, which stuck to me. My sister and I had both thrown our quilts off.

Then the howling began.

It started low. It sounded almost like whistling. I might have mistaken it for that, in my old life. But I knew it now.

When the flood came back home, there had been no warning. Not for us. An alert had flashed across TVs, which we didn't watch; the internet, which we didn't have; and the radio, which my parents wouldn't let us listen to.

But for us in the still woods, the only sign came in the form of the water itself, dark and creeping as an army, moving over the driveway. There it stopped, halfway up the gravel, having swelled the beds of the stream my sister and I had loved so much, had trusted in, believing it would stay calm and shallow. For days, we couldn't leave the farm. We were trapped until the water receded, creeping backward like fog. I thought I had never felt so cut off. Inside the house, water spread like disease from the ceiling tiles. Water dripped from the light in the kitchen, into the sink.

It was worse in town. Worse for others who lived in lower places. Our house was high on a hill, and from there, we could survey the changed landscape. Overnight, fields had turned into pools, trees into islands. My dad kept saying it felt familiar.

When he had woken us up that night, the night of the flood, he had said, "It's happening."

Everything from his dream.

Now in the valley came the warning wind. I sat up. Across the aisle in our room, Amelia lay above the hot sheets. Her limbs looked stiff and scared. Her eyes were open, white in the darkness. She was awake too.

"We have to close the windows in the house," I told her.

"It's so hot."

"It doesn't matter. It'll be worse if the dust gets in."

She sat up and went to the sash. I hurried into the hallway, checking every window. The wind rattled the front door on its hinges like a robber trying to get in.

I turned to see Amelia behind me, rushing to the back door. She let the dogs into the house. She counted them as they rushed by, herding them into the kitchen where she could prop a baby gate against the doorframe. We had learned the laundry room wasn't big enough. We had learned a lot about getting ready, weathering these storms.

The wind had woken my parents. We headed to the living room, where the windows latched the most securely and we could all fit on the floor.

I worried about Ellee. They were camping by the river. I didn't know if that meant a tent or a cabin. Knowing Ellee's dad and his tendency to be frugal, I imagined it was rustic. Had they retreated to the minivan when the wind came upon them? Did they know to close the vents? To wait and wait?

I had read about people on Black Sunday. They tied handkerchiefs over their mouths and breathed through them for days. Did Ellee's family have masks? She had told me their strategy during the first part of the pandemic was to stay as far away from people as possible.

But that didn't work with dust. Dust was everywhere. Dust followed you.

Dust found you.

This was the moment to tell someone about my dream. To tell my parents. My dad might believe it meant something. He had his own dreams and he trusted them, sure as facts. The sky wasn't red outside. It was mud-colored, but that didn't mean it might not worsen at any moment, morph into something else.

"Dad," I began. "I feel like—"

He silenced me. "Not now, Thea. I can't hear myself think over these damn dogs."

Amelia exchanged a warning look with me. We both knew he could change his mind and kick the dogs out of the house. His mood shifted so suddenly, darkening. I thought of the storm glass in Gus's house, the crystals overtaking the orb like a world filled with ice, and fell silent.

We passed another night as if in a snow globe, howling and swirling in the storm that crashed over the house. It seemed to last for hours this time, all night. I couldn't sleep, too worried about having another dream.

In the morning, we dumped the dust out of cups in the kitchen. Amelia swiped a rag across the table and coughed, staring at the blackened rag in her hand. She coughed so much, I hardly noticed it anymore. It was part of her now, a cough that had not been there before.

It didn't matter that I had double-checked the windows. Still, the wind got in, working its way through the cracks. Each small hole it widened. Each opportunity it tore through. And with the wind came the dust.

"It's darker this time," Amelia said. "Have you noticed?"

"Dirt is dirt," my mom said, sweeping.

We were always sweeping.

When it came time to leave to meet Ellee, I grew worried. Without calling or texting her, there was no way to know if she was all right. I wouldn't know for sure until she did or didn't show up.

"I wish we could have reached Ellee, to warn her," I said.

"I know. But there was nothing we could do," my mom said.

"If we had a working phone, we could have told her family about the storm."

My mom grew silent. She worked intently with the broom, trying to brush the grit out of the corners; it liked to cluster there. I thought she was just concentrating, but then she rammed at the corner by the cookstove, and shoved the broom away from her as if she was disgusted. It clattered to the floor.

"The phone works," my mom said.

"It works?" I said. "Why can't we use it?"

"We didn't pay the bill. We ran out of data."

Amelia stopped wiping the table and looked up at me. I thought of my attempt to use my dad's phone. It wouldn't have mattered if the battery had been charged, without data and without Wi-Fi.

"I'm sorry," I said to my mom. "I didn't know."

"We have to make decisions. We have to choose which bill is the most important to pay right now."

"A phone isn't important?"

"Not when we have to pay for water." She picked up the broom again.

I thought about my words. I always had to think before I spoke, had to make sure I had heard correctly before responding—and I knew my parents often didn't do this. They just talked; they didn't think. They didn't have to prepare like I did. They controlled the conversation, always.

I said, "I think Sam might be able to help you."

"A handout? Your dad won't _____."

"No, not a handout. But Sam knows about grants for farmers. He knows these programs. We're not the only people who are struggling."

"Your dad wants to do things his way. He wants to make it alone."

What do you want? I might have asked my mom. Instead I said, "We're not alone. There's community out here. It's just hard to find."

"But you found it," my mom said.

"With Sam and Ray, I did. And you could too."

She had paused her sweeping but now she resumed it again. Hard, as if brushing me off. "You girls and your dad, that's all I need."

"Everybody needs more than that. You need your own thing."

"And what's your thing, Thea?"

"I don't know." I thought of the pictures in the history books. I kept thinking about them. The way the images froze their subjects' expressions, captured them in time, and captured light and shadows. To make something that was both art and a record—it seemed like time traveling. "But I want to find out."

It was time to leave. I was afraid we wouldn't go, not after the conversation we had just had, my mom's admission about the phone. But she placed the broom against the wall. She smoothed her hair and took off her apron. "Time to go, girls. Amelia, fix your braids."

We didn't talk in the truck.

I was relieved. Not only could I not hear above the road, I didn't know what I would say. I could always talk to my mom in a way I never could to my dad. But it exhausted me, trying to keep up. I already had a headache from listening so hard in the kitchen. And now I didn't know what to think. She had told me the truth about the phone, but then dug her heels in about not needing anyone, not wanting community.

Getting through to my mom was like carving sand. I thought I had made headway, but the structures of my arguments kept collapsing, my feet slipping out from under me. She had to follow my dad; she had been for so long. She couldn't go out in her own direction, not with the strength to carry us too. And she wouldn't leave me and Amelia behind, not ever. I knew that much.

Dust colored the sides of the highway. Debris had landed in the road, fallen branches my mom swerved to avoid, and bales of tumbleweeds. My nervousness grew as we came closer to the café. I didn't know if my friend would be there, if she would be okay. I didn't know if Louisa would want to see me again or if she was mad at me for not showing up.

The café and gas station looked both the same and different. They were cloaked in dust. It made the buildings appear even smaller, as if they hid under heavy coats. Or maybe I had just been away for too long. I had forgotten how shabby the café appeared from the outside: Louisa's handwritten signs, the yellow windows.

"Can we go in?" Amelia begged from the back seat.

"I don't see Ellee's minivan, so I guess so," my mom said. "But just for a minute. We're not buying anything."

We didn't have to. As soon as Amelia entered the café, the bells jangling their familiar song, Louisa was there, her arms open. Amelia held back, in that sudden uncertain way she had.

She could be so bold in her questions and brave with animals, but around strangers, she shrank. She was so unused to them.

Louisa hugged me. Her arms were warm and soft. She smelled of coffee and cinnamon, and faintly, of gasoline from the station next door. "I have missed you," she said. "Are you holding up okay?"

"Yes." I was conscious of my mom, who had entered the room behind me and Amelia and stood watching. "Is the café doing all right?"

"Don't worry about that. But us—me—I miss you something _____." She had released me from the hug and turned to Amelia. "Is this your darling sister?"

"I guess. This is Amelia."

"Nice to meet you, ma'am," my sister said.

"Have you girls had lunch?"

Amelia and I paused, uncertain what to say or if we should look at our mom.

Louisa didn't wait for an answer. "Go over to the case and pick out what you want. It's on me. And I've got cookies for you up here at the counter. You like cookies, don't you?"

Amelia just nodded. When my mom went with her to the refrigerated case, I had a moment alone with my boss.

Louisa seized it, touching my arm. She made sure I could see her lips. "How are you doing, really?"

"I'm okay. I miss everybody."

"Have you been able to reach Ray?"

I shook my head. "We don't have a phone."

"Do you want me to give _____ a message?"

Before I could speak, the bells clanged again and Ellee entered the café with her mom. She rushed forward and hugged me. It felt like forever since I had seen her, even though it had only been a night. The dust was like that. It exhausted us.

"It was the strangest thing," Ellee's mom said. "The dust came out of nowhere. Like a giant wall across the plains."

"It roared and the sky got all dark," Ellee said.

"What did you do?" I asked.

"We went to the showers building at the campground. It's concrete and doesn't have any windows. Our tent is basically destroyed. The wind just ripped it _____."

"I'm so sorry."

"It's all right," Ellee's mom said. "We're heading out tonight and we'll stay at a hotel this time."

Tonight? I had thought I would have more time. "But you just got here," I said.

"Cross-country road trip. We're on a schedule. You know men and their schedules." She and my mom shared a smile.

"It's okay," Ellee said. "We have today."

After lunch at the café, my mom and Ellee's mom strategized about the rest of the afternoon. We wanted to go to the Alien Watchtower (my mom was careful not to call it that, only the *observation deck*), but Ellee's mom had to return to the campsite and help her husband finish packing up. My mom agreed to take us all. Louisa asked if the women wanted to see her garden first, those plants that had survived the locusts, and I saw my opening.

"I'd like to show Ellee the library," I said.

It was a loaded sentence and I knew it. Would my mom refuse me, in front of my friend and her mom? In front of my boss?

My dad seemed to have no problem expressing his views

before company or strangers. He didn't care what people thought. He believed he was right. But my mom was different. It had been his dreams that had sent us to the desert, not hers. And even though she trusted him enough to pack up our lives, she was starting to bend, like the walls of our house, to show the tiny cracks. I thought I might be getting through.

She tightened her lips. We all waited. I didn't look at Ellee, who had no idea what was going on—or Louisa or my sister, who did.

My mom said, "Be careful crossing that highway."

We were careful. I held my sister's hand, even though she resisted, my heartbeat thudding in my chest. I felt my heart was as loud as the night wind had been. Would Ray be at the library? I didn't see Sam's truck in the parking lot.

But it was hard to know for certain because the parking lot was packed. I had never seen so many cars and trucks in the little gravel lot. Trucks had parked out front along the highway. The post office lot was full too.

"What is it?" Ellee asked.

"It's just not usually this popular," I said.

"Maybe there's an event."

But I had never known there to be an event at the library. Not here. I didn't think there were enough patrons. I opened the library door and saw people everywhere, their voices joining together in a low buzz. Each computer was occupied, each of the low and worn chairs. People slept in them. People dozed on the floor or sat with their backs against the shelves.

"Whoa," Ellee said. "Happening place."

"It's not usually like this," I said.

"This is so cool." Amelia hurried into the young adult section. She did her shy, hanging back thing, then she plucked a graphic novel from the end display. I couldn't tell if she was pretending to study it, to not be embarrassed in front of the other kids, or if she was really absorbed.

"I can see why you like it here," Ellee said.

"I'm telling you, something strange is going on."

Finally I saw a face I recognized: Captain. He appeared more pale than usual, harried. The wisps of hair on top of his head trembled, looking ready to fly away.

He saw me standing by the front desk. "Oh, thank heavens. I heard you'd been kidnapped."

"Kidnapped?" Ellee said.

"I told you, I got in trouble." To Captain, I said, "It's not that bad."

"Your parents won't let you come here?"

"My dad won't."

"They might be the only people *not* here at the moment."

"What's going on?" I asked. "Why are there so many people?"

"Because it's so hot, and we're one of the only _____ with air conditioning."

I glanced around again. I didn't see anyone else I knew. A man bounced a baby. There was a woman curled in Elmer's chair, her hands covering her face. I never knew there were so many people in the valley. It hid its inhabitants like jackrabbits. "People are sleeping here?"

"Just napping during the day, but because of the heat wave, we're opening the library all night as an emergency shelter. To do that, we need beds. _____. Sam is on it. And Ray." Captain looked warily at me, as if he didn't want to upset me.

"He's been asking about you every _____. If I've seen you, if you're all right. It's not your fault you disappeared. He knows _____."

Ellee elbowed me obviously. I used it as an excuse to introduce her. "This is my friend Ellee, from Ohio. And that's my little sister, Amelia, over there."

Captain shut a drawer of his desk with a snap. "Library cards for everyone."

"Oh no," Ellee said. "I'm just visiting."

They talked and I tuned out, only catching some words. I was remembering how people in the 1930s slept in parks, spent the scorching summer days leading up to the Dust Bowl in movie theaters, which were air-conditioned. But we had no movie theater. The library must have been the largest building for miles.

"Captain," I asked, "do you have enough space here for a shelter?"

"Not on this floor." Captain indicated a door that I had not paid much attention to before, a gray metal one behind his desk. "But there's _____ the basement. It's nice and cool down there, and spacious, if a bit dusty."

There was an emblem on the door, a yellow square with a black and yellow circle with upside-down triangles in the middle. I had seen it twice before. Once, on the outside of the library walls. And once in the history books.

It was a fallout shelter.

21

Amelia walked up to the circulation desk, a stack of books teetering in her arms. "I want to check all of these out."

"And you can," Captain said.

"I don't know." I paused. "Dad's not going to like that."

"I can keep them for you here, if you like. _____ at the desk. You can read them when you come back."

I knew Captain was just trying to be helpful, but it seemed impossible, too complicated, involving so much sneaking around and coincidences. Just to read books. Just to see Ray. And I had learned what happened when my parents uncovered my secrets. They took even more of my freedom away.

My mom would be expecting us back at the café. "Captain," I said quickly. "The heat wave and all the dust storms. Do you think it's building up to something?"

"How so?"

"Last night's storm lasted longer."

"Our tent broke," Ellee said.

"_____ of the windows of the post office did too," Captain said sympathetically.

"Today is one of the hottest days in the valley on record," Amelia said. When I looked at her, she pointed at the computer table. "I read it."

"And the wheat fields," I said. "My dad told me a lot of people planted wheat around here last year."

"Practically the whole valley," Captain said. "It was a bumper crop, but you know what they say about bumper crops. They end."

"Those fields are dead," I said. "They were eaten by locusts. And the dirt isn't rooted by grass or plants anymore. It could just blow away. It *is* blowing in the wind already. Do you think this might mean a bigger storm?"

"A bigger _____?"

"Like Black Sunday."

"Another Black Sunday?" He pushed up his glasses.

"What's Black Sunday?" Ellee asked.

"What do we do if a storm like that comes again?"

"I'm not sure," Captain said. "What did people do a hundred years ago? They hid."

I thought of my dream, the wrong-colored cloud filling the world. I thought of the pictures from the library book, which seemed to look so much like today, like no time had passed. Like we were frozen, making the same mistakes. "We didn't change how we farmed since then or used water. We didn't listen."

Listen. It was the thing that was the hardest for hearing people to do.

I remembered something, the first question I should have

asked him. I said it desperately, "Captain, do you have a phone I could use?"

But it was too late. My mom had entered the library, her eyes widening as she took in the crowd. "What a popular place."

"Thank you," Captain said.

"Time to go," my mom said.

Amelia protested, "But Mom—"

"If you want to see the observation deck, this is your chance. Ellee and her family have to _____."

My sister turned away from her stack of books. They looked bright, promising and suddenly so small, waiting on the desk for her. Her eyes looked like my dad's eyes, and it wasn't just their color. It was the dawning in them of disappointment. It wasn't really that many books she wanted. It wasn't that many at all.

"Wait," Captain tried to call after us. "Didn't you want to use the _____?"

Like the café and gas station, like the library, the Alien Watchtower looked different upon our return. The items people had left on the ground, the letters and teddy bears—even the rocks had been moved. Disturbed and displaced by wind.

"They just got carried away," Stevie explained to my mom. "Some of them for miles."

On the drive to the tower, we had passed clothing tangled up in tumbleweeds. A plastic doll lay in the middle of the highway. Branches were tossed by the road like a giant had blazed a path, throwing trees this way and that. The wind had just dropped the items once it was through with them. And everywhere the dust piled up in orange snowdrifts.

"It's like being able to see the wind," Amelia had said as a gust kicked up a fine powder, scattering it across the road.

It was the first thing she had said since the library. Leaving that stack of books behind had done something to her. Drained her.

My dad's eyes had turned white when there wasn't any water at the well. My mom had paled when she realized we didn't have enough food for Ellee's family to stay for dinner. My family was haunted by these disappointments, these small revelations that maybe weren't so small. Amelia hadn't even asked my mom if she could check out the books. She knew the answer would be *no*. That was a big understanding for a child to come to, that her parents didn't want her to read. Not these books.

We were the only people at the watchtower. Stevie was vacuuming when we arrived. She paused her work to talk to my mom, and while the adults were busy, Amelia, Ellee, and I climbed to the deck.

Up high, the wind felt stronger. We held on to the railing like we were on the prow of a ship. The wind pushed the hair away from our faces, tossing it behind our heads. If I did wear a hearing aid, there would have been no hiding, no covering it up in that wind. What would that feel like, I wondered, to not be able to hide? If people knew, just by looking at me—would that be easier or harder?

They might ask me questions. I didn't know if I had the answers.

From above, we could see what the dust storm had made, how it had shifted and rewritten the land. It was like an Etch a Sketch. You could draw all you wanted, but once the toy was shaken or dropped, your image was ruined, forever gone. The land below the watchtower was changed. I saw humps of sand where the dust covered tires. Flowers had been torn from their bouquets and scattered all around. It reminded me of how the dogs would pick up a stick and shake. It seemed so careless, the wind.

Of course it was. The wind had no pattern, no meaning or intent. It just *was*. It was bad for us, but it didn't mean to be. But also, like the water that had flooded our last home, the wind and the dust wouldn't just stop.

"What's that shape over there?" Amelia pointed.

In the distance, sand covered a huge heap. I could make out two black loops, a silver disc, a shining bumper . . . "I think it's a car."

"The dust covered up a car?"

"The dust covered houses, back in the day."

"What day?" Amelia asked. But then her voice broke off as she coughed, letting go of the railing with one hand to cover her mouth.

Ellee was asking me a question. I turned so I was facing her.

"Are you happy here?" she repeated.

"Oh." I turned once more toward the railing and the wild expanse of dust. It looked like Mars, I decided. Like a brand-new place. "I think I was? I think I was happy. It took a while and it was hard. My dad makes it harder, though. He just makes us stay at home. I don't know what he's so afraid of."

"Maybe you being hurt?" Ellee knew about my friends before, how they had bullied me.

"I've already been hurt," I said. "I don't know why my dad's so focused on protecting me when he won't even acknowledge what I am. Hard of hearing. Deaf." It felt good to say it. To say it aloud and loudly. The wind carried my words away, taking them to someone else to hear, if they could hear. "It's not something to be ashamed of."

"Maybe he's trying to make it better? Easier on you?"

"He doesn't have to make it better. I'm not something to be made better. Nobody's trying to make Amelia's freckles better."

Amelia looked back at me, pointedly.

"Or telling me I have to deny the color of my hair. It's like that."

Ellee was silent for a moment. "Have you tried telling him _____?" she asked.

"He doesn't want to talk about it. He doesn't want to talk at all."

"Especially not to us," Amelia said. There was sharpness in her eyes.

"But what do *you* want, though?"

"I want to talk."

"Don't tell me," Ellee said. "I'm not the one who needs to hear it."

Amelia swung on the deck railing. "I want to talk!" she screamed at the wind.

Ellee and I burst out laughing.

"It feels good," Amelia said. "You should try it." She stood on the middle railing, her stomach pressed against the top rail, and shouted again, "I want to meet Patience!"

"Who's Patience?" Ellee asked.

"Try it," Amelia demanded.

"Okay." Ellee approached the railing, and called as if shouting into a canyon, "I want to learn to drive."

"Louder!"

"I want to drive! I want to go to school!"

"Yeah! Me too. I want to go to school!"

"I want to meet a guy! Or something!"

Amelia leaned over the railing, laughing, then she and Ellee noticed me. "Your turn, Thea."

"No thanks," I said.

"Come on," Ellee said. "There's no one out there."

"No one but Mom."

"She's downstairs _____. Nobody can hear us up here."

No one heard me anytime. No one listened to what I had to say. What I wanted, needed. I stepped closer to Ellee and my sister. Beyond the railing, the world fell away, swept clean like after a heavy snow. "I want to go to school," I said.

"Louder!" Ellee and Amelia said.

"I want to go to school! I want to meet people!"

"I want to meet people!" Amelia echoed.

"I want to hang out with Ray!"

"I want another dog!"

"I want to learn to sign!"

Ellee and my sister had been laughing, Amelia trying to one-up me, Ellee giggling at both of us. But now they stopped.

"You . . . what?" Ellee asked.

"I know," Amelia said. "And I want to, with you."

"Want to _____?"

My mom's voice. I looked away from the railing, from the landscape of softly rolling dust. It was almost comforting how everything looked so clean, smoothed over by a fine coat of light orange. It disguised the trash, the garden of offerings all around the watchtower which my mom had called "unsightly" on our first visit. It hid. That was what the dust did.

But some things shouldn't be hidden.

My mom stood at the top of the stairs. "What is it you _____?"

Amelia hopped off the railing. Quickly she stopped playing and rushed to our mom. "Oh nothing. We were just joking around."

I didn't want my sister to cover for me again. It wasn't her place to try to protect me. And I shouldn't have needed protection for what I said. "I want to learn sign language."

"Sign language?" my mom said.

"Ray knows. He's hard of hearing too. Only he learned to sign when he was little from his friends. Some of his family know too."

"What do you want to do?" My mom didn't seem to understand.

"Ray's been teaching me a little sign language, and I want to keep learning. There's a community I could be a part of, but I'm not. And I want to be."

My mom stared at me. She didn't look angry. She just looked confused, and like all the energy had gone out of her as she stood at the top of the steps. "I didn't know things were so hard," she said.

"They could be better. We could make them better here."

"And I want to go to school!" Amelia said quickly.

"Excuse me?" my mom said.

"I'm sick of learning from Thea."

"*I've* been teaching you too, Amelia," my mom said.

Ellee's mom came up the steps behind my mom, cheerful, unaware of the tension on the platform. "The campsite's all packed and your dad's anxious to get on the road," she said to Ellee. "Ready to go?" She had no idea what had just transpired between me and my mom.

I wasn't even sure I knew. I had spoken up, said what I needed. And my mom had listened? At least she hadn't said *no* outright. She hadn't said much at all.

But now came the worst moment, when the friend I had just been reunited with would leave again. It might as well have been Mars, the sands beyond the railing of the watchtower. An ocean of space would soon separate me from Ellee.

She said, "I'm not ready."

"Oh, come on, girls," her mom said. "You can email each other."

No one said anything.

She asked uncertainly, "They can email, right? I know you don't have internet at _____, but the library?"

"Of course," my mom said. "They can write. Email."

Did she mean it, or was she just trying not to be embarrassed? Ellee's family unschooled and grew some of their own food. But they had internet. Ellee could watch TV. And they never had a basement stocked like my dad's. Her dad didn't have dreams, not that he shared. Not that they acted upon.

I had asked Ellee once, without volunteering my own information—I was too ashamed and confused—*Did her dad keep guns?*

Oh no.

Did they stockpile a lot of food in the pantry for emergencies? Or somewhere else—like in the basement?

No way, she said. Her dad would eat it. Her mom couldn't even buy too many Girl Scout cookies at one time.

My family had crossed some kind of line that even the other line-crossers wouldn't go over. We were the sand that had traveled from across the country, across the world. Too far. We went too far. Could we ever come back?

Ellee turned until she was looking right at me. "I will write you every day. And I know you probably can't answer me every day but I'm hoping for at least weekly."

I glanced at my mom. "That sounds like a good goal."

"When are you all going _____ to Ohio for a visit?" Ellee's mom asked. "You're due _____. You can stay with us. Even if you just want to send Thea back, we'll host her." Amelia must have made some kind of sound, because Ellee's mom stressed, "*Both* girls. We'd love to have them both."

"That's a big trip," my mom said.

"I know. But it's important that the kids get to see each other."

It's important, it's important. I repeated these words in my head as Ellee and I hugged. I tried to keep it light. "Stay cool in the desert," I said to her.

She winked at me. "Go get that guy."

More hugs, then Ellee and her mom were leaving, descending the stairs. And then my friend was gone, like the wind had blown her away. We were alone together, my sister, my mom, and me. If I thought she was going to bring up what Ellee had mentioned, that throwaway remark about a guy, I was wrong. But if I thought we were going to talk about what

Amelia and I had asked for, about sign language and school, I was wrong too.

My mom looked worn out. She said, "A few windows broke downstairs in the last storm. A lot of dust and debris got in, and Stevie is all alone here."

"We should help her," I said.

Work meant not talking. And the work was hard enough, it meant not thinking too. I tried to put those moments on the deck, when we had screamed into the wind, out of my head. Those were wishes, that was all.

Stevie said we should be using a vacuum cleaner, not brooms, to sweep up the dust. She said brooms only spread the dust around, flinging it into the air where we might breathe it in again.

She didn't say anything—no one said anything—about Amelia's cough.

I don't know how long we cleaned. I lost track of time. As the sun moved through the windows, becoming hotter, I concentrated on scrubbing countertops, windowsills, and doorways, focused on making one clear swipe after another. All that waited for me at the farm was emptiness, anyway, and more work. I would not think about Ellee, I told myself, about Ray. I was so intent that when the phone rang in the gift shop, I just assumed it was the wind again.

Stevie left to go answer it, and when she returned to where we were wiping down toys, she came straight to me. "It's for you," she said.

"What is?"

"The phone."

My mom and Amelia looked at me.

"The phone in the gift shop," she repeated.

"Why would anyone call Thea?" my mom asked. "Who knows she's here?"

Ray, I thought immediately. Foolishly. He was kind, thoughtful—but not magic. He hadn't followed me. Even the small rocks he had used to spell out my name had blown away, useless under the force of a storm.

"It's the girl who was here earlier. Your friend," Stevie said. "She took a brochure about the watchtower. It has our _____. She seemed very interested in aliens."

"Why is she calling?"

"I don't know. But she sounds upset."

I put my rag down. It was black now, stained. I hurried to the gift shop. On the counter beside the cash register and a spinning rack of UFO keychains, a landline phone lay off the hook. A red button blinked on the console.

I picked up the phone. "Hello?"

"Thea?" Ellee sounded far away.

"What's wrong?"

Her answer came back staticky and broken. I could only pick up snatches, like a television on too low. "On the road . . . a cloud . . ."

"What?" I asked. "Ellee, I can't hear you."

"Connection . . . safe . . . but . . ."

"But what? What's going on?"

Her voice burst into sudden clarity, as if she had exited a tunnel or stepped closer to the phone, if only for an instant. "There's a storm coming. A giant cloud." Just as quickly as the connection improved, it dropped again. Ellee's next words were fractured in a burst of static. "Shelter . . . fine . . . but . . ."

"Ellee, are you okay? What's happening?"

"Headed your way."

I couldn't understand her next words, or the next. Then I heard a word clear as water.

"Dust," Ellee said.

22

Our connection was lost, Ellee's voice disappearing. I waited a moment, despite the sharp static hurting my ear. I hoped for her voice to burst back in one last time, to tell me she was okay. When she didn't, I hung up.

Amelia, Stevie, and my mom were cleaning like nothing had happened. I tried to make sense of the warning I had received, a warning clouded in feedback and a roaring sound that I might have thought was just a bad connection. But I knew that sound.

It was wind.

I glanced quickly out the windows. We had covered the broken ones with cardboard. The windows that remained intact showed a clear, if dirty, sky. There were clouds but they looked low and white. It was hot. But it had been hot for days.

And so, so still.

"Mom?" I said.

She looked up. "What did Ellee want?"

"Mom, where were Ellee and her family going?"

She thought. She wiped her face, leaving a streak of grime on her forehead. "Moab."

"That's a long drive," Stevie said.

"I'm not sure they're going to make it the _____. They might stop."

"When did they leave here?" I asked.

"I don't know. A couple hours ago?"

"You've been working for a while," Stevie said.

My mom said something else, a question, but I had already turned from her.

There was a framed map of Colorado hanging on the wall. I went to it, tracing my finger from the Bloodless Valley to Moab, over the state line into Utah. The road dipped down, beyond the rim of the national forest. There was just the one major highway. How fast did her dad drive? How far had they gotten? They were near the Southern Ute Reservation, maybe.

"Thea?" My mom put her hand on my shoulder. I jumped and she apologized. She never apologized for sneaking up on me. She never remembered to. Then she asked, "Is something wrong with Ellee?"

"They got caught in a storm," I said. "I think they found shelter. It was hard to hear. But it's headed this way."

"What is?"

Stevie directed her question to me. "A dust storm?"

I just nodded.

She didn't wait for me to say more, didn't wait to make sure. She opened a door revealing a supply closet, shelves with rolls of brown paper towels, tape, and printer paper. She said to Amelia, "Can you help me seal the windows?"

"What's going on?" my mom asked.

"The storm sounded big," I said. "I can't explain it. But Ellee was scared. And the wind—it was so loud on the phone."

Stevie clenched her jaw. "Tape the windows and doorframes, sweetie. We'll stuff towels from _____ under the door."

"Are we trapped here?" my mom asked.

"There's a cellar we can wait it out in," Stevie said. "No windows. It's secure."

"Ellee said the dust is there now," I said.

Amelia clutched a roll of tape to her chest. "What about Dad? He's outside. He doesn't even listen to the radio. He won't know."

"We'll help seal things up here, and then we'll head home to get him," my mom said.

"Are you sure?" Stevie asked.

"I'm sure. We won't leave till you're safe."

I knew what I had to do. I hurried away, my mom calling something after me, but I didn't stop. In the gift shop, I picked up the phone again. I dialed the numbers I knew by heart. To press them, to enter them into the phone, felt like the combination of a secret.

It rang only one time.

A voice came on the phone. A voice I knew.

"Ray," I said.

"You called."

"Of course."

"You remembered the number."

"I couldn't forget it."

"I've been trying to get messages to you," he said.

"I saw the stones. I'm at the watchtower now."

"What?"

"Ray, there's a storm." I didn't know if he didn't hear me or he didn't understand, but there was silence on the other end. "A storm is coming," I repeated. "A dust storm. It's big and headed our way."

"Hold on."

Muffled sounds in the distance. Then Sam got on the phone. "Thea, what's wrong?"

"My friend is a few hours away, and she just called and said there's a dust storm heading for us."

"Where are you _____?"

"At the watchtower."

"Okay. We're coming for you."

He hung up the phone before I could answer or say goodbye to Ray. I had to think about the conversation, as I often did, for moments after the call had ended, the dial tone dull in my ear.

They were coming for me. Ray and Sam, my friends, were coming.

We had taped the window frames and were stuffing rags in the corners—what Stevie called "packing the windows"—when a knock on the front door made us all start.

I was closest. Otherwise, I might not have heard it. We had covered the windows with more cardboard, blocking the view. I had no idea what it looked like outside anymore, what color the sky was or what the clouds were doing. Or that Sam's yellow truck had pulled up close.

I opened the door—still unsealed; we needed one route of

escape. Two figures blew inside as if a hand had shoved them in along with a gust of wind which felt hot, peppered with grit. The sky behind the figures still looked blue, but the clouds hung low and the air felt oppressive.

But here was Ray before me, swiping the dust from his hair and grinning. His hands leapt at his sides. Mine did too, as if we couldn't contain our energy around each other. We wanted to hug, but in front of my mom? Sam closed the door. He stomped his boots on the rug.

"Thea," Ray said.

And then I didn't care that my mom was right there, that Amelia stared and Stevie was coming down the hallway. I fell against him. I fit in the space below his chin, where his hair dipped down and brushed across my forehead. His arm went around me.

"Stevie," Sam said. He glanced around, taking in the preparations we had made. "Looks like you're getting ready."

"Doing our best," Stevie said. "Grateful for the help."

"It was my idea to use the shirts." Amelia pointed to the window wells, stuffed with T-shirts from the gift shop. Most of the shirts were bright green. Stevie said they glowed in the dark.

"What a fine idea." Sam tipped his hat to her, then met my mom's eye. "Mrs. Taylor, I hope you don't mind us just showing up like this."

"Caroline," my mom said. "And I'm glad you're here. I'm sorry it's taken me so long to _____. I know you've been a good friend to Thea. You both have been. My husband—"

Sam cut her off. "You don't have to apologize."

"How bad is the storm?" I asked.

"Not much yet. The sun is still _____. But your friend is right. Something's coming."

"The clouds are moving fast," Ray said. He broke out of the hug so I could see his mouth when he spoke. "They're low and they have these weird colors."

"_____ setting up an emergency shelter at the library."

"Do they have enough cots?" I asked.

Sam shook his head. "No time for it now. Sleeping bags and blankets will have to do. But we've got a phone tree _____. Those without shelter or who feel unsafe are to come to the library."

"To the fallout shelter."

"That's right."

"I can help," Stevie said. "Give me a list of people to call. As long as the landline works, I'll do it."

"You sure I can't take you to the library?" Sam asked.

"I'm sticking it out here. It's all I have. I've got the cellar to shelter in. And this place is battened down pretty tight."

My mom looked stricken. "We don't have a phone to call anyone. I'm sorry."

But Sam held up a hand. "That's not a problem. What about you, though? You don't have a phone out there on the farm? Is your husband home?"

"Yes," Amelia said. "He's all by himself."

"I'm going to take the girls back," my mom said. "We've got a storm cellar."

It was the first time I realized my mom planned to return me, to whisk me away from Ray again. Instinctively, I felt my fingers move at my side. His hand found my own and held it. I couldn't be parted from him. Not so soon.

"Can you do me a favor?" Sam asked my mom. "Can you take Ray too? Keep him safe with you? You're not the only family without a phone. Some of these homesteads don't have radios even, or don't listen to news that tells them anything useful. I've got to warn some folks about the storm, see if I can _____ to town."

"No way," Ray said. "I'm coming with you."

"Me too," I said.

His fingers tightened around mine.

"Thea," my mom said.

"I can help. Some people won't want to go, and I can talk to them. I *know* them and they know me. Gus's neighbor, the one with the signs?" I looked up at Sam. "I talked to him."

"You did?" Sam asked.

"Sort of. I wrote a sign to him. He saw me. It might help."

"I don't _____," my mom said.

"I can help. Please. I want to do this. We'll bring someone in, then come home."

I could feel my mom relenting. Her face seemed to smooth, the lines around her eyes and mouth—when had my mom gotten wrinkles? Was it the harsh sun out here? The stress of the move, or something else?—disappearing for a moment.

My mom had learned so much: about me and Ray and sign language. About Amelia and school. So much of what she had trusted was collapsing, like soft rotted wood on an old staircase. It wouldn't hold you. It only had the illusion of solidness, which splintered once you tested it with any weight at all. I had tested her. Amelia had too. Those stairs my mom had followed, all these years—they led to nowhere.

"I can help," I said firmly. "I want to."

"All right," my mom said. "Be careful. And then come straight back to the farm."

"I'll keep them safe," Sam promised. "You get your little one home."

Sam gave a list to Stevie, numbers of farmers and families to call and warn about the storm. I was surprised at how many there were, all these people who had been living in the valley this whole time.

Stevie and Sam gave instructions to my mom. Get the animals secured at the farm. Tape the doors and pack the windows if there was time. The most important thing was to get into the storm shelter, where the walls were solid, windowless, and the doors closed tight as a metal trap.

I remembered my dad checking the storm cellar once when we first moved in, that the doors sealed tight, that they opened despite their squeaks and rust. I felt worried when I saw him do it. Another basement, another dark space where he could hide guns and food, hide the worst, paranoid parts of him.

For supplies? I had asked.

It was a vague enough question that he might not know I knew, that I still thought about the long guns, the shelves of food he had stockpiled. We had blown through a lot of it already in Colorado, using the emergency water right away. It seemed the emergency was just living.

My dad only said, *No. The storm shelter's for tornados.*

Great, I had thought. *Something else to worry about.*

Nobody had said anything about dust. It crept up without

warning. It was something you stepped on, sneezed at, brushed off your shoes. But great clouds of dust, masses of it, dust sucked from the ground and spit out by the sky—that was like bullets. Even a thing, small by itself, could be powerful if joined together with more.

My dad had never dreamed this, I thought as I rattled along in Sam's truck, Ray close beside me. Never been given this warning: that we could flee all the water in the world but a different surge would find us, just as powerful and punishing. I wondered if this coming storm would change anything, as the other dust storms had not.

This storm felt different. The air was leaden like the sky was just waiting: blue for now, but it seemed like it was building. Pressure mounted behind the clouds. They twisted and roiled, as if they couldn't stand to stay still.

And I couldn't, either. I had never been so anxious, riding with Sam and Ray, not since I was late getting back to the café, where my mom sat waiting. That afternoon seemed like years ago, when I had worried about ordinary things. Now I just prayed for the truck to hurry. For the tires to fly down the road, faster than the storm coming behind us.

We left the watchtower behind. Soon, the viewing platform grew small in the side mirror. Then, like a mirage, it disappeared. The few trucks that passed by us on the highway drove the opposite direction. I wondered if they had learned about the storm and were heading toward the shelter.

Soon enough I knew where we were going.

Down Elmer's driveway, Sam accelerated. We had never taken the dirt, potholed stretch this fast before. In a spin of gravel, we swerved to a stop at the end of the driveway. Elmer sat on the stump of the tree we had felled together, whittling something with a pocketknife. He looked up calmly, mildly amused at the truck.

"Elmer, what are you doing?" Sam said through his opened window. We didn't get out.

"Avoiding writing."

"You have got to get the internet out here."

"Nope. The internet is a worse way of avoiding writing. You can avoid it forever online." He nodded at the truck. He didn't stop whittling. "Where's the fire?"

"It's not a fire, you old fool. It's a dust storm. A big one headed this way. Folks are gathering at the library, at the fallout shelter."

"Well shit," Elmer said. "Is it that bad?"

"Pretty bad."

"All the signs are there," I said.

Elmer pointed his sharp stick at me. "I trust this one."

"Get in the truck then," Sam said. "We'll take you to town."

"Oh, I'm all _____."

"Come on, Elmer."

"I've made it this far."

"Yeah," I said. "Time to make it some more."

Elmer gave in. He ducked into his cabin quickly and I was worried we would waste time, waiting for him to batten up the place or pack his things. But he returned in only a moment with a briefcase slung over his shoulder. It was strange to see. Elmer wore a faded plaid shirt and wasted blue jeans. His boots were more dirt than boot, and at least some of his breakfast was in his beard. And he carried a leather briefcase with scratched gold clasps. When he tossed it in the bed of the truck, I noticed initials embossed onto the front. *EGL.*

"What's in the briefcase?" I asked.

"My next book." He lowered the gate of the truck bed. "And some beef jerky."

"Elmer, you're not riding _____ there," Sam said. "We've got a back seat. The kids can squeeze in."

"Well, all right," Elmer gave me a look. "But I'm not fancy."

I was especially glad Elmer wasn't in the bed of the pickup once we got on the road. Sam drove fast, even faster than down the driveway because the highway was flat and deserted. Word had gotten out about the storm. Ray switched on the radio and above the static, an announcement broke in. *Visibility less than one-quarter mile . . . Hazard: blowing dust . . . life-threatening . . . shelter.*

He couldn't get it in tune, and neither of us could hear much of it. He turned off the radio again, and then I was not sure which was worse: the warning or the silence, just as heavy. We passed farms whose windows were boarded up with plywood. We passed pastures empty of animals, just the wild and silent sedge, ruffling in the wind.

In the back seat, Ray and I were pressed tight together. The truck galloped and the fields flashed by. Sam drove through tumbleweeds, their branches smashing beneath his tires. Out the window, the clouds kept churning.

They were starting to change color.

At the watchtower, Ray had said that the clouds had a

strange shade to them, and now I saw it too. They looked brown in some places, orange in others, even a kind of purplish-blue. It was like the sky had been bruised. But the clouds moved so fast it was hard to get a good glance at them. Just when I thought they had decided on one color, they shifted again, the shade hid by a turbid mass of *another* cloud, silver and thick.

Closer to the library, we saw vehicles. A few trucks passed us, speeding up, their tops laden with suitcases, gas cans, and water tanks.

"Where do they think they're going?" Ray asked.

"Folks think they can outrace the storm," Sam said. "Eventually, you run out of places to run to."

I thought of the flood back in Ohio, how much of that experience might have influenced my dad, caused him to dream of its opposite. Dry, hot Colorado with its yellow fields. It would never flood here—but dust would fill the land. Disaster had followed us. It was just a different kind.

The parking lot of the library looked full, so Sam pulled in front and we all got out. A blond woman in a sundress was walking into the library, her arms wrapped around an older woman, supporting her.

"Helen?" I asked.

She turned and saw us. "Oh, children. Oh, you're all okay."

"Just making a special delivery," Sam said.

"They needed someone to snore in the shelter," Ray said.

"Yeah, yeah. You all think you're so funny," Elmer said. "Where are you when I have to write dialogue?"

"Everything _____ at your house?" Sam asked Helen.

"It's fine. This is my neighbor Ana." She indicated the

elderly woman who tried to smile, but her skin looked clammy. Circles of red had appeared on her face and her glasses were fogged up. "It's so hot. We thought it would be safer here."

"Get inside. Get into the air-conditioning."

"Let me help you." Elmer stepped forward and between him and Helen, they walked Ana carefully toward the building. Someone held the door open for them. It was Louisa. As soon as the trio were inside, she came over to us.

"How packed is it in there?" Sam asked her.

"Oh, Captain's trying to sign everyone up for library cards, but other than that, fine. I dropped off some food and coffee. We have enough blankets and _____ to make it through the night, as long as some _____ don't mind sleeping on the floor."

"How long will the storm last?" I asked.

"There's no way to know."

"How long was Black Sunday?"

Sam lifted his hat to scratch at his forehead. "The total darkness? I think only an hour. But it can be much longer."

"Total darkness?"

"You can't go out in it," Louisa said. "You can't see at all."

Most of the dust storms I had lived through had been in the evening, when the clouds were already dark, and the sun down or headed there. I hadn't seen the clouds turn even blacker. I hadn't seen them blot out the sun. Could they do that, like in the books?

"We better get you home," Sam said to me. "We promised your mama."

I asked, "What about Gus?"

"Gus will be fine," Sam said. "Gus has internet and he definitely knows what's coming."

"What about Gus's neighbor? There's no way he has Wi-Fi and I bet he doesn't have a phone. His house is not going to survive another storm." Elmer's cabin had been closest to the library, but the neighbor was one of the reasons I had wanted to come along in the first place. Someone living so remotely, so sparsely, would have no warning.

"I'll make a call." Sam pulled out his cell as he turned away.

"It'll be okay," Ray told me, signing the last word.

I wondered for how many people it wouldn't be, though. People had died in the first Dust Bowl. They died when dust buried their houses or cars. People had choked on the dust, died of suffocation. And people had died later. That was perhaps the worst part, the sneaky dark heart of it. Not everyone died on the day. Dust, like mold, festered. It lingered, showing up later in the lungs, in the heart.

Sam came back to our group on the sidewalk and his eyes looked clouded with concern. "Gus isn't answering. Something's wrong. He always picks up when I call."

"Maybe he's _____ the house?" Louisa said.

Ray said something about Gus helping the neighbor, but Sam shook his head. "Something's wrong. I have a feeling. I've been working in this valley my whole life. I've learned to trust my instincts." He looked at me. "Like you should."

"Me?"

"You called Ray. You had a bad feeling when you talked to your friend. You were right to trust your gut."

No one had ever said that to me before. That my feelings

were a thing I could act on, believe in. My dad could act on his dreams—so why couldn't I respond to something more, something based on experience and study?

And a dream, a small voice said in my head.

"I'm going _____," Sam said. "You kids, go with Louisa."

"I should talk to the neighbor," I said. "That's what my gut says."

Sam seemed harried, rushed and pulled in too many directions. People were streaming into the shelter. He must have felt responsible for so many here. The wind pushed trash, a piece of newspaper, against his shoe. It was a slight gale, only a preview of the force to come, but hot and dry. It was already hard to breathe in that wind.

"All right. Fine." Sam indicated the truck. "Both of you, get in. I know you're a package deal."

"Be safe," Louisa told me; Louisa, who had stayed after her family had gone. She stayed at the library now. And anything else she might have said was lost in the noise of Sam starting the engine. But I held on to the image of Louisa in front of the library, clutching an empty basket and waving. I looked behind my shoulder for her, the blackness of her hair against the darkening clouds.

On the road, the change in the atmosphere began. In the truck's side mirror, I watched the clouds. There were so many now, they filled the whole mirror like a pool of dirty water. I started to hear the wind more. It was low. It sounded far-off. But it was coming.

Back home, I had learned how to tell if a storm was

approaching. I would watch the trees. When the leaves flipped over, exposing their pale undersides, as if offering their bellies to the sky, I knew it was going to rain.

I thought the leaf flipping had to do with the trees readying themselves to soak up a storm's moisture. That didn't make sense, though. Trees drank from the ground, from their roots. Maybe the turning leaves was instead something about wind. How wind pushed the leaves around as it pushed all of us, urging us to go.

The wind didn't want us here.

And why would it? We were obviously bad for the land, my family and all the families who had come. All the families who had *kept* coming since the 1930s, since even before. Building our houses, tearing up the prairies and planting crops that we tore up again once they ever—if they ever—sprouted. We razed. We dug out everything. Maybe the wind had been trying to send us a message. Failing that, it was shoving us along.

I had wanted to go. Almost my whole time in Colorado, I would have been happy to say to the wind: *Fine. We're leaving.* I would have been thrilled to.

But now, something was happening to me. Something had gotten under my skin like a grain of that sand that swirled in the air. It didn't irritate me like the sand did. Strangely, it soothed. It was like a question kept posing itself, over and over, in my head. *Could I build a life here?* But how could I and my family without hurting the lives already here?

I had thought nothing grew in the valley. Not even grass, really. The land looked so yellow and brown all the time. Those were the colors of death, I thought. Of life drained away, dying of thirst. But even amid the dirt and pale weeds there were bursts of green: cacti, which stored water in their swollen fists. The cacti were small but they were there. And if I looked closer, I saw wildflowers: dark purple, pale yellow, pale pink.

The longer I looked, the more I noticed that was alive in the desert. Rabbits hid in the sedge. Chipmunks would scurry along the ground, their wiggling plump bellies the same color as the earth. Dragonflies twisted in the air and occasionally a hummingbird buzzed by like a doorbell. Or a magpie catapulted through the sky. The natural world unfolded like a hand. If my dad couldn't coax beets or tomatoes from the ground, were there other plants that liked to grow here, that had been growing already? What was a way to raise them that didn't use too much water?

On the horizon, Gus's dome appeared, silver and glinting like tinfoil. The rearview and side mirrors of the truck had been overtaken by clouds, and after we made it down Gus's driveway, parked and got out, I could hear the wind had risen too.

We had been lucky with Elmer; he had been sitting right in front of his cabin. But Gus was nowhere to be found.

We called for him. Sam went to the front of the house and rang the bell. Ray and I walked around the dome's opposite sides, into the backyard. I couldn't help but glance into the neighbor's yard, seeing the small, crestfallen house. There was no way it would hold up under another big storm. It looked like it had barely survived the last one. The roof seemed to be sliding and several windows were broken.

The neighbor had made new signs, I could tell, even if I couldn't read most of them from where I stood. But one sign was huge, the red letters screaming.

THE SKY IS COMING DOWN.

It was, stranger. It was. We just had to get everyone to shelter in time.

I heard shouting from the backyard. Ray.

I hurried through the weeds to reach him. He stood by Gus's instruments that whirled and recorded, collecting data from the air and sky. Gus leapt from instrument to instrument. He had been taking notes on a spiral pad. When he saw me, the pen flew out of his hand in excitement.

"Thea! Do you know what's coming?" He didn't wait for an answer. "It's a storm. A big one. History-making, I think."

"Well, it's coming *soon*," Ray said. "Thea's friend _____ through it. She said it was headed this way."

"It is. I think it is!"

"Gus," I said. "Is your house all right? Is everything sealed up and ready?"

His mouth fell open. "My house! I completely forgot about my house!"

Ray and I looked at each other. I wished we could have signed, that I knew enough to. But I could still read his eyes. Huge and worried.

I asked, "What about your neighbor?"

Now the energy, the giddy delight about the storm, left Gus. He crashed, like Amelia after the sugar of a birthday cake. Reality came swooping down and he saw it: the world beyond his instruments. It was dark and looming. Gus said, "I forgot about him too."

Sam wouldn't let me and Ray go over there. "The man has a shotgun."

"Maybe if I do it?" Gus offered.

"I'm not putting you in danger, either."

"We don't have much time."

"He's over there now." Ray stood at the edge of the property line with Gus's binoculars.

"Let me see." I tapped Ray and he handed the binoculars to me.

I saw the neighbor walking around outside. He didn't seem to be hurrying. He didn't seem worried about anything. He bent to something on the ground, cast a small thing aside then picked up another thing. He was weeding, I realized. Working in his small garden as if this was an ordinary day.

"He doesn't know," I said.

There was no way he would be moving this slowly if he knew about the dust storm. Not this man, who warned of the end-times in sign after sign. Now the end was coming and he wasn't ready. None of us were.

I lowered the binoculars. Close to me, in the grass, lay the sign I had written to the man before. I BELIEVE YOU. I picked up the cardboard and turned it over. No rain these last few days—no rain for many, many days. Nothing had warped the cardboard, and the other side was blank.

"Do you have your marker?" I asked Gus.

The hardest part was trying to get the man's attention. Ray, Sam, and Gus all shouted, jumping up and down. I kept my hands on the sign, on which I had written a message about the storm coming, and held it high.

Finally, the shouting worked. The neighbor looked up. Ray had the binoculars and he waved with his free hand. I lifted the sign, pumping it in my arms.

"What's happening?" I asked. I let go of the sign with one hand to touch Ray.

"He's gone," Ray said. "Back _____ the house." But the man returned only a moment later with a large piece of plywood and his own binoculars around his neck. Ray said he sat on the concrete step at the front of the house, balanced the sign on his legs and wrote something. Then he stood up and hoisted it.

WHEN? The man's sign read.

I took the marker and wrote: SOON.

The man crossed out the words he had written. He wrote: WHAT DO?

"I can't believe my neighbor is asking me for advice," Gus said. "I don't even know him. I've been afraid to introduce myself."

"What do I tell him?" I asked. "Do you have another big piece of cardboard?"

Gus went into the house to look.

I didn't have much space left on my sign. I wrote: SHELTER.

The man wrote: WHERE?

Ray watched through the binoculars. He said the man held up his sign for a while. Then, when we didn't respond, he threw it on the ground. The man paced, shaking his head. Ray said he seemed nervous, upset.

"Hurry," I called to Gus through the open door.

"I can't _____ anything," he yelled back.

I crossed out all the words on my sign. "There's not enough room to tell him about the library. Maybe we should just go over there and talk to him?"

"Kids," Sam said, "we're running out of time. We have to get somewhere safe, with or without him."

"We can't just leave him," I said.

Ray looked through the binoculars and said the man was holding up his sign again.

WHERE?

WHERE?

"Give me the sign." Gus had returned from his house empty-handed. He took the cardboard from me. He wrote, HERE.

23

Gus wanted all of us to stay. He had a storm shelter and the neighbor—Hugo—was shy. He stood quietly, bashful about being invited over. He had brought his cat with him, an orange striped tabby in a backpack. The cat's name was Ketchup.

But I was worried about my mom and Amelia. There was no way for them to contact me, to let me know they were all right.

"I should have given your mom my number," Sam said.

"It doesn't matter," I said. "They don't have a phone anymore."

Sam's face didn't change. "We'll help you deal with _____ when this is all over, I promise."

"We should just go to Thea's," Ray said. "It's close."

Gus told us to wait and rushed somewhere else in the dome. When he returned, he had goggles in his arms and three masks. "Just in case," he said. "Don't breathe the dust. Don't get caught out in it. The sky will turn colors. Orange, bloodred, then black as night."

Bloodred?

"You won't be able to see," Gus said. "And the total darkness might last an hour. Or longer."

The two men watched us leave from the doorway, Gus and his neighbor with the cat. The wind had changed in the small amount of time we had been inside. It felt even heavier, and in a way I couldn't really explain: purposeful, like the air before a hard rain. It was moving toward something. It was bringing something up from the ground. Soon it would fall down upon us.

We got in the truck. Sam rolled all the windows up and I closed the vents. He passed out the masks and goggles. Ray and I slung them around our necks.

The farm wasn't far from Gus's dome. But only a few minutes into our drive, the clouds started to give chase. The color of the world was changing. It was like a watercolor stain, like a drop of ink from a fat brush had exploded in the sky. A burnt orange color spread through the area all around us, behind us and on both sides of the truck. Sam drove fast, so fast the truck began to shake. I couldn't look at the odometer, couldn't bear to see his hands vibrating on the wheel.

Ray held my hand tight. With my other hand I slipped the mask over my mouth. It was the type of mask with headband straps. The goggles clattered around my neck.

The light became tea-colored, dust-colored.

"I'm sorry," I said, muffled through the mask.

Ray turned to me. He had put his own mask on. I knew he couldn't hear me, with the mask and the wind, and I had watched him take out his hearing aid on the side facing me, to protect it from dust. He let go of my hand.

He signed to me, *I love you.*

He turned back before I could answer. But I knew that one. I knew it.

Amelia and I had practiced. *My name is* _____.

Sister.

Dog.

Love.

I never thought I would use it.

Ray reached for my hand again. Quickly gaining on either side of the highway were walls of clouds. They were a color that made me feel queasy, I couldn't describe it any other way. An uneasy, broken color. The color of the earth, not of the sky.

But the sky had taken up the earth. It had swallowed it and now it was preparing to swallow us. The clouds came faster than we could drive. They rolled like an ocean wave, churning and turning. The surf on the bottom of them devoured, and the tops spiraled over, a rotating whirl of dust.

I thought inexplicably of a movie I had loved as a child. *The Last Unicorn.* I had found an old VHS tape of it at a garage sale. In Ohio, we still had a VCR, my parents clinging to older technology long before they made us give it all up. I knew the story because I had read the book. So my parents let me watch it, again and again. The tape started to fuzz, I watched it so much. I watched it alone or with my sister. Then my dad came in the room during the harpy part, when a grotesque winged character with human breasts wheeled through the sky and attacked the witch of the Midnight Carnival. Soon we weren't allowed to watch TV or movies on our own anymore.

But I remembered the unicorn, disguised as a girl. When

the magic of her disguise fell away, she was chased by the Red Bull who, in the end, disappeared into the surf.

The Red Bull approached us now, angry and orange. But there was no ocean to walk into. No hero to give chase. There was only us in the small yellow truck.

"Hang on, kids." Sam said.

Ray's fingers squeezed mine.

The Red Bull was in the road. It was right in front of us, creeping low on the ground like fog, but dark and murky. A shadow fell over us.

Then we were inside it.

I heard a spitting crash, pebbles and debris striking the sides and roof of the truck. Visibility decreased through the windshield to only a few feet. It looked like a blizzard but with earth-colored snow, snow that swirled around us, over us. The wind roared. The sky, just visible from the top of the windshield, emerged blue every few seconds, a flash in the whirling dust clouds. A stuttering reminder. The clouds were like flames.

I squeezed my eyes shut. Ray's grip pulsed in my hand. I imagined it was his heart. I imagined I was sending my own heartbeat to him, a reminder: This is how you keep beating. This is how you keep going. *Keep going, keep going*, I said it in my head to Ray, to Sam, white-knuckled on the road.

Sam shouted.

My eyes flashed open as he jerked the wheel to the right, the truck swerving off the road. Something swam out of the dust toward us, huge.

It was a car.

"Somebody just left it," Sam said. "Abandoned it in

_____." He jerked the wheel again, overcompensating, getting us back onto the asphalt, but barely.

Ray and I knocked against each other. The flashes of blue sky I could see were growing farther and farther apart. Telephone poles loomed out of the brown clouds, pole by pole, every few feet like the masts of sunken ships. Sam was navigating by them, our only markers.

But a wider distance was mounting between each one.

No. It was the dust storm, becoming too thick, masking everything. Soon we wouldn't be able to see at all.

"Honey, we're going to have to stop," Sam said. "We're going to _____ pull over."

"No, please," I pleaded. "The house is almost there."

At home, on clear days, I could see the twinkle of Gus's house on the horizon. At lonely points, I had imagined walking over there. I pictured the dome rising out of the fields to greet me. The round roof made a shape like two people hugging. Leaning forward in the truck, I couldn't see anything, not the dome that had become so familiar. Then—

"That's the weathervane on top of our house!" I sat on the edge of my seat and pointed.

The clouds parted for a moment and we passed an object on top of a crooked post.

"The mailbox!" I said. "That's the mailbox. Turn here. Turn right here."

Sam cut the wheel and we turned into dimness. I could only tell that we had made it to the driveway by the crunching under the tires, the shift from asphalt to gravel and dirt.

Everything was orange, like my family's farm had been transplanted to another, mysterious planet. Familiar shapes loomed out of the clouds: the truck, parked crookedly off to the side (so my mom and Amelia had made it home), the pasture fencing. But all of it was cast in orange.

There was no sun. No sky.

Sam had slowed the truck way down but did not park, uncertain where to stop. I felt like we were underwater. Underwater—or in space. Drifting, rudderless, we crept forward.

Something else was moving out of the orange. Moving toward us.

They came closer and we came closer.

It was my mom.

"Stop!" I said.

Sam hit the brakes. We shot forward, then he shoved the truck into park. My mom walked right to the truck, clutching its sides for support. She came to my door. When she reached the window, I saw she had a handkerchief tied around her nose and mouth. It was not enough to protect her from the dust. I knew it wasn't.

"She'll get us to the house," I said, even though I did not know if it was true. I didn't know if anyone could find the house in the orange that surrounded us. I made a move for the door handle.

"Wait!" Sam said.

He signed something that I didn't understand, but Ray pulled on his goggles, then he tapped my own, around my neck. I put them on too.

We opened the truck doors.

A howling I could only call *hungry*. The wind was in pain and that was why it beat down on us. It was sharp, each driving gust carrying grit. As soon as we opened the truck door, the wind took it, trying to tear it back, to rip it from the truck. Ray, my mom, and I all pushed the door closed, then my mom clutched my arm. Through my goggles, she looked wavy, indistinct. But I could tell her eyes burned, streaming with tears. She squeezed them shut, trying to shield herself against the knife-sharp wind. Her mouth moved, motion below the handkerchief.

I couldn't hear her.

I couldn't hear her.

The wind beat at my back, trying to tear off my shirt. My hair felt sharp, stinging against my face. Another figure joined the three of us at our side of the truck. Sam. He grabbed my mom's shoulder and she leaned into him. They were shouting, but it made no difference. The wind robbed their words. I felt as if we were in the orange mouth of a tiger, inside the Red Bull.

Sam leaned forward and touched my shoulder. Ray and I both looked at him.

He signed *sister*.

He signed *dog*.

He signed other words but I knew those two. Those words were important to Amelia, and those we had learned together because of her.

My sister who was missing.

Who had gone to look for one of the dogs. Or, all of the dogs.

I didn't understand everything but I knew it was bad. Bad enough that my parents were outside searching for her. Not safe in our storm shelter. Not protected even though the air was changing. Even as we stood by the truck, it was deepening. The color of the air shifted.

I heard Gus's words in my head.

The sky will be orange, bloodred, then black as night.

It was red, the eddying air, like the clouds were filled with blood. Like my dream. If this was the storm Gus thought it was—if this was my nightmare, come to life—we had only one stage left before the storm deepened. Before we *had* to be in a shelter, when the total darkness would slam down upon us.

The thought of my sister out alone in that nothingness caused my heart to beat rapidly. My chest felt tight. What did Amelia love, where would she go to hide? The chicken coop. The ruined shed . . .

"I know where she is," I said to Ray.

He couldn't hear me. I couldn't hear myself in the wind's roar. My lips felt cracked beneath my mask. But Ray saw something in my eyes.

Everything was starting to lose its edges, as if the storm were rubbing us away, erasing us. The wind pounded, trying to tear us apart. Sam took my mom toward the house. She leaned into his shoulder and he braced his arm across both their faces, trying to shield them from the worst of the wind, trying to push a path.

I knew they thought we were following. I knew they expected us to and would be horrified when they turned and found we were not behind them.

But Ray and I had to go a different way. I had to find my sister.

I went first, leading Ray along the opposite side of the house. I knew where Amelia was; I believed I did, but how would we get there? I couldn't see three feet in front of my face. Everything was a swirl. I couldn't see the house, the crops, even the truck anymore.

The crops.

The fields of crops had been fenced in. Otherwise, the dogs wouldn't stop trampling them. One of my hands clasped firmly into Ray's, with the other I reached out and felt around in the air. My fingers grazed something solid at the height of my chest. It felt hard and splintered.

A fencepost.

I remembered reaching for the lightbulb in the darkness of our basement in Ohio. I remembered feeling around in the creek for rocks—the water so murky, my hand, arm, and shoulder disappeared below its surface. I grasped the fencepost, held tight. And pulled.

I followed it. I let the fence lead me and Ray let me lead him, hanging onto me. We crawled along, beaten back by the wind but shoving ourselves forward with the posts. I pulled us closer and closer. It felt like I was yanking us up a mountainside, like pulling a rope that pushed back. I didn't know what I would do when the fence ended, what we would hold on to.

Then we were there. I reached out my hand for the next fencepost and felt nothing, only space. The fence turned sharply to the right, where the fields continued. But we needed to go *left*, toward the house. I couldn't see the house, only a world of crimson. If we stepped out into it, we would disappear.

I flung my hand out, stretching my fingers as if I could hit something, anything, familiar. My shoulder burned from extending so far. The wind struck me in the back, the face, everywhere at once with biting and burning grit. I thought of our basement again. Why did I keep going back there in my mind to that darkness, to the light?

The light.

I didn't need to reach out. I needed to reach *up*.

I thrust my arm into the sky, my fingers striking an object thin and taut. The clothesline. It sprung upward, elastic, and before I could lose it again, I clutched it firmly in my fingers.

So many times I had cursed this house, cursed everything about our lives here, including that we had to dry all our clothes outside on the line. It took forever, snapping the sheets, smoothing them, pinning dresses and shirts, waiting for them to dry. Then the double chore of taking everything down, ironing, folding, putting away.

I had hated this clothesline. Now I clung to it for life. I knew exactly where it led. From the fence, it stretched about fifty feet to the house. And just before the house were the remains of the old shed.

I kept my hand raised high and inched us along. The wind buffeted me and swung at the clothesline, moving it wildly, but I kept my fingers grasped so tightly around the cord my wrist ached. Ray kept holding on to me.

We were almost at the house. I could see a corner of it emerging out of the amber fog. But where was the shed? I would have to let go of the line to find it, let go with nothing to hold on to, no way to steer. I wasn't able to shout Amelia's name. I tried to yell and the wind took my words. I wasn't able to see her. I could barely make out the side of the house through my goggles.

I had to release the clothesline. It sprung back up, away

into oblivion, and was instantly lost to me. Ray kept one hand on me and the other one on the line, but his arm would only reach so far. I would have to let go of him, if I couldn't find her. Or he would have to release the line too, our only tether. I stepped forward, not knowing what I was walking into. My hand felt around in the blowing, hot air.

Then my fingers sank into fur.

Matted, soft fur.

Small arms came out of the darkness and wrapped around me. It was Amelia. In her arms, she held a tiny dog, whose white fur seemed to glow in the storm. I had never seen the dog before. Amelia had her face screwed shut against the wind, and she was trembling all over but all right. All right.

I pulled off my mask, the elastic slapping my face, and secured it over hers. The wind tried to push inside my mouth, my nose. I fought to breathe. Keeping Amelia close to me, and clutching Ray, I had no hand left to guide us back. Ray seemed to know. Instinctively, he turned and pulled us back along the clothesline. We filed in behind him, Amelia holding the dog. But the wind had changed direction too, pushing right in our faces.

It was red. How could it be so red? The red of blood. The red of my dream.

The red of the Red Bull.

It howled like an animal, a wounded one. And hurt, wild beasts were capable of anything, I knew that, lashing out, devouring you with sharp teeth, a coyote caught in a trap. I tried to hold an image, to order it in my mind: the farm and all it contained, the layout of everything on our small acres. Old Cuthbert's house.

I could picture the house's screen door. The back window with its shutter hanging off. And to the right of the screen door, buried in the earth were two steel double doors.

The doors to the storm cellar.

I tugged on Ray, hard. He turned, and I pointed. I was not sure if he could see anything through the red dust, even my hand right before him, but I pointed again, emphatically. He felt my body move, sensed the urgency.

It was hard to leave the clothesline. It felt like a mistake, stepping into the blizzard of red. We had nothing left to guide us. Launching forward into the storm, we walked haltingly, seizing one another and pushing against the wind. The gusts threatened to knock us off our path, to knock us away forever.

We pushed toward what we thought was the storm cellar, but I had no idea which direction was up or down anymore. I had no thoughts but the wind. Like a drowning person, I didn't know which direction I faced, which was the air, which was the killing sea. My foot struck something hard enough to hurt.

I crouched, letting go of Ray to feel around. He didn't let go of me, still clinging to my back as my fingers found an edge on the ground. It was the metal door, the bottom of it. My free hand traveled up until I felt the seam where the doors closed. Higher, higher, I found the handle.

I pulled.

Nothing.

I pulled and pulled.

Ray pulled too, letting go of me to yank with both hands.

The doors were stuck tight.

They were locked.

The three of us were trapped. Trapped outside in the raging storm, so close to a safe place. And the red of the world was going away. It was shifting, as the wind had shifted so many times already. It was deepening, turning to black.

It will be black as night.

Black Sunday.

The wind pitched both higher and deeper. On my worst nights, it sounded like this inside me, the howling of absence. I didn't only know silence. Sometimes I knew ringing, a keening of pitches just not right in my ear, a jumble of noise in my head. But the wrong, awful sound was everywhere now and we were all inside it.

I held Amelia tight. Ray's arm went around me and we buried our heads, trying to hide our faces from the storm. My hand was cast off hard as one of the doors flung open from the inside. We backed up, pushing ourselves away from the entrance to make room.

Sam stood below us on the stairs, holding the cellar door open.

24

We hurried down the steps into the cellar. Amelia and her small, bundled dog went first. Once inside, Ray and I hung back at the door and pulled with Sam, forcing the storm back so we could get the door shut again.

When it finally clanged closed, a weird silence descended upon the cellar. We could still hear the wind, roaring, but it was muted, like we finally *were* underwater. Or, like we were witnessing the storm from behind thick glass. It was strange not to see red anymore.

But we were coated in it. I took off my goggles. Ray did too. He had orange dust around his face, his skin exposed in the circles the goggles and mask had protected. I smiled at him and he laughed at me. We must have looked the same. His hair had blown out from his head in matted whorls, stiff with sand. I reached up to touch my own hair and felt grittiness beneath my fingers.

My ears hurt. So did my whole body. It felt like I had been

pounded by waves, dashed against rocks. Amelia pulled off her mask and started coughing as she walked down the steps. The sound echoed in the basement space, and a strange bleating answered it.

When she reached the bottom of the steps, the white dog leapt from her arms and began running around. Animals came from the corners to greet them. It was a smaller space than our basement in Ohio, but the shelter was full of them: dogs, goats, and chickens. I became aware of other sounds: clucks, the goats' bleating, the worried whine of the dogs. There were no shelves along the sides of this cellar. I saw no canned goods, no camping supplies, no guns. Just a few mounds of blankets.

And my parents. My mom rushed forward and took Amelia in her arms. All of us looked the same: sandblasted in orange and stiff-haired. Tears had made clear streaks on my mom's face.

"Thank you, thank you," my mom said.

Shadows moved at the back of the cellar. I had seen so many things emerge out of the storm today—telephone poles, the mailbox, the shed, a car—and now I saw my dad come forward from a corner. His beard was dredged with orange, and his eyes leaked. Was my dad crying?

"You're safe," he said. "We thought, I thought . . . we had lost Amelia. Lost both of you. I thought I had ruined everything."

I climbed down the rest of the steps to the bottom. I was breathless, like I had traveled down a dry riverbed, battered by boulders the whole way. I tried to find my voice. My throat burned as if I had been screaming and my words felt raw. "It's a storm. It wasn't your fault, Dad."

"Bringing you two here was. Taking you from your home. I ruined everything."

"It's not ruined," Amelia said. "We found another dog." She patted the little white one, running around the others with its tongue hanging out. It had a crooked jaw, slightly crossed eyes. Like us, the dog's fur was messy. "Her name is Saturday. I just decided."

"Your favorite day," I said.

"I'm sorry," my dad said. To hear the words coming from his mouth, it was almost as strange as seeing him covered in orange. I thought maybe it was me, maybe I had misheard, invented it in my head—but he kept going. "Your mom told me, about school. About ... learning sign language?" The words seemed hard for him.

"What do you think?" I asked.

"I think we should talk about it."

Sam came down the cellar stairs and sat heavily on the bottom one. He had somehow managed not to lose his hat. He took it off and tipped it, like a shoe full of water. Sand dribbled out of the rim. It made a neat pile on the ground.

It was funny to look at it there. It was just sand, just a small, soft pile of dust. If I reached my hand down, I could scatter it. I could crumble it to bits. It was already crumbling, already almost nothing. Sam could squash it with his boot.

But I knew that in the first Dust Bowl, some people had died months—years—later of dust pneumonia, of cancer. The dust lodged itself in the lungs, making slow and certain cracks, breaking a person from the inside.

Amelia could breathe the dust in and it could hurt her. It could hurt any of us. If enough of it gathered together, assembled into a storm, it could crush us, bury our farms. Just this little pile of dust. Outside the cellar doors, the wind howled, angry at being shut out.

"What now?" my mom asked.

"Now we wait," Sam said.

I held Ray's hand. I said to my dad, "Let's talk now."

25

Captain straightened the books. A table of them stood by the circulation desk, though I wondered when he had told Elmer he could bring his whole back catalog, if the librarian knew it would be this large. I counted at least thirteen books, mostly thick paperbacks, arranged in stacks along the table. They had titles like *Gentlemen Prefer Bullets*, *Death Comes a-Courting*, and *Mother, May I Murder?* I took a picture.

Amelia picked up a copy of that last one, whistling in appreciation at the cover: a glossy, embossed illustration of a girl in a blue dress standing in a doorway, a long and glistening chef's knife in her hand.

"Okay," my mom said, whisking it out of my sister's grip and placing it back on the table.

"Elmer's name is bigger than the title," Amelia said.

"I think that means he's famous." I checked out the image on the LCD screen of the old digital camera Helen had given me. The stack of books was in focus, but the lighting looked wrong. Not as dramatic as I would have liked. I took another shot for Elmer's website.

"We have a famous neighbor?" Amelia's voice was awed.

"Amelia," my mom said. "Why don't you and Patience help Louisa with the refreshments?"

Amelia joined the other girl across the room where my boss was setting up trays of cookies and carafes of lemonade. It was startling to see the girls side by side. They were almost the same height, though Patience's hair was blond and fell freely down her shoulders and Amelia had her tight, reddish braids. My sister clutched her new rescue inhaler. It was always with her now. That was a difference between them too.

The girls would ride the bus together to school in a few weeks. My mom was nervous about it—more nervous than Amelia—but it made them both feel better knowing that Patience would get on the bus just stops before her, that she would save a seat for my sister.

My bus would come later, the bus to the high school.

Ray wouldn't be on it.

I would ride alone, go to a new school alone where I would know no one. Not yet. But I was going. We had convinced my dad, Amelia and I, to let us try. And it was easier to do new things together. Patience was going to school, after all, for the first time too.

A lot of things were happening for the first time.

The farmers of the Bloodless Valley were not planting wheat or corn. Those crops required too much water, hungry for a snowpack that just wasn't coming. Not anymore. It might never come again, not like it used to. Instead, some pastures would be left wild, growing up into grass whose roots would hold down the soil. Chokeberry would be planted, sumac.

But those were the small farmers, family farmers like my dad and the Mistys. It was easy, though it took a lot of meetings down at the Grange, a lot of coffee kept warm at Louisa's, for them to agree on some things. Especially once they had a common enemy: the big companies, the farms that were more corporation than farm.

I think for a long time my dad and men like him thought the earth was their enemy, that they had to wrestle it into shape, form it into an order they thought was right. I think he believed that about me and Amelia too. But we were our own shapes. We grew our own way, and so did the land. It had grown before us. It would grow after us, probably better. We had to listen to it, especially now when it shouted at us with the force of dust walls a thousand feet high, with the anger of gale winds sixty miles an hour. We couldn't ignore what the earth was saying any longer, how we had hurt it.

It was hurting back.

An animal in a trap, I kept thinking. We had made the largest trap of all. We had turned the whole *world* into a trap, and we were stuck inside too, rattling the bars of the cage we had made. Trapped inside with the Red Bull.

It had taken weeks to dig out the valley. Electrical trucks and big construction vehicles came from across the country to mend the power lines and help unearth buildings. Dust had buried semitrailers. Dust had covered houses, but the people inside had escaped to the shelter.

Dust had been blown by the wind to the top stories of

houses and sculpted itself into dunes. They sloped downward, sleek sledding hills. It was strange how the storm did so much damage, and yet it smoothed things out in the end, as if wanting to leave a nice canvas, a tidy field in its wake. Barns looked like they had been tucked into bed, covers of dust silky at the rooftops. Trees were covered up to their tips, wind-stripped of leaves. Dust froze tumbleweeds in time, trapping those rolling travelers, stilling them.

Some people had abandoned their cars, like the one Sam, Ray, and I had nearly hit on the road. The tops and hoods of discarded vehicles poked up like those dinosaur bones Amelia loved to imagine. It was like discovering a fossil every time a breeze revealed another truck on the side of the road, a silent giant in someone's yard.

Dust still blew in the wind for a long time, carrying grit and debris. We wore masks when we went outside. My dad and Sam built a new shelter for the goats. Sam and Ray helped us dig out our fences, and Sam found a grant so we could have a phone again and internet on the farm. It was going to be hard, living in the valley.

But it was going to be hard living anywhere.

"This is what you wanted," I told my dad that night in the cellar, as the storm howled outside as if it was alive. "You wanted us to live here and now we live here. So we get to do a little of what we want too. Because that's what a family does."

"You're children," my dad said. "You don't know what you want."

"I know some things. I know I want to go to school. I want to have friends. So does Amelia. I want to learn to sign."

"We tried school before and that didn't work."

"Well, let's try again," I said. "This is a new place. With new people."

"I just wanted a safe childhood for you. I want life to be simple, for _____ us. I didn't want you to feel different."

"I am different, though," I said. "Maybe it's all right if I feel it sometimes. Maybe it's wrong to just ignore it."

"And it isn't simple," my mom spoke up. "Our life here. It isn't easy. We make it harder than it needs to be." She paused. "You make it harder for me."

One of the goats was bleating desperately. Amelia went to it, the new little dog trailing her like a dirty shadow. She knelt and put her arms around the goat's milky neck. The goat fell silent, licked her hair with its long tongue.

Nobody said anything, until my dad said haltingly, again, the words still sounding so strange coming from his mouth, "I'm sorry."

I tried to remember the other times I had heard him apologize. I couldn't think of any. Not when he pulled us from school, not when we moved. He was so certain, so convinced. His dreams came true. His way was the way.

"Dad," I said. "You're not the only one who has dreams." The storm was loud enough, even I could hear the shifts in the wind outside. "On the farm, you can pretend like nothing is wrong, nothing is happening. That you're isolated. But the world is changing."

"We don't live just on the farm," my mom said. "We live in a whole world too."

I thought of Helen and Elmer, helping the woman into the library. I thought of Gus and his neighbor, Hugo. I thought of the baskets of food from Louisa and the books from Captain. And Sam sitting at my side. And Ray right beside me, holding my hand as if we still walked through the orange, then red, then black night of the storm. My dad didn't know any of those people. He spent his days alone, in the bubble of the fields, his dark thoughts reflected back to him, with no one to question him, no one to ask for advice.

"We live in a community," I said. "A community can help."

"No handouts. You know that, Thea. I have to stay firm _____."

"It's not a handout if you help too. Maybe that's what you're missing." I thought of how my mom had volunteered to clean up and help Stevie, and how it seemed to make both of them feel better. "You're missing helping other people."

"I barely have time to get the work of this farm _____."

"Well, we're going to have a lot of time after this storm," I said.

There would be no crops to water after, I knew. There would be no harvest. Not this year. Nothing living would be left. As if on cue, the wind gusted outside, beating at the cellar doors with a new burst of energy.

"Maybe it's time to try a different way," my mom said.

My dad was running out of excuses. It seemed like he wanted us to tear them down for him, to expose how thin his reasons really were. To give him an out. "You know I don't like new ways," he said.

"Not new ways," I said. "Just different."

So, it was different, selling eggs, goat's milk, cheese, and soap at the farmers' market in the library; the valley had decided to hold the market inside until the dust died down. It was different, making candles, and designing a website with Captain's help to sell a lot of the items online. It was different, my dad going to farmers' meetings at the Grange, and my mom meeting Stevie, Helen, and Louisa for coffee, when she wasn't studying for her night classes; she had decided to finally finish her degree. And me driving my mom to and from the café. I finally had my learner's permit and my parents let me take over on the long, flat stretches of the highway sometimes.

And it would be different in the fall with Ray gone.

I righted one of Elmer's books that had fallen to the side of the table. This one had a cover with a holographic image. If you tilted the paperback to one side, you saw a blond woman's face. If you tilted it to the other, the face turned into a flaming skull.

"Wow," Ray said from beside me. "A skull *and* flames?"

I set the book down and kissed him. I pulled away so he could look at my mouth when I said, "I can't believe you're spending your last afternoon in the valley in the library."

"Nowhere I'd rather be. Anyway, we have tonight. My mom's not coming until the morning."

We would email, we had promised. We would text, now that my parents had a working phone, and they promised to finally get me my own. And we would visit.

"You're coming to Denver in a few weeks," Ray said. "And we'll be back in the valley for Thanksgiving."

"Maybe I'll know how to sign *pass the turkey* by then."

"Maybe," Ray said. "But you know, it's okay if not. You're okay the way you are."

"Yeah," I said. "You're okay too."

In the rush of the dust storm, in the danger and dark night, everything had seemed so urgent. Surviving—that bonded you to someone. And meeting the first person who was hard of hearing like me, of course I would be drawn to them. I was afraid that tight thread would sever once we weren't together every day, once Ray was back at school with his "real" deaf friends, back at home in Denver with his mom. Maybe I was just convenient. Just there.

But maybe not. I still felt warmth flutter through me when we sat down beside each other on the folding chairs before the podium, my bare arm brushing Ray's. I still felt hope and excitement as our legs became tangled, arranging ourselves on the chairs, and then, once we were seated, when Ray reached for my hand. The audience filled up around us. Helen and her neighbor Ana sat beside me. My parents were in the crowd somewhere, Amelia and Patience with the cookies at the back.

Captain took the podium. There was brief applause. Someone whooped, "My Captain!" and everyone laughed.

"Now, now," Captain said. "Our next guest needs no introduction. But I'm going to give him one anyway. Elmer Luck is a longtime resident of the valley, and a frequent resident of that chair over there." He pointed to the atrium, and people laughed again. "And when he's not snoozing in the library, he's writing. Elmer is the author of twenty-five works of fiction, _____ of which have been adapted into major motion pictures, and one a limited _____. He is a national bestselling author. The *New York Times,* in a review, called his work 'weirdly compelling.'"

"_____ me," Elmer muttered from somewhere in the audience.

"We're fortunate to have so many creative artists in our community, and we're honored that Elmer is one of the greats. And that he agreed to share his latest work _____."

"Wasn't given much of a choice," Elmer said.

"Please welcome Elmer Luck."

Clapping and cheers as Captain indicated the podium and Elmer took his place. I snapped a picture.

"All right, all right," Elmer said from the podium. "Hold your applause until I know I actually have something _____. Now, this book is publishing in the _____. It's called *Private Die* and it's about a detective who leaves her job to become a vigilante hunting serial killers."

"Excellent," Ray said.

I smothered a laugh.

"Chapter one." Elmer cleared his throat and began to read. I was grateful his reading voice was different than his speaking voice, loud and clear, resonant as the wood he liked to carve. Elmer, for all his protests, took his writing seriously. "'Detective Carmichael peered at the body splayed on the floor,'" he read. "'Blood splashed the nude form like an abstract painting, one that would fetch a high price at auction, bought by some collector, the kind of rich, disinterested man who would never look at the piece of art again, not once it graced the wall of his bathroom—the kind of man Carmichael had to admit she was attracted to the most.'"

"My mom might regret letting Amelia come," I said to Ray.

He smiled at me. I didn't think he heard me, but I would tell him later, after the reading. We found our ways to communicate. You just had to be thoughtful. You just had to be comfortable being uncomfortable sometimes.

You just have to listen, I had explained to my dad.

And I thought he heard me, finally, in the cellar with the wind swirling all around. Underground, it felt like we were in the eye of the storm, the calm center, and there he could hear me. There, he could be patient enough to try.

After the reading, Sam, Louisa, and Ray came over to the farm for dinner. Patience was spending the night again, and after the men cleaned up (that was something new we were trying: whoever cooked didn't have to clean), the adults retired to the front porch to drink iced tea with mint leaves from our new garden. Louisa had given us starts from her herbs that had survived and now they were ready to be harvested. Sam sat awfully close to Louisa, and I watched long enough to see his hand reach over the side of her chair to grasp her hand. She squeezed back.

Amelia and Patience went off to give the goats their nightly pets, and Ray and I wandered beyond the house, past the doors of the shelter that had saved us, past the broken shed that would never be unburied. We didn't have a use for it, and besides, Amelia said it really *was* like a fossil dig now. Wood planks stuck up from the dust like the flags of a lost expedition.

There was a lot the valley had lost, I knew. There was a lot my family had lost.

All of the fields, for instance, the crops my dad had watered and tended to so obsessively, giving the plants the time he couldn't give us. The dust choked all of them except for a few rows of potatoes. Enough to eat, but not enough to sell.

But my mom had her job and I had my job again, and would continue at the café most days after school. We had the farmers' market and the new website, and the valley made up the difference. We all made up the difference in potlucks and community suppers and the food pantry.

After warning me, Ellee's family had weathered the storm just fine and hurried back to Ohio. Though we emailed and called regularly, I was not sure when I could get back home.

I was not sure I even knew where home was anymore, what the word meant to me.

I had always thought it was a solid, sure thing, like bedrock. Home was a road that would lead me back. The road always led to the same place: Ohio, the humid holler where I was born, the black earth where I would return. That earth had flooded, disappeared under water, but the water had receded. I still loved Ohio.

But now I thought of the earth as red. And the sky as wide and cloudless and blue—most of the time. Except when it was red too. Even then, even during the storm, I hadn't wanted to run. I wanted to stay and protect. I wanted to learn how to live here with my friends.

Maybe home wasn't as simple as one place—or even a place at all. Maybe it was only a feeling, and maybe it was always temporary. I had felt at home in Ohio, splashing in the creek with my friends and my sister, the cicadas droning in an afternoon song and the kingfishers rising all around. But I felt at home now too, sometimes, in the valley, the land low and dry but teeming with cacti and flowers, each wild blossom like an egg cracked open with secret color, humming with bees.

Ray's hand rested in mine as we stopped at the last fencepost at the edge of my family's property. We looked at the mountains, side by side, and watched the sun do its slow setting.

The world had changed colors during the dust storm. But the world changed colors every night. Tonight, it was lavender-soaked, like cotton candy from a fair. I let the last sun rays seep into my arms. Tomorrow, Ray would go home. This was also his home. I was too. Maybe home could be more than one place. Maybe it was a feeling, a sense of safety, and maybe it was changing—growing—all the time, expanding to include more.

I turned to see he was staring at me. "What?"

He grinned, tucked his hair. "You're okay, is all."

I signed the words I knew. *OK.* "You're okay too. And I love you." I knew the sign for that. *I love you.*

"I love you too, Thea," Ray said. "Do you know there are lots of signs for love?"

"How do you know which one to use?"

"Depends on the context."

"I guess there are lots of spoken words for love too."

"Ways to say it, sign it, show it," Ray said.

"Can you show me *home*?"

Ray turned so we were facing each other, the sunset over the mountains to our left, bordered by the fence. I watched him closely. The sinking light illuminated one side of his face. He closed the fingers of his hand with a space between his thumb and other fingers, and brought his hand from his ear to his mouth in a curve.

"Ear to mouth," I said, my voice cracking a bit.

"What's so funny?"

"Nothing. It's just . . . that's what I've been trying to do this whole time. Hear people, get them to hear me, get them to listen."

"I listen," Ray said.

"I know. I listen too."

"I know you do." He brought his hands back down to his sides. "Now, show me *home*."

I turned him by the shoulders, rested my head below his, and together, we watched the sun set beyond the mountains.

Author's Note

I'm like Thea. I'm half deaf due to a congenital disability, and I was born into a hearing family. I've struggled for a long time with what to call myself, how to describe myself, and where to belong. I hear some, read lips some, and miss a lot. Those blanks when Thea doesn't hear something are like the absences in my own hearing. Unlike Thea, I did not begin to learn sign language until I was an adult.

When I was a teenager, a sign language interpreter—who was hearing—told me, *You don't belong in any world*, the hearing or the deaf. She said it with sadness. I think the seed for *Dust* was born right then. Because I knew I wasn't the only one who had been told there isn't a place for them.

But years later, a deaf professor of ASL told me something different: *You're both,* he said. *And neither. And that's a beautiful story.*

Also like Thea, my family's story took me at the start of the pandemic from my home in rural Ohio to Colorado. The

Bloodless Valley isn't a real place, but the struggle for water is very real. *Dust* tells some true stories, including the displacement of farmers of color in Colorado, and the story of the 1930s Dust Bowl, a series of severe dust storms that ravaged the west. The worst one in Colorado was called "Black Sunday," and dust did blanket the Statue of Liberty.

Dust is alternative history in that in the book, destructive farming practices weren't changed after the 1930s Dust Bowl. In real life, they were. But like other speculative fiction based on climate that I've written, the events in *Dust* are not far-fetched. Most scientists believe that because of climate change, we are due for another terrible Dust Bowl. It's only a matter of when.

What I hope you take away from this book is the desire and energy to protect Earth and all its inhabitants, and also the knowledge that your story, whatever it is, matters. It's sometimes hard being both/neither, but there's a lot of joy too. And you're okay the way you are.

Acknowledgments

No book happens without community, and the community for *Dust* has been as vast as a storm. Thank you always to my agent and champion, Eric Smith. Thank you to Vanessa Aguirre, Lisa Bonvisutto, and Alex Brown, who competently and unflaggingly stewarded this story through its many stages. I'm forever grateful for the support of Sara Goodman and Eileen Rothschild.

Thank you to Rivka Holler, Brant Janeway, Alyssa Gammello, Ana Ariane, Kerri Resnick, Eric Meyer, Chris Leonowicz, and Cassie Gutman for their creativity and smarts. I'm grateful for the words and wisdom of K. Ancrum, Olivia Chadha, and Lillie Lainoff. Thanks to Andrew Villegas and family. Thank you to my kin in the deaf and disability community, especially Stacy Jane Grover, Lara Ameen, and Meg Day, and thanks go to Jenna Beacom for reading an early draft. Ellee Achten is the first and best reader for my stories, always.

Thank you most of all to my family, especially Henry, best writer's kid ever, who learned to sign alongside me and who listens to all of my dreams.